M000206038

VICTIM 14

A DETECTIVE EMILY TIZZANO VIGILANTE JUSTICE THRILLER

KJ KALIS

This is a work of fiction. Names, characters, places, and incidents either are the products of the author's imagination or are used fictitiously. Any resemblance to actual persons, living or dead, or locales is entirely coincidental.

Copyright © 2021 KJ Kalis
eISBN 978-1-7352192-8-8
ISBN 978-1-7352192-9-5
All rights reserved

Without limiting the rights under copyright reserved, no part of the publication may be reproduced, stored in or introduced into a retrieval system, or transmitted, in any form, or by any means (electronic, mechanical, photocopying, recording, or otherwise including technology to be yet released), without the written permission of both the copyright owner and the above publisher of the book.

The scanning, uploading, and distribution of this book via the Internet or via any other means without the permission of the publisher are illegal and punishable by law. Please purchase only authorized electronic editions, and do not participate in or encourage electronic piracy of copyrighted materials. Your support of the author's rights is appreciated.

Published by:

BDM, LLC

ALSO BY K.J. KALIS:

The Kat Beckman Thriller Series

The Cure

Fourteen Days

Burned

The Blackout

The Bloody Canvas

Sauk Valley Killer

The Emily Tizzano Vigilante Justice Series

Twelve Years Gone

Lakeview Vendetta

Victim 14

The Jess Montgomery Thriller Series

The Trident Conspiracy

The Patriarch Code

Never Call Home

1

Dampness hung in the air over the trees and scrub around Little Bayou Pond. There'd been rain on and off for weeks, enough so that Ollie parked farther away from the edge of the water than he was used to, otherwise, the wheels from the van might get stuck. On a normal day, it wouldn't have mattered.

But today was a special day...

Along with the darkness and dampness, the sounds of toads calling out to each other, the night birds awakening, and the rustling of small unseen creatures in the brush, filled Ollie's ears. With each step, he could feel his boots sinking into the muddy ground, the wet soil squishing up around the tread. More rain was predicted in the next few hours, probably enough to wash away any tire tracks or footprints. At least, that's what Ollie hoped.

Ollie's breath came in waves, his lungs sucking in as much oxygen as they could absorb with each step. He wasn't used to carrying such a heavy load this far from the van. Parking farther away meant he had to lug the body a longer distance than usual.

"At least it's not a whole body," he muttered, getting close to the water's edge. Ollie stopped, setting it down near the water's edge. It was a tradition of sorts, taking a moment to think about what he'd done. He realized if someone asked him if he felt bad about killing, he'd say no. The weight of that realization laid heavy on him, knowing that he felt worse about not feeling bad than he did about what he'd done.

Ollie straightened up, pain shooting through his body. His lower back was aching, the weight of the torso he'd been carrying having stretched and pushed his muscles past what they were used to. Each one of them weighted at least a hundred pounds, he figured. Ollie stood at the edge of the pond. There was only one last step. It was his favorite part of the entire process, the part that gave him freedom, a release. He lifted his arm, using his sleeve to wipe the sweat off his brow. Summers in Louisiana were hot and humid no matter what time of day it was. The thick air hung over the pond like a cloud, the dampness almost enough to create rain.

As he glanced down at the body at his feet, or at least what was left of the body, Ollie flashed back to just a few hours before, when the man he'd captured tried to beg for his life. What the man didn't know was that begging would do him no good. But Ollie wasn't someone that got joy out of watching people suffer. He just wasn't that way, but his memories had to be appeased. There was no choice about that.

On the ground, Ollie saw a rock near the edge of the water that reminded him of the brick he'd picked up and smashed into the man's face, rendering him unconscious. There was mercy in that, Ollie thought, bending over to pick up the torso for the final time. As he did, his fingers nearly slipped into the bloody edge of the cut where one of the man's legs had been severed. Taking two steps forward, Ollie knelt, allowing the edge of the man's dead skin to caress the water before letting it go. Heaving with his arms, Ollie pushed the torso away from him, watching it as it disappeared under the surface of the water, noticing the color of the skin pale and gray in what moonlight could get through the passing clouds overhead. The surface of the skin was sleek and smooth, hairless, all features removed. It didn't look much different from one of the sides of beef that Ollie's father used to bring home from the butcher when he was a child.

As Ollie stood up, he wiped his hands on his pants, leaving reddish stains on the front of his jeans. He bent over again, rinsing his hands in the pond water, red droplets releasing from the tips of his fingers as he stared at the pond for another moment.

It was time to go home...

2

Miner barked, a high-pitched yelp that let Emily know someone was at the back door. It was followed by a click and then Mike's lanky frame making his way into the kitchen. "Good morning," Mike said, dropping his backpack down on the floor, ruffling Miner's fur, and then pushing a few long hairs out of his own eyes. "What's going on with you two?"

"Nothing new here," Emily said. "I wasn't expecting you this morning. Everything okay?" After the last case Mike and Emily worked on together, their relationship had changed. When Mike abandoned her in the middle of a case and took Miner with him, there was a pause in their relationship. That lasted for a month or so, and then Mike started coming around more again. Emily hadn't pushed it, but somehow Mike seemed different now. As Emily stirred creamer into her coffee, she realized she never asked Mike why he started coming around more. The metal from the spoon clinked against the edge of the mug as she set it down. Mike was probably coming around more because he was lonely. Mike lived by himself and didn't have much family. He had a loose group of a few friends and now his girlfriend, Alice, the molecular geneticist who had helped them analyze some tricky DNA information in a previous case. That was it.

"Yeah, everything's fine. Just wanted to come and check in on you and my favorite dog." Mike rifled through his backpack and pulled out something wrapped in a plastic shopping bag. Miner trotted over, his ears pricked and his gray tail wagging behind him.

"Another toy for Miner?" Emily smiled.

Mike grinned, "Yeah, just a little something." From out of the bag, Mike pulled a blue stuffed T-Rex. Miner grabbed it and trotted off. From behind her, Emily could hear the toy squeaking as Miner figured out where the small plastic bubble was sewn into the fabric. She knew Miner would spend the next several hours pulling and tugging on the cloth until he could get the squeaker out. Why, she wasn't sure. It just seemed that if the toy had a squeaker, Miner wanted it out.

After watching Miner trot away, protecting his new toy, Mike sat down at the table. Emily looked at him. His lips were pressed together. There was something on his mind. "Want a cup of coffee before you tell me what's going on?"

Mike nodded, "Sure."

From her years with the Chicago Police Department, Emily could tell when someone had something to say. Emily walked over to the kitchen cabinet, pulled out a mug that said "Eat More Cookies" on it and filled it, watching the steam curl in white tendrils above the cup. She set the cup in front of him, waiting, wrapping her fingers around the edge of the mug. Not that she was cold. It had been one of the hottest summers on record in Chicago. Emily crossed her legs and pulled the hem of her running shorts down as she waited for Mike to start speaking, the scar from where she'd gotten stabbed during one of the cases they worked showing underneath. There was no need for anyone to look at it.

Saying nothing, Mike got up and pulled his laptop out of his backpack and set it on the table. Emily could hear the fans start to whirr as it opened. "New laptop?"

Mike nodded but didn't look up. "Yeah, the last one I had didn't have enough memory to run all the encryption and firewall stuff I need."

Emily nodded, not surprised.

For about two minutes, there was no other noise in the kitchen other than Mike typing on his keyboard. After another minute passed, Mike sighed and leaned back in his chair, turning the laptop toward Emily. "See this guy?"

"Yep. What's his story?" Emily leaned forward to stare at the image of what looked to be a middle-aged man with a short mustache, a round face, and even rounder eyes. From the resolution of the picture, Emily wondered how old it was. Her experience in the cold case division made her sensitive to the advances in digital resolution. The picture looked to be close to ten years old.

"This guy's name is Corey Hawkins. Or it was..." Mike said, turning the laptop back towards him and punching a few keys. He spun it back around toward Emily. "He died almost exactly seven years ago."

Emily leaned forward, staring at the image Mike had pulled up on his screen. "Is that Louisiana?" she asked.

Mike nodded. "Sure is. Glad you have your geography straight."

Smiling, Emily picked up her mug and took another sip of coffee. "Glad you packed your sarcasm this morning. What's his story?"

"Well," Mike said, his tone changing to sound much more like a college professor than a tech geek, "Seven years ago, Corey Hawkins disappeared. A few days later, his body was found."

Emily frowned, "And why do I care about this particular

case?" Mike knew about the volume of requests Emily got for her help — families and friends and husbands and wives whose loved ones had disappeared or been killed, and they got no satisfaction from their local law enforcement, or for some reason, local law enforcement was unable to prosecute the perpetrator successfully. That was Emily's specialty — dealing with cold cases off the books, getting justice for family and friends who would otherwise be left with the haunting memories of the person they knew without any closure.

"It's a weird one, that's for sure." Mike spun the laptop screen back towards Emily.

Her breath caught in her throat. "Is that..."

"A torso? Yes, that's exactly what it is. That's all they ever found of Corey. No head, no arms, no legs. Seven years ago, DNA was in its infancy. While most labs can now process DNA evidence in twenty-four to forty-eight hours, unless you know someone, back then, it took weeks to do the sequencing."

Emily knew what Mike was talking about. Mike's girlfriend, Alice Chang, had done some off-the-books DNA work for them and managed to find a link to their suspect in the short span of two hours, not even two days. Emily chewed her lip. Mike was right, DNA testing had come a long way. "So, the only way they figured out this was Corey Hawkins was through DNA?"

Mike nodded.

Emily got up and walked over to the coffee maker, her bare feet padding on the wood floor. As she refilled her cup, she looked over her shoulder, "Why show me this?"

"Turns out, there's been a string of these in the same city for the last seven years. Every six months, somebody goes missing and a few days later, a torso is found. That's all, nothing else."

"When was the last body discovered?" Emily knew Mike was leading up to something, but she wasn't exactly clear where he was going. Was it just an interesting case he wanted her to see? She wasn't sure.

"Almost six months ago." Mike leaned back in his chair. "Can you imagine living there? I mean, think about it, you're going about your daily business, but in the back of your head, all you can hear is tick-tock, tick-tock. You know the six-month mark is coming up and you're just wondering if you or someone you love is the one that's going to get nabbed. Crazy, right?"

Emily sat back down at the table, setting her coffee aside. She leaned her elbows on the edge and looked at Mike. "Yeah, that would be crazy, but why are you telling me this?" It was time to stop dancing around. She knew Mike had a purpose in telling her all of this information.

"I was just thinking since it's been a while since you've taken a case, maybe this is one to look at."

The words hung in the air.

"Yeah, it's been a while. What was the last one?"

"Marlowe Burgess. Heard anything about her?"

The name caused the hair on the back of Emily's neck to rise a little, "Last I heard, Marlowe got the twenty million in funding returned to her from the man that stole it, finished the original project, and is now working on another one in downtown Chicago. You know Vince's body showed up a couple of days later, right? The Mob took care of the problem so I didn't have to."

Mike nodded.

The last two cases had taken a toll on Emily. Every time she agreed to help someone, it was at her own risk. She no longer had a badge. If she got caught, she'd be prosecuted like any other criminal. Her desire to help others outside of the law get justice had created a strange tension in her life. She was now avoiding the very people who'd taught her to do the job she used to love. A tingle ran up her spine. "I'm not sure I want to do any more cases, Mike. I told you that."

Before Mike could answer, Miner came trotting into the

kitchen, carrying the T-Rex in his mouth. The white stuffing was jutting out of the back of the toy. Emily reached down and felt around to find the plastic squeaker, pulled it out of a tuft of stuffing, and then handed the toy back to Miner. Looking a little dejected, the dog grabbed the toy and trotted off again. The last thing Emily needed was her dog swallowing it. That would be a problem.

"I know that's what you've been thinking," Mike said. "But I found this case on a forum. You should take a look at it when you get a minute. The cases on there are more brutal than any I've ever seen. And most of them have gone unsolved. It's like the criminals have managed to outsmart law enforcement again and again."

"I'm not law enforcement anymore. You know that."

"Yes, I do," Mike nodded. "But what we've been able to do for families, that's important. Alice and I were talking about that. It might not be the traditional way to make a positive impact, but it sure does help people like Vicki Schmidt, right?"

The minute Mike mentioned Vicki's name, Emily thought of Sarah Schmidt's mom, sitting in her yellow kitchen, drinking pot after pot of coffee, waiting for news about her daughter that took twelve long years to come. After Emily had taken care of Benny Walters, the man that abducted and killed Vicki Schmidt's eighteen-year-old daughter, Vicki had finally moved on. Last Emily had heard, Vicki had remarried and relocated from Stockton closer to her younger daughter.

Emily got up and walked to the window, staring out toward the garage. Even though it was summer, and the weather was nice, Emily kept the garage door closed. The little house she and Luca had bought when they got married was all hers now, after their divorce and then Luca's overdose. There were no traces of him left in the house.

At the back of the yard, Emily could see the tomato plants at the edge of the fence, growing tall. She'd need to get outside and check them for suckers and any ripe fruit at some point during the day, a day that Mike seemingly wanted to upset like apples rolling off of a pile neatly stacked at the local grocery store. It might look like only one would fall, but when one went, they all went.

Taking on a new case was something Emily wasn't sure she was ready to do. She folded her arms across her chest and stared. All the people around her always seem so eager to have her take on a new case, but it wasn't that simple. It might seem that way on the outside, but each and every time she went out to try to get justice for someone else, she was reminded she'd hardly gotten justice for herself.

Unfolding her arms, she rubbed her wrists without thinking about it, the sting of the cold metal of the handcuffs somehow embedded in her skin. After her arrest, her husband left her, choosing drugs and other women over his wife. Emily hadn't ever dated after that, the hurt and betrayal too deep. A couple of months later, mysterious envelopes filled with five thousand dollars in cash appeared on the first day of every month in her mailbox. Though she never confirmed it, Emily believed it was Luca's father, Anthony Tizzano, who gave her the money. Emily figured it was Anthony's way of apologizing for his son's behavior. Anthony was well known in Chicago, but probably not for the best reasons. Nonetheless, he'd been helpful in her last case with his connections to the other crime families working in Chicago.

Taking on another case meant taking on more risk. The odds of anyone helping her on the case — whether that was Mike or Alice or Anthony — getting arrested were slim. Even if they did, they'd only suffer minor charges. That wouldn't be the case for Emily. She'd dropped enough bodies in the name of justice that the feeling of steel handcuffs could become a daily reality for her. A shiver ran up her spine. "I just don't know if I want to take on any other cases. And, if these are happening every six months, then they aren't exactly cold." Emily only took on cold cases. It was what she was good at and how she made her name in the Chicago Police Department. It also helped her avoid any chance of bumping into local law enforcement while they were hot on the trail. The last thing she needed was to end up in jail.

"That's not exactly true," Mike said, chewing his lip. He stared back at his computer for a moment and then brushed the hair out of his eyes. "Think about the families who lost loved ones at the beginning. It's been seven years for those people. Whoever this serial killer is, he takes someone new every six months. To date, thirteen people have been killed in the same city, in the same way, every six months. No one has been able to solve it."

"You're talking like I could make a name for myself if I figured it out." Emily frowned. The last thing she wanted to do was make a name for herself. Anonymity was her friend.

"You could, but I know that's not what you want. I was just thinking more along the lines that you could help a lot of families all at one time."

To that point, Mike was right. There was a good side to what she did. Delivering justice wasn't always easy, but if it allowed the people who'd lost someone to move on, then it couldn't be all bad. Unless you got caught, of course.

Before Emily could say anything more, Mike interjected again, "I was thinking about how it might be to live in that town. It's called Tifton. I wonder if people have the months marked on their calendars so they know when to hide in their homes. It's got to be terrifying."

Emily turned back to Mike and sat back down at the table. "Where did you find this case?"

A couple of keystrokes later, Mike turned the computer towards her, showing her an online forum. "It's called Unsolved." He dragged the cursor down the left side of the page. "These are all cases that have gone unsolved for at least five years. I was bored one night and decided to take a look. That's how I found the story of Corey Hawkins. Six months later, another guy from the same town disappeared. His name was Junior Owen. His family posted on here, too. Can you believe that's how these families spend their time?"

Emily almost laughed at the question given who it was coming from. Unlike most people, Mike spent an inordinate amount of time on conspiracy websites and the dark web. The fact that he'd even asked brought a chuckle up the back of her throat. "I suppose so. That's part of the problem, though. These people haven't asked for my help."

"They would if they knew you were out there. They would if they knew how good you are."

Before Emily could say anything else, there was a knock at the back door, the sound causing Miner to leap up and charge, barking, leaving his stuffed T-rex behind in the corner of the kitchen. A wave of concern washed over Emily. She wasn't expecting anyone, and the only person who went through the back door was Mike.

"I'll get it. I know who it is," Mike said, unfolding himself from the chair.

As Mike walked to the door, Emily noticed he'd put on a little weight. His normally skeletal frame didn't look quite as thin as usual. That was good. Emily quickly chalked it up to Alice. She must be good for him, Emily thought, still wondering who was at the door. Taking a sip of coffee, she waited for a moment, knowing the drawer behind her had a loaded pistol in it. All she would need to do was twist and grab it if whoever at the door was a threat.

Listening, she could tell by the low murmuring that Mike knew who it was. Emily relaxed. Mike walked back in the kitchen first, followed by another guy that could have been his brother, just a shorter version. He had wire-framed glasses and carried a backpack that looked a lot like Mike's. He had the same brown hair, although it was cut a bit shorter, and was wearing beat-up jeans and a White Sox T-shirt. No one in the entire city of Chicago would give him a second look.

"Emily, meet my buddy, Flynn Cunningham."

Inviting someone to her house guaranteed Emily had to say yes to meeting Flynn. Emily swallowed, trying to be as graceful as her personality would allow. "Nice to meet you. I'm Emily." From behind her, Miner let out a bark, still trying to determine if Flynn was a friend or foe. "And this is a Miner. He's very friendly but gets a little nervous around strangers. Just give him a couple of minutes before you reach out to him, so he doesn't bite you, okay?"

Flynn's eyes widened, "Okay." He gave Miner a sideways glance as he pulled up a chair at the table. "So, Mike said you're interested in the Tifton killings?"

Emily raised her eyebrows and glanced at Mike, whose cheeks reddened. "Mike was just telling me about them."

From his backpack, Flynn pulled a laptop and set it up next to Mike's. Sitting next to each other, they looked like a couple of college kids trying to finish their homework. Staring at his computer screen, Flynn said, "It's an interesting case. I'd be happy to share what I know."

Emily glanced back at Mike and raised her eyebrows again. "Sure. But how about if you start by telling me how the two of you know each other?"

Flynn looked up, sighed, and then looked at Emily as if she was interrupting the information he was trying to access on his computer. "We met on a forum. I can't remember which one..."

"It was one of the firewall forums, where that guy blathers on about encryption every day," Mike said.

Flynn nodded. "Right. Anyway, we started chatting on the side and discovered we have some stuff in common."

"What do you do when you're not busy researching firewalls and serial killers?" Emily asked, re-crossing her legs and running her fingers across the scar on her thigh.

Flynn glanced at Emily's leg and then rapidly looked away as if he was staring too long. "I'm a forensic accountant. People hire me to dig through their books or the books of people they don't like," he chuckled.

"We could have used you on the last case," Mike said. "Trying to figure out what happened with all that money for the Lakeview project was a pain."

"You guys helped out with that? That building is beautiful."

The last thing Emily wanted to happen was for the two guys to get off on some tangent. She didn't want them sitting in her kitchen at all. Mike wasn't any bother, but she didn't want her house to end up being a hangout for any secret hacker society. They all had their own houses and apartments to hang out in. "So, let's get back to the discussion at hand," she said, straightening in her chair. "The Tifton killings."

"Yes, yes," Flynn said. "To give you the high-level view, seven years ago, someone started dumping parts of bodies into Little Bayou Pond just outside of Tifton, Louisiana. For some context, Tifton is a rural community. No real industry. Not big and fancy like Baton Rouge or New Orleans. Definitely rural. But the fact that torsos were being dropped in the water every six months garnered them national attention, and not in a good way."

"It's only torsos?" Emily asked, feeling bile rise in the back of her throat. The idea of chopping bodies up like a butcher at a meat shop twisted her stomach in knots.

Flynn turned his computer towards Emily so she could see the screen. On it was the chest and waist of a person, cut off at the legs, the skin pale and shriveled, only covering the torso in part. "This is the torso of Joe Day. He's body three-one."

"Three-one? What does that mean? Emily said, frowning.

"Sorry. It's how crime enthusiasts have organized the

killings. Three stands for the third year. One stands for the first body killed that year. Whoever the killer is, he's like clockwork. Every six months, someone disappears, and then a few days later the body pops up at Little Bayou Pond. Sadly, local law enforcement has gotten so used to the pattern they send the dogs and the flat-bottomed boats to the pond about a week after someone disappears to see if there's anything in there. There usually is."

The nerves in the back of Emily's neck tingled. That someone was killing that regularly disgusted her.

"Do they have any leads on the killer?"

"No. That's the thing about it," Flynn said, his eyes narrowing. "You'd think that after all of these years, the killer would make a mistake. He'd leave something behind on the body that would help identify him." Flynn tilted his head to the side, "I am assuming it's a male. It could be a female perp, though. Unfortunately, women as serial killers are becoming more common."

Emily blinked. What Flynn was saying was interesting, but she didn't need him going off into conjecture. "This is fascinating, but what does it have to do with me?"

Flynn's head spun towards Mike, "I thought you said..."

Mike interrupted him before Flynn had a chance to finish his sentence. "Emily, I know how much you don't like to see people suffering. There are a whole lot of families in Tifton that are doing just that. I found another post from this guy named Bradley. His brother, Sean, was body five-one. He was taken a couple of years ago and then his body resurfaced six days later in the Little Bayou Pond. Bradley, his brother, seems to be pretty obsessed with the fact that Sean was taken and killed." Mike glanced at Flynn. "Can you show her the picture of Sean?"

Flynn twisted his computer towards Emily. It was virtually indistinguishable from the first image they'd shown her. Just a torso with no arms and legs, no distinguishing features, and the torso only partially covered by skin. "What happened to the skin?"

Flynn tilted his head to the side and blinked, "Little Bayou Pond is filled with fish and other critters. I'm sure they make a nice meal out of the torsos that are dropped in there."

"Did they ever recover the rest of the body?"

Flynn shook his head, looking at Emily. "No. The FBI has gotten involved in the cases, but no one has ever recovered the heads or limbs of anyone that the Tifton killer has taken. It's always the same. Just the pale torso left over, like a chunk of meat."

The way Flynn said it made Emily swallow, hard. She stood up and walked to the sink, rinsing out her coffee mug and setting it inside the dishwasher. Wiping her hands on a towel, she said, "This is all very interesting, but I don't know if Mike told you, but I'm not sure about taking any more cases."

Flynn shot a look at Mike. "That's not what you told me. You said you thought this might be something Emily would be interested in."

"Well, that's technically true. She might be interested in it."

Emily shook her head. What had been a serious discussion about a serial killer had now turned to the bickering of two boys. "One thing I always look for in my cases is someone who reaches out to me directly, so they know my story. I'm not sure that fits here."

For a second, Emily wondered why it was important to her that someone from the family reach out to her, but in her gut, she knew she wanted them to understand what she'd been through and what she'd been accused of. It was important to her they knew she was good at what she did, but that it didn't come without baggage. It wasn't her style to reach out to anyone to offer to help them. They needed to come to her.

"I think if the families knew who you were, they'd want your help," Mike said.

"That might be true, but the reality is, they haven't asked."

"What if I could make that happen?" Flynn said.

Emily felt a flood of anger run through her body. What were these two guys trying to pull? It wouldn't be their life on the line if they got caught. They wouldn't be the ones in jail if they had to kill someone. It would be her. Her freedom would be taken away. She glanced towards Miner who was curled up on his dog bed, still chewing the T-Rex. What would she do with Miner if she got convicted or killed? A chill ran down her spine. She thought by now Mike would understand the risk that was involved. Maybe he didn't.

She said nothing for a minute, waiting for her anger to subside. "This is an ambush. That's all this is," she said, walking away. As she made her way through the house, the wood floors creaking under her feet, she remembered that it was the beginning of the month. She opened the front door, just in time to see a Chicago Police Department cruiser drive by. She felt prickles on her back. Even after all these long years away from the department, she felt she couldn't get away from what happened the night she was arrested. She bent over, picking up the mail that had fallen on the front step and reached into the mailbox, finding the envelope with five thousand dollars in cash sitting in it.

Emily took the steps two at a time to the second floor, going into her bedroom. On the wall, there was a photograph of Lake Michigan. She swung it to the side, revealing a wall safe. Punching in the code and putting her finger on the reader, the door popped open. She tossed the envelope inside on top of a pile of other envelopes she barely touched. "I'm going to have to do something about that," she mumbled, realizing the safe was nearly full.

Emily closed the safe door and pushed the picture back

against the wall. Sitting down on the edge of her bed, Emily sighed. In a way, she felt bad telling Mike and Flynn they'd ambushed her. But they did. The cases she took should be her choice, not theirs. Was the story they were telling her important? It was. But was she ready to take another case? She didn't know.

Standing up fast enough that it startled Miner, Emily darted out of the bedroom and down the steps. Flynn and Mike were still huddled over their computers, leaning so close together that their hair was practically touching. Two steaming cups of coffee were in front of them. Mike must have gotten one for Flynn, Emily thought. She slumped down in the third of the four chairs at the kitchen table, leaning forward and staring at Flynn, "You said you might be able to make contact with one of the families?"

Flynn's eyes widened. He turned to look at Mike and then looked back at Emily, "I think so. I mean, some of these people post on the forums pretty often. This case is legendary."

Legendary. The idea that it was a famous case made it all that much more dangerous for Emily. The skin on the back of her legs crawled a little bit. Was she doing the right thing? Emily didn't know. But something in her gut told her that if law enforcement hadn't been able to solve the murders in seven years, someone needed a fresh look at the case. Someone who was outside of the local law enforcement and the FBI. That would be her.

"Make contact. Let's see where this goes."

The musty smell of the cellar was what Ollie always remembered first about the small storage space below his house. Most homes in Louisiana were built on a slab, or even better, on posts. Too much flooding. But, for some reason, the old house Ollie lived in had a small cellar. As he walked down the creaky planked wooden steps, he realized it probably wasn't for storing much more than root vegetables someone wanted to hold on to over what winter Tifton had. But to him, it had become something more.

There wasn't a lot of light in the space. The little light there came from a few dangling bulbs in the ceiling. Ollie pulled the chain on the first one that covered the path down the steps. There was a second bulb right at the bottom of the stairs and a third at the back of the small space. The uncovered bulbs cast sharp shadows in the space no matter the time of day. Ollie's body ached with the long day he'd had working at the machine shop, his body hunched over a metal press, making fittings. It seemed like he was never able to straighten up anymore, a permanent ache between his shoulder blades. It just added to the pain he carried with him.

Standing at the bottom of the steps, Ollie noticed the cellar seemed particularly dark. There was no reason why, except that it was nighttime and the small window that wasn't bringing in any daylight. During the daytime, it would let a tiny bit of light in the space, but now, at night, there was only darkness. Ollie blinked a couple of times and then looked at the chair that was bolted to the floor just opposite the window. The first time he brought someone into the cellar, it wasn't bolted down. The whole scenario was completely unplanned. A rare opportunity, in his mind. Ollie had been at a bar and saw a man that looked an awful lot like his wife's new husband, Ned, the man that had become a father to his girls and had taken them away from him. That same night, Ollie had too much to drink and found the man in the parking lot as he was trying to leave. The man that looked like Libby's new husband never made it home.

In the cellar off to the left, there was a workbench made of dry, dusty wood. It was nothing more than some scrap wood nailed together by whoever had owned the house before Ollie bought it. Ollie imagined the previous owners used it as a place to set their baskets of potatoes and onions so they were at least off the floor. For a moment, he wondered how that worked, given the fact that nothing in Louisiana ever really cooled off. Most root sellers needed to be chilly enough to preserve the food and prevent mold. He shook the thought away as he took the few steps to the workbench. Potatoes and onions were the least of his worries.

On the right side of the bench was a pile of tools. Nothing fancy, just a few saws, a chisel, and a couple of hunting knives. Ollie bent over, his body complaining as he reached for a small shoebox that was on the lower shelf of the workbench. At one time, the box had been a glossy pink and white, holding a pair of roller skates that his then five-year-old daughter Willow had wanted for Christmas. Once she and her twin sister had left with their mom, there were very few traces left of them. The shoebox was one of the few things that remained. Ollie opened it up, turning to the side so the little light there was in the base-ment could penetrate the contents of the box. Holding it up, he gave the box a little shake, looking inside. A couple of wedding rings, a necklace, a watch, and a couple of pairs of earrings rattled at the bottom of the box. Seeing them brought back memories of each of the people that visited the cellar. None of them made it out alive.

Closing the top of the box, Ollie set it back on the lower shelf, making sure it was in exactly the same spot as he'd found it. He took a deep breath in, exhaustion covering him, staring at what was around him. The only other item in the basement was a tattered olive-green upholstered chair in the corner. Ollie lumbered over to it and slumped down, extending his long legs out in front of him, his feet still covered by the boots he'd worn to work. He didn't know why he was so tired all the time. It was as if he was carrying the weight of the world on his shoulders no matter where he went. It was probably because of Libby, he thought. That had become a common refrain in his mind, blaming his ex-wife for the condition of his life that was as tattered as the old chair he sat in.

A moment later, Ollie felt his eyes close, his mind entering the haunted place that normal people would have called sleep. His mind went black for a little while — how long he couldn't tell — but soon after, images of Libby and their twin daughters, Willow and Sage, started to emerge in front of him. He saw them smiling and laughing, but they were far away, just out of reach. In his dream, he ran after them, trying to catch them. When he finally did, out of breath and frustrated, he dragged all of them to the cellar. He yelled as he plunged a long serrated hunting knife into Libby's chest. The yell brought him out of sleep. Ollie realized he was awake, his fingers wrapped tightly around the arms of the olive chair he'd nodded off in.

Using the back of his sleeve, Ollie wiped his forehead, sweat pooled on his body from the dream. He pushed up out of the chair, pulling the strings for the light bulbs behind him, giving the chair in the corner one last look. Glancing at the calendar posted on the wall, a picture of his smiling twin girls at five years old attached with a rusty paperclip, he realized it was almost time. Five months and twenty-three days had passed since the last torso entered the water. Ollie pulled the last string on the bulb suspended above the ceiling and went up the stairs, plunging the cellar into darkness again.

4

E mily hadn't slept well. The basic details of the torso killer case rattled in her head. Miner had gotten so frustrated with her twisting and turning that at some point in the middle of the night, he'd jumped off the bed and found a spot laying on a discarded blanket on the floor. Sitting up on the edge of her bed, Emily mumbled, "Sorry about that, buddy. It was a rough night."

Standing up, Emily stretched for a second, trying to work the kinks out of her body. Her regular boxing workouts had made her body longer and stronger, but she also had more soreness than before. Might be time to schedule a massage, she thought, heading into the bathroom. Brushing her teeth and pulling her hair back into a long ponytail, Emily tugged on a pair of sweatpants and headed downstairs. Mike was crashed out on the couch, his mouth wide open, clearly deep in sleep. Miner walked over to him and nudged at Mike's nose with his own, startling him. Mike's eyes half-open, Emily said, "Where's Flynn?" wondering where Mike's friend had gone. When she went to bed the night before, Flynn and Mike were still sitting at the kitchen table. She was a little surprised that Mike was still at her house. Alice must be working on a project, Emily thought, wondering why Mike didn't want to spend time with his girlfriend.

Mike coughed a little, blinked, and then looked at Emily, "He took off late last night. Said he'd be back this morning."

"He's not working?"

"He's got a couple of days off. Just finished a big client project."

Emily nodded and went into the kitchen, the wooden floorboards creaking under her bare feet. She walked to the back door, disabled the alarm system, cracked it open, and let Miner outside. It was early enough that the full light of day hadn't descended on Chicago yet. Cool air touched Emily's face. Though humid, it was a nice start to the day. Slipping into a pair of flip-flops, Emily walked into the backyard, her toes quickly covered with cool dew on the grass. She bent over and found two ripe tomatoes. Better to get these before the chipmunks do, she thought to herself, giving the fruit a little twist to get it off the vine. She got back to the door at the same time Miner did, the damp from the yard leaving small wet paw prints on the floor as she followed Miner into the kitchen.

Just as she was starting a pot of coffee, there was a knock at the door. Mike passed behind her. "Flynn," he said, holding up his phone. "Just texted me."

Emily nodded, reaching into the cabinet for the coffee. After a night of bad sleep, she needed a cup of coffee to shake the cobwebs out of her head.

Before she had a chance to start thinking about the dreams that plagued her, Flynn walked in. Unlike Mike, he looked properly prepared for the day. Clean shirt, clean jeans, his hair still damp enough to show the comb marks in it.

"Good morning," he said, setting a bakery box down on the kitchen table and shrugging his backpack off next to the wall.

Miner growled for a second and then sniffed Flynn's knee. Flynn plopped down in one of the kitchen chairs and looked at him. "You remember me, right? I was here last night. Remember? The one feeding you pizza?" Miner agreed to have his ears scratched and then turned away, walking towards Emily, giving her a look that said there were too many people in the house for his liking. He walked off, the noise of his nails tapping on the floor. Emily figured he was going to lay down on the dog bed in her office to get some peace and quiet. She wished she could do the same.

"I come bearing good news and food," Flynn said, standing up. The plastic bag around the bakery box rattled and crinkled as he pulled it off, lifting the lid.

Mike leaned over, "What'd you bring?"

"Donuts from Presti's."

Emily smiled a little. Presti's was one of the best Italian bakeries in the area. They were known for their bread and their cookies, but particularly their doughnuts. One Friday night a month, the bakery opened at midnight, as soon as the first doughnuts came out of the fryer, restaurant and moviegoers headed there for a sweet snack before a nightcap. Emily had done that one time with Luca, she remembered, pouring the first cup of coffee from the pot. She pulled two more mugs down, one for Mike and one for Flynn. Her stomach clenched. Flynn had come in, saying he had food and good news. Was it really good news or was it news that would set her off on an adventure she wasn't sure she was ready to have?

Might as well get to it, Emily thought. "Thanks for the doughnuts," she said, looking down into the box, the sugary smell of vanilla glaze catching in her nose. As she took a bite, she said, "You said you have good news?" The words coming out of her mouth made it hard to eat, her throat tightening at what he might say.

"Yep," Flynn said, sitting down on a kitchen chair.

"Remember how you asked me if there was a way to get in contact with one of the family members?"

Emily nodded, walking over to the counter to get a paper towel for her fingers.

"Well, we got lucky. Bradley Barker was online last night. I made contact. He's game. Said he'd be grateful for the help."

Emily frowned for a second. "Who is this? What do we know about him?" The reality that Flynn made contact with some random person attached to the Tifton torso killer case made her uncomfortable. She chewed her lip. Could this person be trusted?

Flynn licked the glaze off his finger and pulled out his computer from his backpack,. "Remember what we were saying about the case yesterday?"

Emily nodded.

"Bradley's brother, Sean, was body five – one. Same MO, same body drop in the Little Bayou Pond. He was found as the first body of the fifth year."

"Did they find all the bodies or are people assuming that all of the killings belong to the torso killer?" The question had occurred to Emily the day before, but she had forgotten to ask it. Seven years of killing seemed like a lot to get away with.

"I'd have to check on that," Flynn said, typing on the keyboard of his laptop. "At any rate, Bradley messaged me back within a few minutes. We went back and forth a couple of times last night. I explained the situation — that you sometimes will travel to help families get the justice they need. He's open to help. Said local law enforcement and the FBI have done nothing. They tend to show up when a new body is found, rumble around for a week or two and then everything goes back to normal for the next five and a half months until another person is taken."

"You didn't tell him who I am, did you?" The idea that

Flynn might have given away her identity caused Emily's stomach to clench into a tiny ball. Staying under the radar was one of the only ways she'd managed to keep out of the way of law enforcement. Many times, when she traveled to a case, the families didn't even know she was there. She'd spend about twenty-four hours on the ground at the location, doing some research, before she let the family know she'd arrived. It was better that way. Once she had a chance to dig around locally, she'd meet the family. If they seemed overbearing or too controlling, she'd simply get in her truck and disappear.

Flynn scrunched up his face, "Your identity? No way! I know better than that. Too many trolls on the Internet." He looked at Mike, a half-smile on his face. "You know, hanging out with this guy has made me completely paranoid."

Emily smiled and felt her body relax. Knowing that Flynn was on the same page as Mike made her job a little easier. "Okay, so tell me a little bit more about the conversation you had with this guy last night."

Flynn reached into the box and pulled out another dough-nut, taking a bite. "Well, he said the whole town is on edge because they are at the five-month and twenty-three-day mark. Everyone knows what's coming. They just don't know who it will be. When someone is taken, law enforcement and the FBI turn everything upside down for a couple of weeks, create a lot of chaos in Tifton, and then they leave. The people that live there are left to put the pieces back together as best they can." Flynn put his doughnut down for a moment. "It's a sad thing. I was thinking about that when I drove over here this morning. Can you imagine living in that town knowing that every six months someone is going to disappear? And then the disrup-tion — law enforcement and the Feds all over everything, making a mess, and then they leave." Flynn shook his head. "It's gotta be hard."

Emily nodded. After working in law enforcement for as long as she did, she knew that though most officers were there to help, some just liked to create a commotion and then go back to their own lives. That was one of the things she had learned to love about working in the cold case division. It was a place she was able to make a real difference. But no longer. Emily turned her head to the side for a second, staring out the window. She turned back to Flynn, "When these murderers have happened, does law enforcement take a fresh look at the old cases? Did Bradley happen to say anything about that?"

"From what he said, it doesn't sound like it. Sounds like for the first year or year and a half after someone disappears, they check-in when a new body is taken., But after that, they just walk away."

"So, in essence, they are only working the active cases. Anybody who disappeared more than a year or so ago, they aren't that interested in."

"That's what it sounded like to me," Flynn said, nodding. "I mean, I kind of understand that. Not that I think it's right," he said, tilting his head, "but, I can understand how they might think it would be easier to solve fresh cases. You know, fresh leads, new evidence, that kind of thing."

Emily tilted her head, suddenly wondering how much about law enforcement Flynn knew. It didn't matter. She didn't need Flynn for the case. All she needed was Mike for tech support. "Let me see the message."

Flynn's fingers ran over the keyboard and a few clicks later, he turned the screen toward her. On it, Emily could see the black border of the forum page, the title "Unsolved" at the top. In a little box in the lower right-hand corner of the page, Flynn opened the direct messages between his account and Bradley's. Emily squinted at the screen as her eyes adjusted to the small type. She found where Bradley Barker replied to Flynn. It read,

"Sure, we'd be grateful for any help we can get. Sounds like your friend knows what they're doing. Can't say the same about local law enforcement. Can't speak badly about them either — not sure anybody but the Feds could crack a case like this one. Been going on for too long." On the next line, Flynn asked why people stayed in the city. Bradley responded, "It's home. I've lived in Tifton my whole life. I guess we could run scared and move away, but we'd leave everything we've built here including friends and family and work. There's trouble no matter where you go. At least we know what kind of trouble we have here." On the next line, Flynn asked Bradley if there was anything he should tell Emily, though it didn't specifically mention her name. It was the longest response from Bradley, "Just tell your friend that we'd be grateful if they would look into the case. It's hard living this way. Almost like living in a war zone. And since no one's been caught all these years, we have no justice. The worst part is we have no idea who might be doing it. No leads, at least none that any of us can find. It's like sadness has taken over the city. Several families have moved away, worried about their loved ones, but I just can't. My whole life is here, and I know other families feel exactly the same way. If your friend is interested, make sure they look me up when they get here. I'd be more than happy to show some Southern hospitality. I live on the outskirts of town." There was an address listed on the next line.

Emily leaned back in her seat. By the way that Bradley wrote the response, she could tell Flynn hadn't divulged anything about her — including whether she was a man or a woman. That was good. Just the fact that Flynn had been that respectful felt like he gave her room to breathe. She didn't say anything for a moment, her mind clattering on its own. Was this the kind of case where she thought she could make a difference? Flynn and Mike were right to some degree — there were parts of it that were definitely a cold case, particularly some of the earlier murders. In defense of the local law enforcement, she agreed with what Bradley said. The locals were hardly equipped to deal with a serial killer that had dropped a whole series of bodies. That was definitely work for the Feds.

Standing up, Emily walked over to Miner's food bowl, bent over and picked up the bowl, and took a few steps down the hall, opening the closet door to refill it. Her mind was still working. So was her gut. She was waiting for the feeling that said to stay in Chicago or make the drive to Tifton. The dry dog kibble rattled in the bottom of the metal bowl as she scooped it up and poured it in. Emily straightened, closed the closet door, and walked back into the kitchen, feeling her eyes clear. "All right," she said standing in front of Mike and Flynn, who were watching her from over the top edge of their laptop screens. Emily chewed her lip for a second, "Let's give this one a try." She noticed they both started to smile, but her words stopped them, "I'll make the trip down there and do some digging, but no guarantees whether I take the case or not."

Mike nodded, his eyes wide. He looked at Flynn, "That's normal. Emily never commits to a case until she's there."

"How long of a drive is it?" Emily frowned.

Flynn answered before Mike, "About thirteen hours from Chicago, depending on how much you stop."

Emily nodded. "Okay. I'll go tomorrow. That will give me the rest of today to wrap things up here and pack." She glanced at Miner, "And play with my boy before I go." She glanced at Mike, "You'll stay here with Miner while I'm gone?"

"Sure. And I'll have Flynn on speed dial in case anything else comes up while you're there." Mike looked down at his laptop and then back at Emily, "I think you'll be glad you took the drive down there. Not that I'd want to speak for you," he said carefully, "but I think you'd feel bad if someone else disappeared and you hadn't taken a look at the case."

Emily shook her head, "Because I'm such the sensitive type, right?"

"I didn't say that!" Mike said, getting up from the table.

Emily turned to walk to the other end of the house to start preparing for her trip. "Not that you're right very often, Mike, but I think you might be correct in this case."

5

E arly the next morning, Ollie woke up, his back so stiff
he could hardly sit on the edge of the old bed he used
to share with Libby. He sat for quite a while, staring at
his feet, wishing he could still hear the pitter-patter of his twin
girls in the house, their footsteps crisscrossing from the kitchen
to the bathroom to the television and then up to see him. It had
been one of their rituals before he and Libby had divorced —
the girls would come running into his room and jump on him
while he was still sleeping, waking him up. What they didn't
know is that he was usually awake long before they arrived but
stayed in bed because he enjoyed playing with them so much.
He'd roll over slowly, growling like a lion, and then tickle each
of them until they ran off. Many times, Libby would be
standing in the doorway, leaning on the frame, a sweet smile
across her face. It all ended when she met Ned.

The pure joy of a new day wasn't part of his life anymore.
Hadn't been for years. It had been nine years since Libby left
him. It had happened as suddenly as a slap in the face. Ollie
had been at work one day and had come home, expecting to
find Libby in the kitchen and the girls watching television.

They were in kindergarten that year, five years old. Instead of the normal noise of a full house when he came in from working at the machine shop, there was silence.

Sitting on the edge of the bed, Ollie remembered that day. He walked into the kitchen looking around, his eye catching on something shiny on the kitchen table. It was Libby's wedding ring, a scrawled note underneath. "Ollie," the note started, "I've left with the girls. I'm sorry, I fell out of love with you a long time ago but have been trying to stay to keep us together as a family. It isn't working. I found someone else and have taken the girls with me so you don't have to worry about childcare. I'll be in touch to arrange for you to see them."

At the time, Ollie remembered how the words drained the life out of his body. He slumped into one of the kitchen chairs, staring at the words on the page as they blurred in front of him. Questions flew through his mind about how this had happened. When had Libby decided she didn't love him anymore? What about the girls? When would he see them again?

Curling and uncurling his toes on the floor as he sat on the edge of the bed reliving that day, Ollie realized Libby leaving had set off a cascade of events he was no longer in control of. Libby had promised to let him see the girls, but it had only happened one time two months after she left, as she and her new fiancé were getting ready to move to Edmonton, Canada. Now the girls were fourteen and Ollie wasn't sure he'd even recognize them.

Thinking back to the last time he saw Libby and the girls, it seemed like it was part of a dream. Ollie had met Libby and the girls at a gas station on the outskirts of town. The car they were driving was packed to the gills, boxes, and suitcases pressing up against the back windows of the minivan. Ollie didn't recognize the car. It must have belonged to Libby's lover. Ollie's interaction with Libby and the girls didn't last more than a couple of minutes. He'd tried in the couple of months she'd left to get her to talk to him, to get Libby to come home and start their life again. She wasn't having any of it, "I'm sorry Ollie but I just don't love you anymore. It's not fair to you or to the girls for me to be unhappy." Libby said it in a way that was so-matter- of-fact it didn't seem any more emotional than her telling him what they were going to have for dinner that night.

Standing outside of their minivan, all Ollie wanted to do was grab his girls and run, but they were strapped in tight, bags of snacks and drinks between the two of them. Libby's fiancé at least had the sense to go into the gas station store and pretend to buy some things while Ollie and Libby stood outside with their broken family. Though Ollie tried to remember what Libby said to him, the words escaped his memory. The only thing he had left was the blurry views of his girls and Libby, a broad smile painted on her face. He'd never seen her so happy.

A couple of minutes after the new fiancé walked into the gas station store, he came back out, baseball cap on his head, walking toward the minivan. Libby introduced them, "Ollie, this is my fiancé, Ned."

Ned wasn't as big as Ollie, but he was neatly dressed. In addition to the baseball cap, he had on a pair of nice jeans, work boots, and a short-sleeved plaid shirt. "Nice to meet you. Sorry, it's under these circumstances," he said.

Ollie fought every urge he had to pick the smaller man up and hurl him through the plate glass window of the gas station store. He knew it wouldn't get him any closer to Libby or his girls if he was sitting in jail for the rest of his life. The best he could do was manage a nod, so that's what he did.

An awkward silence fell across the threesome, the only noise was the rattle of a chip bag being opened in the back seat by one of the girls. After a minute, Libby looked at her watch. "Well, we'd best be going. It's a long drive into Canada. I'll send along our new contact information when we get there. We'll be staying with Ned's family while he gets settled in his new job."

As Ollie took a couple of steps back from the minivan, watching Ned and Libby get settled inside, he felt a tearing in his soul watching his family drive away without him. Edmonton was nearly the other side of the world as far as he was concerned, at least from Louisiana. The odds of him seeing Libby or his girls anytime soon shrunk as every second passed. He remembered standing in the gas station parking lot, his hands limp, feeling defeated, the face of Libby's new fiancé, Ned, burned in his mind.

Ollie pushed the thoughts back into a corner of his mind and stood up from the edge of the bed, leaving it unmade. He spent just a few minutes in the bathroom and got ready for work. Taking the steps downstairs slowly, waiting for the ache in his body to subside from working at the machine shop hunched over all day, he picked up his keys and wallet from the kitchen table and walked outside.

The new day had dawned pleasant, though still a little dark, hot and humid, not that the dampness in the air ever left Louisiana. The nearly constant humidity was a gift from living on the Gulf Coast. But, unlike the coastal areas, Tifton didn't get much of a breeze. As usual, the heavy air hung around Ollie and he swatted at a bug as he walked to the old work van parked in the driveway. It was white, with black lettering on the back that said: "New and Used Windows" with a phone number that wasn't Ollie's. He'd bought it secondhand from someone on the other side of town whose name he couldn't remember. He'd never taken the time to remove the lettering. It didn't matter. It was just him. Alone.

Starting the engine, Ollie pulled out of his driveway and drove down the road. There were no other houses in the area, not for a couple of miles. Once he got to the first paved street, he turned right and drove south. The urge for him to visit his next target was more than he could stand.

As he drove, he could feel the pain inside of him building, memories of Willow and Sage in his mind. He hadn't heard from Libby in a while, but as far as Ollie knew, she was still living in Edmonton with Ned. His mind turned and focused on Sage, her long brown hair grown almost to her waist, her little round cheeks and bright smile pressed through his memory. The more he thought about her, the more he hurt. Since they'd been gone, he'd only found one way to relieve the pain, at least temporarily. Though he didn't want to punish other people for the loss of his twins, the ache he felt inside of him was worse than the action he needed to take to relieve it. He gripped the steering wheel a little tighter. It was time to focus on Sage. What he needed to do might temporarily relieve the pain of losing her, but then the ache of losing Willow would come back. He knew it was a strange way to honor his girls each year, sacrificing a life for each of them, but it was the only way he could dull the pain. Memories of the girls cycled through his mind, tormenting him with their absence.

The headlights of the van cut through the dusky morning. Ollie didn't have a lot of time, just enough for a drive-by before work. The house he was looking for was small and white, perched up on posts in case of flooding. Pressure started to build inside Ollie's chest as he turned down the street, his heart beating a little faster. He noticed the street sign read Camelot Way. Kind of a strange name for a street in Louisiana, he thought to himself.

He'd spotted the little girl a month before at the drug store with her parents. They were standing at the pharmacy, a young woman helping them. "Prescription for Lexi Cooper?" the woman called. Ollie noticed the little girl, her beautiful blonde hair cascading down her back, just like Sage's did. It was at that moment he knew. He'd been waiting for the right time and it was almost here.

The dusk hanging over Tifton had caused the people living in the little white house to flip on two bright front porch lights. As Ollie pulled down the street, he noticed them right away, and that the garage door was open. Standing down by the street was a man and a little girl. She had her hair in pigtails with a pink backpack strapped over her shoulders. Ollie didn't realize that school had started. He'd lost track of school days and holidays without the girls. Ollie stopped the van a few houses down, watching. The little girl bounced around, twirling, her father laughing and smiling even at the early hour of the morning. Ollie licked his lips, leaning forward, practically resting his chest on the steering wheel. He remembered when Willow and Sage were that age. When Libby had taken them, the girls had barely started kindergarten. "Sage had a backpack like that," he whispered to no one in particular. He knew he couldn't trust his memory, but he thought that Sage had a pink backpack and Willow had a purple one for their first year of school. All the pinks and purples had left his house when Willow and Sage moved away with their mom. Everything that was left in Ollie's life was drab and gray.

Headlights in Ollie's rearview mirror startled him, and he sat straight upright in his seat, wondering who was coming down the road. To anyone else, it would look like he was just a repairman waiting to start a job somewhere on that street that morning, but Ollie knew better. Glancing in the rearview mirror, he saw the headlights were higher than usual, ones from a school bus. Sighing, Ollie leaned back in the chair, watching as the father smiled at the little girl and hugged her, nearly following her onto the school bus as she carried the backpack that was almost as big as she was. With a wave, the dad stepped back from the bus, the doors closing. He stayed in his spot as it pulled away, blowing a kiss to his daughter.

The fury and pain built inside of Ollie. He watched the man walk back up the driveway and go into his house. The garage door and front lights stayed on. A few minutes later, a car backed out of the garage slowly, the man behind the wheel. Ollie squinted at him, wondering where he was going. Work would be the logical guess. As the car idled in the driveway, the man looked down, his face illuminated by the glow from a cell phone screen. A second later, the front door opened, the figure of a woman silhouetted by the bright lights left on next to the front door. She was wearing running shorts and a tank top, her hair pulled up in a high ponytail. She had a striking resemblance to the little girl who left just a few minutes before. In her hand, she had something. It was too far away to see what it was. Barefoot, she ran down the front walk to the car. The man rolled down the window, a smile on his face. The woman handed whatever she had found for him into the car, leaning over and kissing him on the mouth before he left. Walking quickly, the woman passed across the front of the house, pausing for a minute at the bottom of the steps to wave at the man who was pulling out of the driveway, the garage door sliding closed. The woman went up the steps, her hips swaying, the door to the house closing behind her and the front lights going dark.

There was nothing else to see. Ollie leaned back in the driver's seat for a moment, waiting for the pain in his body to subside. The pain from losing his girls was like a knife cutting him over and over again, knowing that somewhere, they were living a new life with their mother and Ned. Fury rose inside of him. His family used to be like the one he'd just seen — the excitement of kids going off to school, smiles from the parents, evening dinners talking about how everyone's day went. That wasn't his life anymore. Thinking about it made Ollie's whole body ache in a nearly indescribable way. Over the years, the pain that started in his heart had become visceral, his muscles tight as if fighting against the life he was living.

Ollie turned the key in the ignition of the van, putting it into gear and slowly creeping away. There was no reason to alert any of the neighbors of his presence, though there weren't many houses on the street that anyone would even notice. Putting his foot on the gas, he gave the van a little goose, letting it slide slowly down the road and away before the sun was fully up.

THE REST of the day went as could be expected. Frustrated from work, Ollie drove home exhausted. As he walked in the back door, the musty smell of a house that needed to be cleaned filled his nostrils. He went to the cabinet and pulled out a can of soup, and poured it into a pot to heat. He stood by the stove watching it, waiting for tiny bubbles to form at the edge before taking it off the burner. Leaning over, Ollie pulled the spoon out of a drawer next to the stove, used a potholder to pick up the pan, and set it down on the table. He ate right out of the pot, the lukewarm soup filling a little of the hole in his stomach. He didn't even bother to take off his work boots.

As soon as he finished eating, Ollie ran water in the pot and left it in the sink. He had other things that were more important to do than worry about dishes.

The house he lived in didn't have a long hallway, just a stumpy corridor at the intersection of where the family room, kitchen, and stairwell met. The door to the cellar was at one end, locked, a heavy phalange and padlock preventing anyone from going down or coming up. From his pocket, Ollie pulled out a ring of keys. It was the same keyring that had his van keys and house keys on it. He never left the cellar key at home. It was always with him, a reminder of the secrets he had. Fumbling with the key for a minute, Ollie finally jammed it in the lock, his hands shaking. Without giving it much more thought, he pulled the padlock off the door and reached for the first string that lit the bulb at the top of the steps, the rough wood creaking under his feet as he went downstairs. Pulling the string for the bulb at the bottom of the stairs, it cast a dim, murky light over the cellar.

Ollie stood at the bottom of the steps for a minute, taking heavy breaths. His chest felt like his heart might explode. The pain was so intense he wondered if he was having a heart attack. Walking over to the workbench, he ran his fingers over the tools assembled on the surface. His mind and body began to calm, just the touch of the hunting knife and saws helping him to remember the solution to all of his problems. Ollie leaned over the workbench, carefully picking up each one of the implements and setting them in order. From underneath the top of the bench, he reached for a dirty rag and a bottle of oil. From working in a machine shop, he knew that keeping his tools clean and sharp was the best way to get his project done efficiently. Ollie took the rag in his hand and wiped each one carefully, checking to make sure that each tool was in good working order. The last thing he wanted to do was be in the middle of his project and have to stop and repair a tool. That very thing had happened a few years before, the blade on one of his saws breaking in the middle of removing a leg. He had to go upstairs and out to the garage to get a new blade. By the time he went back downstairs, it was as if the magic of the moment had disappeared. He finished his project as usual, but it wasn't the same. It didn't remove the pain. Remembering what'd happened before, he always checked his tools and made sure he had extra parts handy just in case he needed them without having to leave the cellar. It all had to happen there. To stay there in the dark and the damp. That was the only way to relieve the pain and remember his girls.

After wiping each tool carefully, a dull shine from the oil

glowing in the dim light, Ollie sat down in the tattered green chair, wiping his hands on the dirty rag. He rested his hands on his knees and stared forward, his eyes darting from the tool bench to the chair bolted in the corner, and to the calendar on the wall. The time was coming, he could feel it in his chest. "This is for you, Sage..." he whispered.

6

Emily was just about done packing when Mike came up to her room. "Okay for me to come in?" Emily nodded.

"What's up?" she said, zipping her black duffel bag closed. Inside, she had a few basic changes of clothes, clean jeans and shirts, fresh pairs of socks, and her toiletries. She even included a couple of pairs of shorts in case she needed them, though she usually only wore them when she was heading back from a case.

"I know me and Flynn, we kind of pushed you on this case. Sorry about that. I thought about it and I know it's not my place."

Emily raised her eyebrows. After the issues she and Mike had on their last case — Mike accusing her of being disloyal, stealing Miner and taking him to his off-the-grid cabin — the trust between them was almost repaired. Almost. The fact that Mike was coming to her with something of an apology told her the therapy was helping. Having a girlfriend probably didn't hurt either, Emily thought. "It's okay. I don't know how many more of these cases I'm going to do, but there's nothing wrong with looking at a new way to approach them." She stood up, walking into the bathroom, checking to make sure she'd packed everything, and then came back out, Mike still leaning in the doorway. "What you and Flynn said was correct. There are lots of cases out there that need justice, but there aren't many people who know I'm available to help." Emily picked up her duffel bag and slung it over her shoulder. She turned towards Mike, "Like I said, I don't know how many more cases I'm going to do, but if I am, I need to be open to doing them in more than one way."

Mike stared at her for a second, "Thanks for that, I think."

"What does that mean?" Emily said, starting for the door, passing him as she walked down the steps to the first floor.

"Well, I didn't expect you to be so flexible. Thanks."

Emily shook her head and smiled. "Listen, you aren't the only one who has to learn some new things. I do, too." Miner met the two of them at the bottom of the steps, his round eyes staring at them, the tip of his pink tongue sticking out.

Walking into the kitchen, Emily set her duffel bag off to the side, picked up her laptop and the charging cable, and stuffed it into a matching backpack, along with her cell phone charger, a notebook, and a couple of pens. From the kitchen drawer, she pulled out her Sig Sauer pistol, checked to make sure it was loaded and set it next to her backpack along with two extra already-filled magazines and a couple of boxes of ammunition. There was more ammo in the truck, but it was hard to be too careful. Trouble could come at any time. She wanted to be prepared.

A rattle at the back door sent Miner scurrying, his hackles up and his ears pricked. All of the people in and out of the house over the last couple of days, even though it was just the addition of Flynn, had put her dog on edge. Emily called to him, "Easy, boy." For a moment, Emily thought about telling Mike she wasn't going to go. She could stay in Chicago, go to her boxing classes with Clarence, and get back to living her life. As Flynn walked in the back door, Emily sighed, a wave of fear almost stopping her. She hoped this wasn't the trip she didn't come home from.

"You're here early," Mike said.

"Well, I wanted to see Emily off and say hello to my new friend Miner." Flynn knelt, but Miner turned away, only offering a short growl.

"I think he knows his mom is headed out for a trip. He doesn't like those black bags, that's for sure," Mike said, shrugging. He bent over, catching the dog as he walked by, "But, we'll have fun together, won't we? Us and Uncle Flynn."

"Uncle Flynn?" Emily said, sticking her wallet and cell phone in her backpack.

Mike shrugged, "It seemed like a good idea when I said it, I guess."

Although Emily could have stood around and joked with the guys for another half hour or so, she knew there was a long drive ahead of her, due south, to Louisiana. The truck was gassed and ready. Emily took one last pass through both of her bags, making sure she had everything she might need. Her rifle, more ammunition, and an extensive first-aid kit were in the truck already.

Zipping the bags closed, Emily looked at the two young men standing in her kitchen. "Anything else I should know before I head out?"

Flynn rustled through a plastic bag he'd brought with him and then handed it to Emily. "I stopped and got you some protein bars for the trip. In case you can't find a place to eat, you know."

Emily smiled. Mike's new friend was sweet, in an awkward

kind of way. "Thank you," she said, taking the bag from him. Emily stuffed it inside of her backpack. "I'm sure these will come in handy at some point." Emily reached around her back, pulling her long black ponytail around the side of her shoulder. It was a habit, nothing more, one that signaled she was thinking. "Mike, any tech gear I need to take with me?"

Mike shook his head no and handed her a small black bag, "Just take this. It's a bag of goodies. Just in case, you know. Might give us more options if we need them. You should have no problems while you're down there. Flynn and I will stay here, monitoring you and the situation, as well as news out of Louisiana. If anything changes, I'll let you know."

With that, Emily knew it was time to go. Not one for extensive goodbyes, she squatted down and gave Miner a good scratch behind his ears, running her fingers over the white spot on the top of his forehead — the one mark all cattle dogs had in common, the Bentley. She felt his warmth under her fingers and whispered in his ear, "I'll be back soon. Take care of Mike and Uncle Flynn, okay?" The dog wagged as she stood up. Emily grabbed her bag and her backpack and walked out the door, giving the guys a little wave. Turning back for just a second, Emily said, "Mike, take good care of Miner. I look forward to seeing both of you here when I get home."

The color drained from Mike's face, the realization that Emily was calling him out on making sure that her home and her dog were exactly where she left them when she got back, unlike their last case. Sure, she thought to herself, I trust him, but he's also human.

Shutting the door behind her, Emily walked out to the truck. For the drive, she decided to wear jeans and tennis shoes, with a tank top and a flannel shirt over top. Although it was summer, once she got the air conditioning going in the truck, she always felt cold. Emily opened the back door and threw her bag in, settling her backpack on the front seat next to her. She pulled the passenger side seat belt over and clipped it, securing her backpack. It would prevent the bag from falling over while she was driving and also save her the annoyance of the seat belt warning bell from pinging the entire way between Chicago and Tifton.

The first few hours of the drive went by quickly, Emily enjoying watching the city melt away behind her, plunging the truck headfirst into the heartland. She passed miles and miles of corn, soybeans, and wheat, pastures filled with cows and sheep and horses. Emily lost count of the number of dilapidated, abandoned barns near the interstate. A calm passed over her as she started to drive. The calm before the storm, maybe, she wondered.

The temperature on her truck's thermostat steadily climbed the further south she drove. About seven hours into her drive, Emily stopped for the second time, taking a few minutes to stretch her legs and get something to eat at a local fast-food place along the highway. When she traveled, she didn't like to drift too far off her route. She wasn't on a sightseeing trip, so taking the time to stop to go shopping or find a gourmet eatery wasn't on her agenda. Maybe if I was still married to Luca, she thought. Then again, if she was still married to Luca, she probably wouldn't be going to Tifton, but rather home with him and maybe a family. Getting back in the truck, her phone rang. It was Mike.

"How's the drive going?"

Emily started the truck, putting it into gear. As she pulled out of the parking lot and merged back onto the highway, she said, "Good. My GPS says I'm five hours out. How are things at home?"

"Fine. Miner and I went for a walk and we stopped at Carl's on the way back. Miner is laying down. I think he may have eaten too much sausage."

Emily shook her head. Sammy's Butcher Shop was one of

her favorite places to go. Carl, the owner, loved Miner so Emily usually went in the back door and hung out in his office instead of going in the front door. Dogs and the health department didn't always get along. Carl would show up a couple of minutes later, his hand filled with dried sausage. Miner loved it and loved the attention from the big man as well. "Well, at least I don't have to clean up the puke," Emily said, wondering how much sausage Miner had eaten. It seemed strange to her to be talking about the normal things of life. She was driving headlong into a city that very well could be looking at the abduction and killing of yet another person in the next few days. Silence settled between her and Mike for a minute.

"Emily, you okay? Did I lose you?"

She sighed, "No. I'm here. Just thinking. Any updates from Tifton?" It made her feel better to focus on the case at hand. Her life at home was behind her, at least for the moment. There would be time for her to do the things she loved to do, but right now she was on a case. Focus, she thought. Staying focused might be the only way for her to return home alive.

"No, nothing significant. Flynn found an article from the local paper that noted we are five months and twenty-four days past the last killing. There's also been a little chatter on the forums about the timing."

Knowing that the Tifton torso killer was coming up on another deadline made Emily's stomach churn. Would he strike again? Would Emily be able to concentrate on the cold cases? "Is there any speculation on whether he'll take someone again?" she asked. Although she knew neither Mike nor Flynn could answer the question for her, hearing some other voices after so many hours on the road helped to pass the time.

"No idea," Mike said. "Flynn's been monitoring the forums. There's nothing that's changed in the last few months to suggest there either would be another killing or not."

"Any community deaths in the last six months? Have you

guys looked at that?" Emily shifted in her seat, her back getting tight from sitting for so long.

"What do you mean?"

"Well, if I were profiling the person who's chopping people up, I'd say he's male, somewhere between the age of thirty and sixty, probably a longtime resident of the area, with a mediocre job and not much education. Could be somebody well-known in the community, or maybe not. If the guy died, there might not be another abduction. Did you check the obituaries?"

"I haven't, but that's a good idea. Let me look into that and get back to you. Oh, by the way, there's not a hotel in Tifton. Just a bed-and-breakfast. I made you a reservation."

As they hung up, Emily tried to imagine what a bed-and-breakfast in Tifton, Louisiana might look like. Quaint, with decor that probably looked a lot like the things her grandmother used to have in her house on the other side of Chicago — maybe lace curtains with some dusty figurines sitting on display shelves. Emily frowned, shifting in her seat. Though she appreciated the reservation, it might be that she spent the trip sleeping in her truck. At least it was clean.

With five hours of driving still ahead of her, her mind wandered. It seemed like every few miles, the memory of Lou Gonzales, her partner in the cold case division, snapping the handcuffs around her wrists popped up. Now that some time had passed, and she'd made contact with him, she knew it'd been hard on him as well. Her last case was based in Chicago, which was something she normally didn't do. Out of town was better, but because her last case was in her area, she needed some help. What she got from Lou restored their relationship to at least speaking, which was better than it was before. Emily stretched her neck left and right, trying to get the kinks out of it. Maybe solving these cold cases wasn't the best idea, she thought. A knot formed in her stomach. She knew she could turn the truck around at the next off-ramp and head right back to Chicago. She could go back to taking Miner on his walks and stopping at Sammy's Butcher Shop and get in the ring for her boxing lessons with Clarence. Watching another field of corn go by — one of about a million she'd passed in the last seven hours — she considered it, the muscles of her hands nearly pulling the truck onto an exit. It would be easy. Flynn could send a message to Bradley and no one would be the wiser. After all, this was a problem for Louisiana law enforcement to solve, not her.

The thought settled across crossed her uncomfortably, as though it was too tight a fit. Sure, she loved her life at home, but did she want to spend the rest of her days just collecting the five thousand dollars in cash out of her mailbox? Emily felt herself wrestling, the pull to go home just as strong as the pull to do something with her life. Doing something with her life had cost her, and dearly. Trying to get away from the thought, Emily fussed with the radio, looking for a new station. It seemed like every couple hundred miles, the radio would fade out and she'd have to find new music. Even though she was fussing with the radio, trying to distract herself, the question lingered in her thoughts: Was the risk of solving these cases actually worth it?

ABOUT AN HOUR OUT OF TIFTON, Mike called again. Emily hadn't stopped, except to get gas, for the last few hours. The truck had been on a steady downward slope toward the ocean and the flatlands that marked the bayous of Louisiana. "I see you are about an hour out," he said, a bounce to his voice.

"Yep," she paused. "You sound happy," Emily said with more than a hint of sarcasm. All the driving was exhausting, even though the only thing she was doing was sitting behind the wheel.

"Well, you know me. Always chipper and happy!" Mike said, matching her sarcasm.

"I'm assuming you're calling with some news?" Emily grunted. No matter how cheerful Mike felt, Emily's mood declined. She was an hour outside of Tifton and still felt a strong urge to wheel the truck around in a U-turn and head right back to Chicago. What was the problem? Why was she so unsure about this case? She blinked, trying to focus on Mike.

"I researched the local obituaries like you suggested."

"And?"

"Nothing doing. I checked through all the notices over the last six months, figuring there was no point in searching earlier than that. We know the last body was dropped almost exactly six months ago, a man named Gerald Wexner. Since that time, there haven't been any significant deaths in the Tifton area."

"Did you check surrounding areas?"

"I thought you might ask me that, so I did. Nothing there either. I'm guessing, though, that the person you're looking for is probably in Tifton. I mean, everyone he's killed is a resident of the Parish. Maybe this is some weird vendetta against the town? Is that possible?"

"Anything is possible," Emily said. "There's never just one reason people get killed, that's for sure. Tell me about this Gerald Wexner."

There was a pause for a second, as though Mike was looking for something. A moment later, he came back on the line, "I think Flynn will be able to give you more information later. We figured we could conference call tonight after you get settled at the bed-and-breakfast."

Emily grunted again, the idea of staying in a dusty bed-and-breakfast with a lumpy bed not sounding any better than sleeping in the back seat of her truck. "Okay, but do you know anything about Gerald Wexner you can tell me now?"

"Sure. Guy was in his late thirties. Single. Worked in

construction but was out of town a lot according to the article I read about him. He'd leave to go take care of hurricane damage in the area. According to the articles I read, he'd come home from working a job in Texas about two weeks before his disappearance. Was at a bar late at night — that was the last time he was seen — and then disappeared. His torso was found a couple of days later in the Little Bayou Pond, just like the others."

The whole story made Emily's skin crawl. It wasn't so much the history of the people that disappeared, but the way they were found -- chunks of flesh discarded in the water. "Any other information on why this guy cuts his victims up?"

"I think Flynn will give you more background when we talk in a couple of hours. He had to go take care of a few things for work, but he should be back here about the time you get settled. Sound okay?"

Emily nodded to no one in particular. It wasn't as if Mike could see her. "Yeah, that sounds okay. I'm almost there. I'll text you once I get checked in."

Mike chuckled on the other end of the line, "Well, you can, but I can see exactly where you are. I'm trying out some new toys on this case."

Emily shook her head and sighed. Mike and his tech toys. "Sounds good. Stay in touch."

As Emily hung up with Mike, the truck seemed to plateau after spending a few hours descending toward the Gulf Coast. Like many of the southern states, the northern portion of Louisiana was much different in topography than the southern portion. The southern edge of the state is what made it famous, from the jazz bars in New Orleans to the massive hurricanes — including Hurricane Katrina — which could create billions of dollars in damage in just a day or so, forcing the antiquated levee system to try to deal with the rush of waters up out of the Gulf.

Emily had only been in Louisiana one other time. It was with Luca. They'd traveled there together so he could attend an architectural conference. While he was in his seminars, Emily walked the streets of New Orleans, stopping for a beignet and a coffee and watching the people stroll by.

Tifton was an entirely different kind of city, Emily noticed as she passed the signs for the parish. There was low-hanging scrub near the edge of the road, the woods crowded and heavy with the moisture from the tropical winds encouraging the trees to grow dense and twisted together. The road narrowed in front of her, a small area carved out where a tiny house sat. Dense woods quickly took over the area again as she drove, leading to another small carved-out area for another tiny house.

The GPS on Emily's truck beeped, warning her that she was only a mile out from the bed-and-breakfast. She frowned. Although she'd programmed her GPS for the center of Tifton, somehow Mike had been able to log in and change her destination. On the right, Emily saw a small school and the Tifton General Store. She almost laughed. What kind of city still had a general store?

As Emily glanced left and right, trying to get her bearings on the little city that had popped up virtually out of nowhere, she realized the most startling feature of the parish was the amount of foliage. She had honestly never seen such dense woods in her life. Maybe it was the Gulf Coast heat and humidity, she wondered, making the turn into a narrow driveway just off the road into the bed-and-breakfast. Emily looked at the building as she pulled past it, finding a parking spot in the back.

The Tifton Center B & B was a sprawling, white clapboard house with black louvered shutters, a wide porch across the entire front, dotted with the shadows of chairs Emily could see in the dusk. The sun had begun to set, leaving Tifton in an orange glow.

As Emily got out of her truck, she stretched, grateful to be done sitting, at least for now. The heavy, thick Louisiana air covered her before she barely had time to take a breath. It was hot. Hotter and more humid than she'd expected.

Droplets of sweat forming on her brow, Emily started walking around the front of the building, taking in her surroundings, brushing off a bug that landed on her arm. The back of the house was just as neat as the front, the rough-hewn foundation painted a bright white, pots of flowers and vines placed carefully around the perimeter of the house. Emily glanced up, noticing it was three stories with what looked to be an attic at the top. "I hope I'm not in the attic," she mumbled. "With my luck, that's where my room will be."

Emily left her bags in the car, still not sure she wanted to stay at the bed-and-breakfast. She worried they would hover over her. That was the last thing she wanted while she was on a case. Anonymity was her friend. Walking around the side of the house, Emily approached the front, climbing five wooden steps onto the porch. There was a screen door off to the right. She pulled it open, giving the interior door, one with a long oval etched glass window in it, a push open.

As her eyes adjusted, she saw a small check-in desk off to the right, much like what was at a full-service hotel, just on a smaller scale. A young woman was standing behind it, probably someone about Mike's age, Emily guessed. "Good evening. Are you checking in?"

Emily nodded.

Before Emily could offer anything else, the woman interrupted, "Are you Emily Miner?"

Emily tilted her head to the side and nodded again, not sure what to say.

The woman smiled. "Your assistant called about ten

minutes ago to let us know you were almost here so we could have everything ready for you. Welcome," she said, "Let me show you to your room. Did you bring your bags in?"

Mike. He must've made the reservation under somewhat of an alias and then called them to let them know Emily was about to arrive. She'd have to talk to him about that. Not sure if she wanted that kind of help. It seemed a little creepy.

As Emily followed the young woman, she took a look around. The Tifton Center B & B was way more professionally run than Emily expected, with updated decor and the smell of cleaning products in the air. Emily couldn't imagine how they survived. It wasn't as though there was a lot of vacation traffic in the area. Tifton was too far away from main cities like New Orleans and Baton Rouge for that. The only thing they had to offer was the regular killings.

As soon as she thought about it, she realized that was it. The killings. Every six months, a flood of law enforcement would arrive in Tifton, with nowhere to stay, except the Tifton Center B & B. Emily almost laughed out loud at the clever nature of the business. With government expense accounts, the bed-and-breakfast owners could practically charge the Feds any rate and it would be covered. With the regularity of the killings, the owners were virtually guaranteed a surge of income every six months.

But that might change if Emily was successful. If...

The young woman Emily was following pointed out some of the amenities as they walked to her room, "Over here to the left, this is our dining room. We serve breakfast starting at six o'clock and keep it open until ten every day. I think you'll enjoy it. Everything's homemade and if you have any special requests, we will be sure to take care of them."

Emily hadn't noticed the woman's heavy southern drawl as she was so lost in her own thoughts, but it was there. This is definitely the deep South, Emily thought, suddenly feeling like a fish out of water. A tingle began to creep up her spine. She'd have to be careful. A northerner would stick out like a sore thumb in the small town. The only advantage she had was the town was used to getting outsiders in every six months to investigate the newest killing.

As the young woman led Emily up a wide set of stairs, she said, "You'll have a private room at the end of this hallway. It has a lovely, attached bathroom I think you'll enjoy," she said, sticking the key card in the slot. Emily was surprised by that. Most bed-and-breakfasts weren't as updated in terms of technology enough to use programmable key cards.

The young woman pushed the door open and flipped a light switch to the right of the door frame. A gentle yellow glow bathed the room. Straight ahead, there was a large king-size bed, covered in white linens with a blue afghan folded neatly over the foot of the bed. The young woman reached around to the right, "The bathroom is in here," she said, flipping on the light. Emily looked in, seeing a clawfoot tub and a shower in the corner.

The woman stopped in front of her, handing her the key card, "Is there anything else I can do for you? Would you like me to send someone out to get the bags out of your car?"

"No, that won't be necessary. I'll take care of it." As the young woman turned to walk away, Emily stopped her. "Does the key card work on the front door of the building as well?"

The young woman nodded, "Yes. It will be locked unless there is someone at the front door waiting to meet a guest."

"Okay, thank you."

As the door closed behind the young woman, Emily had the first chance to take a look at her surroundings without a tour guide. She walked over to the windows on either side of the bed, pulling the curtain back enough to peek outside. From her room, she had a good view of the truck. Directly below her room, there was a line of dumpsters. What was below was always good to know in case she needed to make a quick escape. Better to jump down and land on the lid of a dumpster than try to jump the entire way from the second floor without something to break her fall. Emily sighed, hoping her trip to Tifton wasn't that kind of case.

Turning back to the room, Emily noticed the air-conditioning was blowing gently, keeping cool, dry air circulating. Nodding to herself, Emily realized she was surprised. The bed-and-breakfast was nothing like she expected. In addition to the bed, there was a small desk in the room, information on their Wi-Fi, and a big-screen TV mounted to the wall. The bathroom had fluffy white towels and bottles of shampoo, conditioner, and small bars of soap. "This might change my mind about bed-and-breakfasts," she muttered to herself, pushing the key card into a pocket in the back of her jeans.

As soon as Emily stepped outside, the heat and humidity assaulted her again. She was still wearing the jeans, tank top, and flannel shirt she'd put on early that morning when she left Chicago. It had only been a thirteen-hour drive, but she felt like she was a world away. As soon as she got to the truck, she stopped for a second, stripping off the flannel shirt and tying it around her waist. From inside the backseat, she grabbed her duffel bag, slinging it over her shoulder, and then reached to the front, unclipping her backpack from the front seat.

As she slammed the door to the truck, she realized she was starving. Though she wasn't sure how long her hunger would last in the heat and humidity, she lugged her bags back inside the front door where the young woman was still standing, working on a laptop. "Are there any restaurants around here? Any delivery services? I haven't eaten in hours."

The young woman looked up. Emily noticed she had a name badge that said Heather. "I'd be more than happy to get a sandwich from our kitchen for you if you'd like, or there's a pretty good Mexican place down the road that delivers. Or, if you want to drive, I could recommend a place that has the best gumbo in the area."

"The sandwich would be fine if you don't mind. You can add it to my bill."

"Yes, ma'am. I'll have it up to your room in ten minutes."

Emily nodded and walked up the steps to her room, sliding that key card in closing the door. Exactly eight minutes later, there was a rap on the door. "Miss Emily? It's Heather from downstairs," a voice called from the hallway.

Emily checked through the peephole before opening the door. It was a habit, probably not one she needed right now in Tifton, but helpful anyway. Heather was standing at the door, carrying a wicker tray with a sandwich and a bag of chips on it.

"I hope a BLT is all right? I added some chips and a cookie just in case you needed it." From underneath her arm, she offered Emily a bottle of water. "A long trip can be dehydrating. Is there anything else I can get you?"

"No, thank you. That will do it," Emily said.

Emily bumped the door closed with her hip. She heard it click behind her. Carrying the tray, she walked over to a small table and set it down. There wasn't a good place to eat in the room, so Emily picked up the plate and sat on the bed, leaning against the headboard and folding her legs underneath her. The remote for the television was on the nightstand next to the bed. She clicked it on to watch the news. Weather, sports, some international stories... there was nothing about Tifton, at least not yet.

Emily tasted the sandwich. Surprisingly, it was good, the bacon salty against the sweetness of the tomatoes. The little bag of chips rattled as she pulled it open, popping one in her mouth, the potatoes crunching and sharp against her tongue as she chewed. Emily took a swig of water from a bottle she brought up to the room and glanced toward the window for a second. Getting up off the bed, she walked back to the door and bolted it from the inside. Knowing that time was ticking before the next person was taken sent a shiver up her spine. No reason to take any chances, she thought, trying to reassure herself that the Tifton torso killer had only killed people from the parish over the last seven years. Emily didn't fit that profile, but for some reason, it didn't make her feel any better. Curling back up on the bed, she tried to take another bite of her sandwich, but it ended up feeling dry and lumpy in her throat. Just as she was pushing it away, her phone chirped. It was Mike. "Getting settled in?" the text read.

"Yes."

"Have time for a call with me and Flynn?"

"Sure. Let me get my computer out. Give me two minutes." Emily slid off the bed and grabbed her backpack. From inside, she pulled her laptop and the charging cable out, setting it up on the bed. She took another sip of water while she waited. The urge to get right back in her truck and head home was strong, stronger than it had ever been on any other case. I wonder why, she thought, trying to look at her surge of feelings objectively. The fear came back even more strongly, erasing the option to try to make sense of it. Before Emily could get lost in thought again, her computer beeped, some secret encrypted video conferencing software Mike had installed on her computer automatically opening on the screen. For a second, Emily almost laughed, thinking about the fact that most people used any commercial-grade video conferencing. Not Mike. He had to use a version that was the super sleuth variety.

As the call connected, Mike and Flynn's faces appeared, Mike in front and Flynn standing behind. "How was the drive?" Mike asked, his face almost taking up the entire screen.

"Long. You know how it goes." Although Emily certainly could have flown down to Louisiana and rented a car, there was something about the secretive nature of her work that prevented her from doing so. Having the option to just get in her truck and leave whenever she wanted to, night or day, gave her some comfort. There was nothing worse than having to travel back to the airport, drop off a car, check luggage and then wait forever just to board the plane and fly home. At least with her truck, Emily had some freedom. "What's going on at home?" Just asking raised a wave of sadness in her.

"Same old, same old. You know, nothing new. Flynn and I spent the day digging through some cases we thought might be helpful for you."

Emily nodded, "Okay, tell me what you've got."

Mike waved to Flynn, who pulled up a chair next to Mike, or at least that's what it looked like to Emily. Their heads were close together on the screen, like strange twins. Flynn started first, "Well, one thing to know is that torso killers are not unique. I mean, Tifton isn't the first time that a serial killer has gone about dismembering bodies. It's pretty normal."

"How that is normal, I'm not sure," Emily grunted.

"Well, I don't mean normal, normal. I mean it's a common practice for serial killers. I have a couple of examples for you. Recently, a torso that was discovered in 1979 in California has just been identified. How they managed to keep the tissue intact, I'm not sure..."

Mike glanced at Flynn, "That would be a good question for Alice."

Emily nodded. With her degree in molecular genetics, Mike's girlfriend was exactly the right person to ask, but it wasn't something she needed to solve the case in Tifton. "Keep going," she said, realizing trying to keep Mike and Flynn on track was going to be a challenge.

"Sure. Anyway, this torso pops up in 1979 in California and sat for decades. Nobody could figure out what happened. Before DNA identification, having no facial features or finger-prints made it nearly impossible for law enforcement to figure out exactly who the victim was. If you think about it, a body that's only a torso doesn't say much, unless there are scars or something like that. And it's fairly common for torso killers to put their victims in the water."

Scowling, Emily said, "Why's that?" The idea that torso killers would leave their bodies in water as a common practice seemed strange.

Flynn shook his head, "Honestly, I've got no idea, but what I can tell you is in doing a review of the cases over the last one hundred and fifty years, it's a common theme. Not always, but frequently. That particular case in California led the police back to the woman's husband. Bad marriage, apparently. Another famous case is a torso killer in Cleveland. That case was in the mid-1930s. Happened all in one neighborhood. That one is still unsolved. The police kept finding torsos of men in the neighborhood, but never figured out who did it."

The idea that torso killers were fairly common surprised Emily. She wondered why there was no mention of that in her police academy training, although she didn't have specialized training like she would've gotten at the FBI's Quantico Academy. "What else do I need to know about the case here, in Tifton?" Emily said, looking at Flynn.

"The torso killer in Tifton has been at it for roughly seven years. I say roughly because in many cases, killers have initial victims that investigators never find and never connect to the case. It could be animals or other people they practice on, for lack of a better phrase, as they hone their craft." Flynn shifted in his seat, "Sorry, that sounded a little gruesome, but I hope you get my drift."

Emily nodded, "I get it. Keep going."

Flynn smiled a little, "Whoever the Tifton torso killer is has a very specific schedule, as we discussed — every six months. Why that is, law enforcement hasn't been able to figure out, though it's not for lack of trying. Based on the information in the online forums, the torso killer seems to have somewhat of a profile, but it's not as narrow as many other serial killers."

That was curious to Emily, "The Tifton killer doesn't have a type?"

Flynn cocked his head to the side, "It's hard to say. First of all, we don't know for a fact that the Tifton killer is male, although as we discussed, it's likely. I mean, think about it. Chopping a leg off of a person isn't exactly an easy job. Even surgeons use power tools."

Emily's mind flashed to a story she'd seen on television months before, profiling the life of an orthopedic surgeon. What most people didn't know was that orthopedic surgery was the bloodiest of all the subspecialties. The noises from the operating room sounded more like a mechanics shop than a hospital. She remembered the image of the surgeon on television. He didn't have normal surgical scrubs on. He was dressed more like a butcher, a long waterproof smock over the top of his scrubs plus knee-high gaiters over his shoes and pants. Emily tried to shake the thought from her mind. "Yeah, I know what you mean. So, what you're saying is you think, based on the size of the project, if you could call it that, it's most likely a man?" Although Emily agreed, she wanted to hear Flynn's opinion. After all, according to Mike, he was the torso killer expert, at least in Mike's mind, for whatever that was worth.

"I had the same question and wondered if you would, too. Mike gave me a hand and we accessed the medical examiner's reports for the torso killings in Tifton. Knowing what we are up against, I thought it would be good to make sure I have all my ducks in a row." He shifted in his seat a little and looked away for a second, as though he was checking something on his laptop. Clearing his throat, he said, "Based on what Mike and I were able to find, the medical examiner reported that the cut marks, or what he could see of them, didn't look to be from a power tool. That's an important point because the sheer amount of strength it would take to remove five different appendages — two legs, two arms, and a neck and head — is a physically exhausting process. Not to be gross, but you'd have to cut through skin, flesh, and muscle before you got to the bone and the flesh on the other side. I'm just tired thinking about it!"

Emily shook her head. She sighed and glanced at the abandoned tray of food next to her. Talking about dismembering a body certainly didn't do anything for her appetite. She pushed the half-eaten sandwich aside but managed to take another sip of water, hoping it would settle her stomach. "All of that said, you believe it's a male that's doing the killings?"

Flynn nodded. "Definitely. And there's something about the timing. Something happened in this man's life that causes him to relive it every six months. Why? I don't know. I'm not sure anyone does. The other option is that law enforcement does but hasn't revealed it yet while they try to catch him."

"Were you able to find out anything about the location where he drops the bodies?" Emily remembered Mike had mentioned a pond, but it would be good to confirm the information.

"Yes, the Little Bayou Pond." The screen flashed for a second, Mike pulling up a map with a star on it. Mike and Flynn had prepared for the call with Emily like they were giving a sales presentation. In some respects, Emily thought it was cute. She just hoped the information was accurate. Her life might depend upon it. Mike continued, "In each of the cases where local law enforcement has recovered a torso, it's been left at the same pond. The first one was found floating."

"Floating?"

Flynn's face emerged on the screen again, "Yes. The first body belonged to Corey Hawkins. According to the case file, he'd been reported missing and gone for about three days when a fisherman went out onto the pond and saw something floating in the middle of it. I guess it took him a minute to figure out what it was and then he called for help. The notes in the case file said the fishermen mentioned the torso was so mangled it was hard to tell if it was human, or a piece of a dead animal, or a dead fish. The man said he almost didn't call it in."

Emily realized that was probably what the torso killer was hoping for. Not only was there a sense of vengeance on a person by severing their limbs from their body in their head, but it made disguising the crime all that much easier. She bit her lip for a second until Mike interrupted her thoughts.

"You're chewing your lip. What are you thinking about?"

"Just thinking that dumping only a torso in the water would make it difficult for anyone to identify the body, especially years ago when there was no DNA testing. Imagine a nondescript chunk of meat floating around in the water, nibbled by critters. That had to be difficult not only for the investigators but for the family."

Flynn nodded, "Yeah, not much to bury. By the way, they've never found any of the limbs or heads of any of the bodies in Tifton. Only the torsos."

Emily's skin began to crawl. The fact that the torso killer had gotten away with more than a dozen murders they knew about and that law enforcement had no leads and was never able to find the remaining body parts wasn't a good sign. This man was dangerous, that was for sure. "Anything else I need to know?"

"I made an appointment for you to meet with Bradley Barker tomorrow morning at eight," Mike said. For a moment his face dipped down as he looked at his keyboard. Emily's phone chirped in the background. "I just sent the address to your phone. It's already programmed into the truck, so you'll be ready to go in the morning. It's a twenty-two-minute drive from the bed-and-breakfast."

Emily raised her eyebrows, "Okay, thanks. Not sure how you hacked into my truck's GPS, but..."

"Now, I can't share all my secrets," Mike said, smiling. The smile washed off his face as his next words came out, "Be careful, Emily. This guy is no joke."

Emily nodded, "I will."

7

Emily woke up in a sour mood. She'd spent the better part of the night tossing and turning, her mind processing all of the information Mike and Flynn passed to her the night before. "Probably talking about hacked-up bodies before bed wasn't a good plan," she muttered to herself as she went into the bathroom and flipped on the light.

A half-hour later, after taking a hot shower and putting on a clean set of clothes, Emily felt better. She checked the temperature on her phone. It was already eighty degrees out. Although she would like to wear shorts, chasing down a case with her legs exposed wasn't a good plan, especially if it involved running around the woods and getting a raging case of poison ivy. Emily pulled on a pair of jeans and a T-shirt, going back into the bathroom to braid her long dark hair. There was no point in drying it, not that she did very often anyway, but in the heat and humidity, she'd probably sweat through it in no time fast. She had to stay focused. Hard to do that with sweat running down my face, she thought.

Getting ready to leave the room for the day, Emily slid the holster of her pistol on her hip, clipping it to her belt. She checked to make sure it was still loaded — she knew it was, but she checked again, a habit she developed in the police academy. "Better to check your equipment than to be surprised," one of her instructors had said. She pulled her T-shirt over top of it. The rear grip was still a little visible, but she didn't care. With a serial killer on the loose, she wanted to make sure she was safe, or at least as safe as she could be.

It was six forty-five. She knew it was too early to leave for Bradley Barker's house. Emily grabbed the key card to her room and stuffed it in her back pocket, deciding to go downstairs and see what breakfast looked like.

As soon as she got halfway down the steps, the sweet scent of maple syrup hit her. Turning the corner, there were two other tables of people sitting in the small dining room. Emily took a table in the corner, facing the doorway. A minute later, a young man greeted her, his name badge reading Matthew. "Morning," he said, with a deep southern drawl. "Coffee?"

Emily nodded.

"Is this your first morning here?"

"Yes."

Matthew nodded, "Let me get your coffee, and then I'll bring you a menu."

A minute later, Matthew came back with an oversized mug of coffee, a glass of water, and a laminated menu under his arm. "The special this morning is French toast, but we have eggs and cereal as well. Pretty much anything you could want."

Emily didn't want to take the time to look at the menu. "I'll take the French toast. That sounds good. Thank you."

Matthew nodded and walked away. While she was waiting, Emily looked at the other people that were sitting and enjoying their breakfast. There was a couple with a young girl with them, probably not more than three or four years old. They'd cut up a sausage for her and she was picking at it with her fingers, the parents discussing something Emily couldn't hear.

On the other side of the room, there was a couple, eating in silence, their heads down; faces buried in their food. Emily tried to guess why the other people were there. She had a moment where she imagined walking up to the tables and introducing herself, "Hi, I'm Emily. I'm here to track down the torso killer. You?" The thought of how preposterous it was almost made her laugh out loud.

A few minutes later, Matthew was back at Emily's table, a couple of plates balanced on his arm. Before he even set the food down, Emily could smell the cinnamon and the bacon and sausage. "Here you go," Matthew said, setting the plates in front of her. Emily took a bite of the French toast, mopping it up with syrup. "I'm going to have to remember to thank Mike later," she whispered to herself. Although her appetite hadn't been all that good in the last few days, the food was so delicious at the Tifton Center B & B it was hard to turn it away.

About halfway through her meal, Emily realized she was full. If she ate anymore, the only thing she'd be able to do would be to go upstairs and head back to bed. Wiping her lips on the napkin, she checked the time on her cell phone. It was seven-thirty. If she hoped to get to Bradley Barker's house on time, she'd need to get moving. Lifting her hand, she caught Matthew's attention. "I need to head out for a meeting. You'll add this to my tab?"

"Is included in your stay, ma'am," Matthew said.

"Okay. Thanks," Emily said, surprised. She wondered how much she was paying per night for the bed-and-breakfast, but then realized it didn't matter. There was nowhere else to stay in Tifton. After the case was over, she'd have to remind Mike that budget was still an issue, even with the five-thousand-dollar monthly envelopes stacking up in her safe.

Stepping outside, the air was thick and humid. Before she even got to the truck, she realized she was sweating. Summer humidity in Louisiana was nothing like anywhere else. Inside the truck, she flipped on the air-conditioner, feeling the cool air bring her body temperature down. How people live here, I'll never know, she thought to herself, suddenly wishing for a brisk winter wind off of Lake Michigan. Living in a hot climate wasn't all it was cracked up to be, she realized.

Pulling out of the bed-and-breakfast, Emily took a better look at the town. It had been dusky bordering on dark when she drove in the night before, so she hadn't gotten a good look at the homes and businesses in the area.

There wasn't much to the center of Tifton, a single big-box grocery and home goods store, flanked by a few smaller strip centers that looked pretty new, a couple of gas stations, and two single-story office buildings. The buildings seem to be clustered together as if they were huddled in one place. It looked like the start of a city expansion plan that never came to fruition.

As she drove out of the center of Tifton, a few homes dotted the sidewalks. Stopped at one of the few lights in the town, Emily could see the sidewalks had heaved in a couple of places, probably from flooding. The homes ranged from small and well-kept to those that looked like they had been built forty years before and never touched since.

About two miles out of the center of town, the woods became thick and dense again, the trees and scrub clamoring for rays of sunlight. Every now and again, Emily would pass a driveway where enough space for a home and a small yard had been cut out. She'd seen the home the night before, but there were even more on the other side of town. The roads were narrow, with no guardrails and not much in the way of striping. A semi-truck passed Emily's pickup, nearly side-swiping her, his horn blaring, "Geez," Emily said, feeling her stomach knot. She instantly wished for the wide, well-striped lanes of the Chicago freeways. "How do people drive around here?" she muttered.

Ten minutes later, the GPS told Emily to turn onto a side street that was barely paved. It looked more like pitch and tar — a combination of gravel and road sealants that made something of a passable street — than it did a properly paved roadway. Her truck's tires vibrated over the sealed gravel. Slowing down, the GPS told Emily to make another turn, this time onto the driveway to her right. Nearly hitting the mailbox, Emily turned the truck onto the sharply angled driveway. Unlike many of the other homes she'd seen in the area, this driveway was still flanked by trees and undergrowth. Emily leaned forward, tilting her head, looking to see exactly where she was going, the truck hit a rut in the road. A moment later, the trees widened, exposing a home low to the ground, perched on an incline, a large garage off to the side. As Emily parked the car, she realized the garage was probably bigger than the house.

Getting out of the truck, Emily checked to make sure her pistol still sat squarely on her hip. She pulled her T-shirt down over the top of it. She didn't know Bradley Barker, but there was no reason to take any chances, especially given the fact that she'd never met him before. Only Flynn had talked to him in an online forum. That wasn't much of a referral in Emily's mind. Locking the truck, Emily walked to the front door, first on a paved walkway, then taking a few steps up to the front door. She pressed the doorbell, but the door opened as soon as she did. A man with thin, balding hair and thick glasses that made his eyes look wide greeted her, "You must be Emily?"

Emily nodded. "Are you Bradley?"

The man nodded. "I'd invite you in, but the place is a mess. Let's go over to the garage — that's where all the information you're looking for is, anyway. I'll be out in a sec."

Emily turned away and walked back down the front walk, frowning. It seemed strange to her that Bradley would send her out to the garage. The back of her neck tingled. Who was this Bradley anyway? Supposedly, he was the brother of a victim, but wouldn't it be clever if Bradley was the one who was doing the killing? Emily shook off the thought, but reached for her pistol, leaving it in the holster.

By the time Emily made it around the side of the house, Bradley had come out. He walked with a cane and had a severe limp in his right leg. That he couldn't move well gave Emily at least a bit of comfort. Unless he was faking it, Emily was faster than him in case he tried anything. As if he knew she was wondering about his limp, he looked at her and said, "Fell off a tractor about fifteen years ago helping a buddy bring in a crop of soybeans. Broke my leg. It never set quite right." Limping ahead of her, he called over his shoulder, "Surgeons say they can fix it, but I'm not much for people cutting me apart if you know I mean."

Emily wondered if his comment was some sort of sick Tifton humor, but she didn't respond in case it wasn't. "Thanks for taking the time this morning. I heard you lost your brother to the torso killer. Is that right?"

Bradley pulled a ring of keys out of his pocket and unlocked the side door to the garage. Emily followed him in. Flipping on a light switch, Bradley said, "That's right. My brother Sean. He was a good guy, too. Everybody liked him. Just up and disappeared one night and never came back. They found what was left of him in the pond a few days later. Can't imagine what he went through."

The words hung in the air. Emily watched for a moment as Bradley stared at the ground, his lips moving, but nothing coming out. It was one thing to kill someone, but to dismember them, that was something else entirely. Bradley was right, the amount of torture and torment the people had gone through before the torso killer ended them was unthinkable. Emily shivered even in the heat, the thought settling on top of her, hoping the dismemberment had happened after they were already gone. The alternative was nearly unthinkable. Hopefully, there was some mercy in whoever was killing the people of Tifton, even if that mercy just meant a quick death.

As Emily's eyes adjusted to the inside of the garage, a bank of dim fluorescent lights hanging from above, she saw there was an old-fashioned chalkboard on a wooden stand against the wall. Next to it was a matching whiteboard. To her left, there were more photographs and news articles taped to the drywall. The smell of mold and mildew, probably from the incessant humidity, hung in the air. As she glanced around, Bradley said, "Well, this is it." He hung his cane on the back of a folding chair and sat down, staring.

From behind, Emily heard some scratching and turned just in time to see a small white and brown dog jump into Bradley's lap. He scratched the dog behind his ears, "I wondered when you'd show up to meet our guest," he said.

Seeing the dog reminded Emily of Miner. The thought made her wish for home. "Is that a Jack Russell Terrier?" Emily asked.

Bradley nodded.

"What's his name?"

Bradley looked confused for a second, "Jack. What else would you name a Jack Russell Terrier?"

The way Bradley said it, with his deep southern drawl and matter-of-fact tone, made Emily laugh. "That's funny."

Bradley narrowed his eyes, "You have a dog, Miss Emily?" By the time he asked the question, Jack had jumped off of his lap and was sniffing around the edges of Emily's boots.

"I do. Australian cattle dog. His name is Miner because he digs so many holes in my yard. All he needs is a hard hat and a headlamp."

The moment of levity seemed to cut through the tension in the dark garage, the images and information Bradley had amassed about the torso killer looming in front of them like grisly wallpaper. "So, tell me a little bit about what I'm looking at here," Emily said, taking a couple of steps forward.

"Well, let me start by telling you that my wife, Carla, thinks I'm plumb crazy for doing all this. Won't come out to the garage at all. But it's the only way I can stay sane, knowing that the killer is still out there. Even after all these years, I can't believe Sean is gone." His words hung in the air for a second. Bradley sighed and then pointed to the boards in front of him and the information on the wall. "I've been collecting information ever since Sean was killed. Articles, images, whatever else I can find. Just trying to get the whole mess straight in my head if you know what I mean. Then, I found your friend Flynn on the forum." He looked at Emily through his thick glasses, "You'd be surprised how many people are out there with unsolved crimes like me. It just eats at you, day after day after day," he said, pulling a handkerchief out of his pocket and wiping his forehead.

It was no surprise to Emily that people were tormented by crimes that were never solved. She tried her best to help families like Bradley's when she was working with the Chicago Police Department and now on her own. But helping others and staying free would only last as long as she didn't get caught if she had to take action, like killing someone. Investigating was one thing. Getting vengeance could look very different than that, though. "You are quite the detective, I see. Tell me a bit more, would you?"

"Yeah, Flynn warned me you're pretty to the point about things," Bradley said, standing up and limping over to the chalkboard. "On this board, I have information about each one of the victims. That one," Bradley pointed to the whiteboard that was stationed next to it, "That one has information just about Sean," he looked away as if it was too painful to see. "On the wall is just general information I found about the torso killer over the years."

Looking more closely at the chalkboard and whiteboard, Emily realized each one of them had to be at least six feet wide and every inch was packed with sticky notes and articles and pictures, some of them marked with questions or arrows. "Flynn brought me up-to-date on the general gist of the case, but why don't you go over it with me?"

"I'd be happy to. For some reason, it helps me when I talk about what happened to Sean." He approached the whiteboard where the information about his brother was located. "As I said before, Sean was a good guy. Nothing fancy. No one in our family is. We're all just your average Southerners. I spent my career as a bus driver for the local school district. Sean was a mechanic. Never married. No kids." Bradley walked over to one of the pictures on the board. Pointing, he said, "This is my favorite picture of him. It was taken a couple of years before he died."

Emily walked closer to the board and stared at the image, the edges wrinkled from the heat and humidity. There was no doubt there was a family resemblance between Sean and Bradley. Sean looked to be younger, with a wide grin and a round face, much like Bradley's. "Was he younger than you?"

Bradley nodded, "Almost ten years. Surprise pregnancy. 'A mistake of the best kind,' my mama used to say." He paused for a moment, "Anyway, Sean was a mechanic. He worked at the only garage here in Tifton. There are a couple of others a little farther out, depending on what you need fixed, but Sean liked being in town, seeing the familiar faces of the customers for oil changes or flat tires. He used to say that a whole lotta life could happen between fixes – someone might get married, have a baby, get a new job. You know, that kind of stuff. One night, after work, he went out to eat. What exactly happened after that, we're not sure. Tifton isn't exactly the kind of place where people have surveillance cameras if you know what I mean. That was a Friday night, so nobody was really looking for him until Monday when he didn't show up for work. By lunchtime on Monday, I got a call from his boss. Sean was always reliable. Always the kind of guy who showed up when you told him to. I thought it was strange too, truth be told. I tried calling him, but no answer. I drove over to his house and checked it. Nobody there. That's when I got to thinking there might be a problem. Right after that, I went to the police station. I wish you could've seen the look on their faces when I told them that Sean was missing. It was like they knew or something."

Emily chewed the inside of her lip. The pain in Bradley's voice felt like a knife sticking into her. Victims like him were the reason she used to love her work with the Chicago Police Department. They were real people with a real loss they suffered from every single day. And Bradley was suffering. "What happened then?"

Bradley sat back down in the folding chair. As soon as he did, Jack jumped up in his lap as if knowing his owner needed some comfort, "Well, as you can imagine, all hell broke loose. People were crawling all over Sean's house and mine. They went through the gas station and the restaurant where he'd been seen last with a fine-tooth comb, those fancy people from the FBI showing up with their matching jackets and all..." Bradley's voice drifted off. "A couple of days later, I got a call that they found something in the Little Bayou Pond, part of a body. I have to tell you, I knew right then and there it was Sean. They didn't have to say any more than that."

Emily walked back over in front of the board where Sean's information was hung. She sighed, wondering how many questions she could ask Bradley without upsetting him. It was his brother after all. "Was there anything unusual about Sean's murder?"

Bradley snickered, "Other than some maniac chopped his body apart and tossed the torso into a pond? Nope." Bradley stood up, shooing Jack off his lap, "Sorry, Miss Emily, I don't mean to be snide. It's just that even two years later, it's hard to believe Sean is gone."

Bradley had come up next to Emily, staring at the pictures in front of them. Emily turned to the side, "Are you comfortable talking about the details of the case with me? I don't want to upset you."

Bradley nodded, "Flynn told me you'd have to ask some pretty pointed questions to get to the bottom of this, but he also told me that if anybody could solve this, it would be you. All I'm hoping is you give it your best shot. Those morons from the FBI have done nothing for us."

"All right then, let's get to work," Emily said.

For the next couple hours, Bradley and Emily stayed in the garage, the morning light filtering in through the open door. Jack ran in and out every few minutes, alternately sitting on Bradley's lap and sniffing Emily's boots. Bradley walked Emily through every detail of the case, starting with the very first person who'd been murdered, Corey Hawkins, all the way through Gerald Wexner, the last victim. Emily paced back and forth in front of the boards in the garage, trying to absorb as many of the details as she could. Bradley had amassed an enormous amount of information, more than most families of victims she'd ever worked with. But then again, she realized, they were dealing with a serial killer, not a one-off or person that had run away. The person they were dealing with was relentless and dangerous. The back of Emily's neck started to crawl. She swallowed, refocusing on the boards.

For a minute, they were silent. Emily walked in front of the images, while Bradley sat on the folding chair. A second later, Emily pointed to the torsos. "Bradley, why do some of these torsos look different from others?"

"What about them?" he said.

Emily stopped in front of one of the torso pictures, one that was red and mottled. There were a couple that looked red and another few where the skin was pale and gray. "This one, and the one over there, the skin is all red. See that? The rest of them, the skin is gray. Any idea what caused the redness?"

Bradley's face paled even in the dim light of the garage, "That? Yeah, the medical examiner thought the killer poured acid on the skin before he dumped them."

Emily swallowed, realizing she was dragging Bradley through all the details of everything that had been done to his brother and others like him. Luckily, Sean's torso wasn't one of the ones that were blistered and red. Emily glanced at Bradley, who was staring down into Jack's fur. She couldn't imagine how hard this was for him. From the corner of her eye, she spotted another folding chair, one that matched the one Bradley was sitting in. She pulled it out and unfolded it, sitting next to Bradley. They sat quietly for a minute, both lost in thought. Emily was trying to wrap her brain around the kind of person who would mutilate others. Part of her was sure Bradley was reliving the days and weeks around his brother's disappearance and his death as they talked about it. If Emily had learned one thing, it was that no one got through life without pain and struggle. Some people's pain looked different than others — could be a divorce, or the loss of a parent, or the destruction of a dream — but everybody had an issue that followed them. This kind of loss was too much, though.

"Are you okay to keep talking about this?" Emily said. The words coming out of her mouth surprised her. Initially, she'd been resistant to looking at this case, but now, sitting with Bradley, she realized it was an opportunity to make a difference, that was if she could find the killer. And that was a big if.

In cases like these, Emily knew the FBI didn't spare any expense, especially if the crimes had gone unresolved. Even if they weren't on the scene, she was sure they had analysts working on the case in the meantime. It was a black eye to the agency that any serial killer could get away with as many murderers as he had. Emily stared at the images again, the chunks of flesh and faces swimming in front of her as she scanned them pinned up on Bradley's boards. The killer almost had to be a him, didn't it? Emily thought about it for a second, the reality of looking at bodies cut up into pieces settling over her.

Bradley looked up from the small dog sitting on his lap, "Yeah, I'm okay. Like I said before, Carla thinks I'm crazy, but this is probably actually what keeps me sane. It's nice that you're interested."

Emily wanted to ask him if other people weren't. That seemed so callous to her, but she avoided the subject. "Okay," she said, standing up and walking over to the images again, this time to the board that held all the faces and the bodies of the victims. There were only a couple of women in the lineup. Other than that, it was all men who looked to be between twenty and fifty years old, maybe a little bit older. Emily stared at the torsos, "Hey, Bradley?"

"Yeah?"

"Did you ever notice there seem to be some pieces missing here?"

Bradley raised his eyebrows and smiled, "Other than heads and arms and legs? Sure. That's one of the strangest things about the case." He got up from the chair, took two limping steps, and stopped next to Emily. "The thing that makes this killer so strange in my mind," Bradley said, lifting a crooked finger to point at the pictures, "is that it's not enough to just chop somebody up." He glanced at Emily, "Not to sound like I'm speaking ill of the dead, or anything," he said. "But if you notice the women's torsos are missing the very things that make them women. The men have the same problem. On top of that, there are a couple of bodies where the medical examiner said there were pieces of bone missing. Now, what on God's green earth would you do with a piece of bone from a dead body? That's one thing I just can't wrap my brain around."

Emily folded her arms across her chest and chewed her lip, "I can't say I understand that either." Her mind was racing. In their call the night before, Mike and Flynn hadn't mentioned any body parts that were missing. It seemed strange to her, given the fact they said they'd accessed the medical examiner's reports. Maybe it hadn't been mentioned? That seemed equally strange. It was the medical examiner's job to detail every last bit of the body, or in this case, what was left of it.

EMILY STAYED with Bradley for another hour or so, talking through more details of the case. By the time they were done, Jack was sitting on her lap as if he'd known Emily his whole life. Lifting the small dog and setting him gently on the floor, Emily looked at Bradley. "I think I've taken up enough of your time today. I've got some more research to do," she said, standing up and brushing the white dog fur off her jeans. "I appreciate your time and the hospitality."

Bradley struggled to his feet, reaching for his cane, "You'll keep me posted on what's going on?" he said. "Time is running short, I'm afraid."

"I'm afraid of that, too."

8

B y the time Ollie got home from work, the rage inside of him had built into an enormous amount of pressure. He'd nearly killed the man he worked for with his bare hands after he rejected a batch of fittings, saying they weren't up to spec. His words sounded just like something Libby said to Ollie, telling him he wasn't good enough and that she was leaving for a better life.

A better life.

Ollie pushed in the back door at his house with such strength that it ricocheted off the wall behind it, leaving a dent. He knew there was only one way to rid himself of the anger and the pressure in his body. There was only one way for him to get on with his life, at least for the next few months. Ollie unlocked the basement door and went down the steps, staring at the calendar, the date Libby had left with the girls glaring at him. He realized it had been so long that he didn't even know what his girls looked like anymore. They could walk by him on the street and he'd pass them as complete strangers. Ollie punched the brick wall of the cellar, nearly shattering his hand. He didn't even feel the pain, only seeing the blood and torn skin after he did it. He went back upstairs, turning the lights off behind him.

9

Three hundred miles away, Cash Strickland picked up a sub sandwich from a deli in the building next to his office and headed back upstairs. It was his dinner. The day had been long, catching up on reports and paperwork at the FBI's Baton Rouge office. The FBI had satellite offices nearly everywhere. The goal was to be able to get to any crime location within the country within an hour. It was an ambitious goal especially in the middle of Louisiana, where hundreds of miles of farmland or parkland could sit empty for years until a crime occurred, but it was the goal, nonetheless.

By the time Cash got back up to his office, most of his colleagues had left for the night. When they weren't out on assignment, his office of FBI agents kept pretty regular hours, just following up on cases, writing reports, and attending training. But, when something happened, the job became nonstop, sometimes for weeks on end.

After eating a few bites of his sandwich, Cash glanced at the calendar on the wall. The dates loomed ahead of him, one, in particular, giving him pause. It was nearly the six-month anniversary since the last torso had been found in Tifton. Would there be another?

Cash used a napkin from inside the bag to wipe his fingers. With a few keystrokes, he was able to bring up the case files the FBI had on the murders in Tifton. Not that Cash wanted to relive them, but there was nothing to suggest the torso killer wouldn't strike again, and soon. In front of him, the screen lit up with hundreds of images taken by the FBI's crime scene experts and their team of medical examiners. While the FBI had resources and expertise much beyond local law enforcement, that wasn't always a benefit. At times, the agents would collect so much data that the real story could get hidden. It became like a needle in a haystack. Cash shook his head, looking at the layers of information in front of him, wondering where that needle in a haystack was. They'd never had a solid lead on the killer. In his mind, it was a miracle they were even able to identify the bodies with how mangled they were by the time the killer was done.

Standing up from his desk to get away from the massive amount of information,

Cash stood by the square window in his office. It had a not-so-lovely view of the parking garage below, but at least he had a window. When he'd been promoted to field supervisor and given a team of his own, the little office came with it. There wasn't much of a view, but at least it was outside. The guy he'd taken over for had retired. Cash remembered the day he'd handed him the keys to his office. "Enjoy it," was all he said.

At the time, Cash thought the promotion was exactly what he wanted — the next step he needed to build his career in the FBI and hopefully end up as an Assistant Director or at least a Division Director at some point. Now, a couple of years later, Cash wasn't sure how long he'd last.

He walked back to his desk, the open files of the Tifton

torso killer still up on his screen. Sitting down, he felt a streak of pain in his calf. He needed to get out for a run, that was for sure. The FBI had stringent fitness requirements and Cash had always been able to supersede them, but the amount of paperwork he had in his job right now made it hard to find time to hit the gym. He'd do that in the morning, he decided.

From inside a drawer in his desk, he pulled out a lined notepad, figuring he might make some notes on the Tifton killings. Before he could write anything down, Janet Crenshaw stopped by his office, her blonde ponytail pulling her hair back from her face, her FBI windbreaker barely covering the bulky sidearm she wore on her hip. "Hey boss," she said, leaning in his doorway. "Know what time it is?"

Cash hadn't looked up. He was staring at one of the reports from the medical examiner. "No," he muttered.

"It's been almost six months..." Janet walked away without saying anything more.

Cash stared at the doorway as she walked away. He could almost hear Janet's voice echo the words again, "It's been almost six months." That couldn't be a good sign.

There was nothing more frustrating to Cash than not being able to solve a crime. Solving cases was what he was good at. He had a focus like very few others, or so his yearly evaluations read. That was one of the reasons he was chosen to lead the team. Leaning back in his chair, Cash felt a surge of frustration and slammed the pencil in his hand down on the desk. There was no way of knowing whether the Tifton killer would strike again. If the perpetrator did and followed his pattern, Cash should be getting a call about a missing person in Tifton sometime during the next couple of days. It felt like a ticking time bomb lodged in his chest.

It wasn't as though he hadn't tried to solve the case. He'd met with his team and specialists, and profilers, and higher-ups multiple times, trying to figure out a way they could protect the people in Tifton. Was there a way for them to find the killer before he struck again? Or maybe they could send in the Louisiana State Highway Patrol to keep an eye on the parish? All the ideas he and his team, the profilers, and his bosses tossed around came to nothing. The words of one of the profilers working on the case haunted him to this day, her words seared in his mind, "Someone like this, Cash, is very hard to find. He's like a mouse in the walls of your house. You know he's there, you know he's eating your food, but you only see the result of what he's done. This guy is going to be nearly impossible to catch."

The phone on Cash's desk rang, breaking his concentration on his computer screen. He stared at it for a second and then glanced back at the computer, the files from the mutilated bodies swimming in front of him. Sighing, he picked up the phone, "Agent Strickland," he said.

"Agent Strickland, this is Sierra Day. Do you remember me?"

Cash swallowed. The timing couldn't be worse. Sierra Day was the sister of Joe Day, body three-one. Joe was taken in the third year of the killings, the first body of the year. It was before Cash had taken on the case, but he'd talked to Sierra periodically throughout the years.

"Of course. How are you?"

"Honestly? I'm nervous. We're getting close to that time again. You have any news on Joe's killer?"

It was as if there is a theme to the day. First, Janet. Now, Sierra. "I'm sorry, Ms. Day. I wish I had something new or different to tell you. As I've told you before, we have some of the best profilers and case managers working on your brother's murder and the murders of the others we think are connected, but there've been no new leads."

"Not even in the last six months?"

Cash quickly flipped through the file in front on his computer screen and saw the face and mangled torso of Gerald Wexner, the last body to be found in Tifton. The situation had been the same as every other time. Gerald disappeared. No one saw him for a couple of days. Someone reported him missing and then a couple of days later after the FBI had been called in again, his body was recovered from the Little Bayou Pond. The FBI had tried staking out the pond, but somehow, the killer managed to get in and out without being seen. How that was possible, Cash still wasn't sure. "No, I'm sorry. As you know, there's not a lot I can say about an ongoing investigation, except that we're working on it." He felt a tension in his chest, wishing he had more to tell her. "I promise, we haven't forgotten about Joe or any of the other victims, but I don't have anything to report right now."

There was silence on the other end of the line. Cash wondered what would happen next. Would Sierra start to cry? Maybe it would be better if she screamed at him? Both options were entirely possible. Victims' families could be unpredictable.

"I'm sorry to hear that. What are we supposed to do now?"

Cash was surprised at her reaction. Sierra was calm and rational, something many victims' families were never able to accomplish. Maybe it was just the passage of time. After all, Joe had been gone for more than four years. "Other than being aware of your surroundings and calling me if you sense anything off, there's not a lot more that I can suggest." Cash's heart sunk at the words coming out of his mouth. There really wasn't anything else he could suggest, but he wished there was. Maybe move out of Tifton? That's what he really wanted to say, but agency policy prevented him from saying things like that.

"And, if the killer strikes again, do you have any new plans or strategies in place to catch him?"

Cash furrowed his eyebrows. Sierra was way too calm. "As

I've said, we haven't stopped working the case. And yes, we've been in discussions with our top people here at the agency to get this solved. What those things are, specifically, I can't discuss." In reality, Cash had nothing new but telling Sierra that wouldn't help. There was nothing more they could do than what they were doing, which was to show up once something happened and hope to catch the killer. So far, it'd been completely unsuccessful. He was praying for a break in the case.

Sierra sighed on the phone. "You know, it's just so hard. It's not too bad for me, but it's awful for my dad. Joe was his favorite. We still don't understand why the killer chose him."

Cash knew Sierra was asking for insight, any reason at all, that the Tifton killer took her brother. Based on the information he'd gotten from the profiler, there was very little physical pattern to the people the killer took. It was almost as if he had a type without having a type, which had made solving the case nearly impossible. "We still aren't clear on that, either. Listen, Sierra, it's late. I do have some paperwork I need to finish before I can leave the office for the evening, but please feel free to give me a call again if you have any more questions or concerns."

As Cash hung up the phone, his eyes settled back on the files in front of him on his computer. He tabbed back through the notes from year three, the year Joe Day was taken. When Cash took over the case, he'd gone back and re-interviewed all the families. He remembered sitting with Sierra and her dad in their home, the two of them sitting ramrod straight on a floral couch, glasses of sweet tea in front of them. Cash had asked them all the standard questions about where Joe had been and whether he had been happy at his work and in his relationships. The reality was the information that Joe's family gave Cash was the same as every other family. There was no common denominator in terms of the place they worked, or being unhappy with their job, or a relationship.

That's what made the case so frustrating.

Unlike so many other cases Cash had worked throughout his career, the serial killer in Tifton left them basically nothing in terms of evidence, unless you could call the hunks of torso behind in the pond as something to go on. With the bodies submerged in almost stagnant water for at least forty-eight hours, the medical examiner and the forensics teams were unable to pull any data from the bodies — no fingerprints, no fibers, no nothing. It was an investigator's nightmare.

And now the nightmare was his.

Cash sat at his desk, drumming his fingers on it, staring at the pages in front of him, hoping for divine intervention, some sort of insight that would help him move the case forward. He had none.

The day his supervisor gave Cash the case, he was excited. His boss, a short, balding man, who was nearly as wide as he was tall, looked at him, "I wouldn't get too excited, Strickland. This one has seen a bunch of field agents. No one has been able to get a handle on it. Not sure you'll do any better, but I've got to assign it to someone."

For the first couple weeks, Cash poured through all the information in the file, sure he was going to be able to find something that everyone else missed. He didn't. One of the most frustrating parts of the case was that the killer always dropped the torsos in exactly the same spot. The FBI and the local police were never able to catch him doing it, even though they had staked it out on more than one occasion.

And now time was ticking. The killer hadn't missed a six-month mark in nearly seven years. Would he kill again? Cash didn't know, but the reality was the case was his until he got a promotion and passed the whole mess off onto some other unknowing field supervisor.

But, if Cash could close it, it could be a career-maker. He stared at the calendar hanging on his wall again, wondering if in just a few days he'd be racing back to Tifton, hoping and praying for a breakthrough in the case. Only time would tell.

10

I t was time.

Ollie sat in his kitchen, stock-still, for what felt like hours, the pressure in his chest growing. Dark had covered Tifton, the open windows in his house allowing for only the slightest night breeze to come in. It was just as hot and humid as it'd been that morning when he'd headed over to visit the little girl he'd decided on, Lexi. She reminded him of Sage at that age, her long hair, her wide smile lighting up everything in her path.

And Libby had deprived him of seeing his little girls grow up.

Ollie stood up from the table, shoving his keys in his pocket and picking up a roll of duct tape from the counter. His heart beat steadily in his chest as he walked out to the van and got it started, giving the engine a little goose as he headed down the driveway and onto the road. Retracing his steps from the morning, Ollie drove the same route as he did before, creeping slowly into the neighborhood where the little girl lived. They had a history, the two of them. She just didn't know it, but Ollie wanted to make sure to tell her all about it if he got the chance.

There was a little park behind the house. Nothing fancy, just a driveway that made a single loop with a few picnic tables in the middle. Why this kind of park was in Tifton, Ollie wasn't sure, but he was grateful for it that night. Unlike his other victims, who he'd been able to grab while they were out and about, Lexi wasn't able to do that, not yet. She was too little. Too fragile. Thinking about it, Ollie gripped the wheel tighter, realizing that Sage had grown up so much that she'd be driving soon. The thought of his daughters being able to go wherever they wanted to go scared him to death. A bead of sweat ran down Ollie's forehead as he parked the van at the edge of the loop.

From the front seat, Ollie picked up a screwdriver, the roll of duct tape, and a pair of latex gloves. He was a simple man. He only needed simple tools, he reasoned. Getting out, he started off in the darkness, cutting through the woods that ran behind Lexi Cooper's house.

The sky in Tifton was cloudless. There wasn't much of a moon, and the ground was uneven. Ollie grunted as he tripped over a half-rotten log in the middle of the woods. After a few minutes of navigating the darkness, Ollie could see the outline of the little white house ahead of him. It wasn't the first time he'd gone through the woods to watch Lexi. She looked so much like Sage it was hard for him to believe. If he hadn't known his own daughter was living in Canada, he would have sworn Lexi was his.

Standing at the edge of the woods, Ollie stared at the back of the house, his heart beating a little faster, his palms sweating. Her window was the second one from the right. He pulled on the gloves and fingered the screwdriver in his hand, rolling it around. A calm descended over him. On some level, he knew what he was about to do was wrong, but it was the only way for him to have peace. Lexi was as close to Sage as Ollie knew he was ever going to get.

Taking a few quiet steps into the yard, the grass muffling the noise of his boots, Ollie made his way to the window, quickly slipping the screwdriver under the sill. The window grunted as Ollie pushed it up and wedged his body through, his boots landing on the young girl's soft carpet.

Ollie stopped for a second, getting his bearings. Lexi was wrapped up in a pink comforter huddled in a ball in her bed. All around the room, there were toys — stuffed animals, and dolls, and a pair of roller skates in the corner. Seeing the roller skates sent a wave of rage through Ollie. He gritted his teeth and in one smooth movement, walked to the side of her bed, quickly covering her mouth with duct tape before she could make any noise. Her eyes opened wide, startled out of her sleep. She mumbled a cry for help, but Ollie paid no attention. He grabbed her wrists and fastened them with more tape and did the same with her ankles. Picking her up, he walked to the window and set her down outside as he wedged his way out, closing it behind him.

Lexi scooted away from him, her eyes filled with tears, pushing as best she could with her bound hands and feet. He ignored her, picking her up and putting her over his shoulder. With a few quick steps, Ollie was across the lawn and back into the cover of the woods.

Once he was out of the Cooper's yard, he slowed down. He didn't want to trip and fall accidentally while he was carrying Lexi. She struggled against him, but he clamped a heavy hand around her back. She groaned and then began to whimper.

When Ollie made it to the other side of the woods where the van was parked, he stopped for a moment, watching. A Tifton police cruiser drove through the park. The car stopped for a second, pausing at Ollie's van parked off to the side. Ollie's heart began to race. He didn't have a plan if the police showed up before he got Lexi back to his house. Watching, Ollie was breathing so shallowly he could hardly get enough air in his chest, the heat and humidity, making him wheeze. He stood silent and unmoving, gripping Lexi's back, his arm arced up and over her, pinning her to his shoulder. He'd gotten this far. She wasn't going to get away now.

Watching from the edge of the woods, the police car inched forward, the sweep of the searchlight touching the ground not more than ten feet from where Ollie was stopped. His breath caught in his throat. But, just as quickly as the police car passed him, it was gone. Making his way out of the woods, Ollie walked to the van, opening the back door and laying Lexi down on her back. Her eyes were already red and bloodshot from crying. Without saying anything, he grabbed a strap from the back and tied her to a couple of metal cleats that were welded to the side of the van. The last thing he needed was the young girl somehow slipping her restraints and opening the back door, tumbling out onto the road.

As he slammed the van door, he wanted to tell her that everything was going to be okay, that what she was doing would help him, but the words wouldn't come. Ollie slipped into the driver's side and started the van, pulling out of the park and back onto the road.

Driving toward his house, Ollie kept glancing in the rearview mirror, adjusting it so he could see her. Lexi had curled up on her side and was still whimpering. Ollie turned his eyes back to the road, driving slowly so as not to attract any unwanted attention, not that there was much traffic in the middle of the night in Tifton. It was a sleepy town, one where people went right home from work and barely left their houses after that.

Pulling in the driveway, Ollie parked the van behind his house, getting out and slamming the driver's side door. He opened the back doors, unclipped the straps, and hoisted Lexi up over his shoulder again, fumbling for a minute with the keys. As he did, Lexi struggled. He nearly dropped her. "Stop that!" he yelled, paranoid that if he dropped her, she might be injured. Her body became limp and silent as he walked through the house, the old linoleum floors creaking underneath his feet. When he got to the basement door, he unlocked the padlock, pulling the string for the first bulb at the top of the stairs. It cast a dull glow in the darkness.

At the bottom of the steps, Ollie turned on just enough light so he could see what he was doing. He set Lexi down in the chair that was bolted to the floor, cutting the tape off her wrists and then re-securing them to the arms of the chair. She didn't struggle.

Standing in front of her, Ollie felt his breath steady, the first time in weeks. He stared at Lexi, reaching out with a thick finger to push a stray lock of hair off her face. She quivered under his touch. He never meant to scare them, not any of them, but somehow, that's what happened. Huge tears ran down her face, her skin pale. Ollie stared at her for another second and then pulled the tape off of her mouth so she could breathe better. "There's no point in screaming. There's no one around," he said, turning away and tossing the used tape in the trash. He pulled off the latex gloves and tossed them as well. As he looked back at her, he could barely focus on her features. He muttered, "I knew someone else in your family. Someone from a long time ago..."

Lexi began to cry, long, deep sobs that ate at the inside of Ollie. It felt like nails on a chalkboard, the sound clawing at something deep inside of him. He balled his fists. None of his other victims had ever cried like that, but none of his other victims had been a little girl, a lookalike for his precious Sage. The other victims whimpered a little. Most of the men just stayed silent, or they yelled at him. "I told you, stop that!"

Lexi looked down as if she was trying to stop, but she couldn't. The noises just kept coming. It felt like someone was sticking needles in Ollie's ears. He couldn't have her sobbing like this. It wouldn't do. Ollie bit his lip hard enough to taste blood and then walked over to the bench, picking up an old brick he'd found in the yard years before. He'd always meant to throw it away — it was a tripping hazard for the girls, but somehow it ended up in the basement. He felt the weight of it in his hand and then looked back over his shoulder at Lexi. Her head was still down, the sobs racking her body, her shoulders shaking. With two steps he moved from the workbench to directly in front of her, raising his hand in the air and smashing the brick down on the side of her head. Her body slumped to the side, the crimson creep of blood soaking through her blonde hair. Dropping the brick out of his hand, Ollie reached for her wrist. She still had a pulse. That was good.

As he turned to go back up the steps, he muttered, staring at the fragile body of the five-year-old slumped in the chair, "I told you not to cry."

11

Emily had set her alarm for five o'clock in the morning, but she got a message from Mike before it went off, "9-1-1." She rolled over in bed, pulling her phone off the charger, quickly dialing Mike. Panic rose in the back of her throat. Was everything okay at home? He picked up after the first ring, "Sorry to wake you, but I think there's something you need to know."

Emily sat up, dangling her feet over the side of the bed. She'd slept with only the sheet covering her, the air-conditioning in her room pumping out of a steady flow of cool air all night long. It didn't matter, she was still hot. "What happened?"

"There's been an abduction."

The words settled over Emily. Scooting off the edge of the bed, she started to pace, "What happened? How did you find out?"

"Just got the notification a couple of minutes ago. I have my computer set to scan for keywords. I'm still trying to piece it together, to be honest, but it looks like the Tifton Police Department got a call about an hour ago that a young girl is missing. Lexi Cooper. I'm still trying to put the details together. I'm not sure if it's related to the torso killer, but I thought you should know."

Emily went and stood by the window, pulling the sheer curtain aside. There was no one in the parking lot and only a couple of cars, including her pickup truck. "It's a child?"

Mike mumbled, "Uh-huh."

"That doesn't match the serial killer's normal pattern, does it? Has he nabbed any other kids to date?" Emily racked her brain, but the fog of sleep made the wheels move a little more slowly than she wished they would.

"No. He's never grabbed a child before. Maybe this isn't him? Maybe it's a domestic issue, like a divorce gone bad, or one of those Amber alert things?"

Although Emily would have liked to believe it wasn't the torso killer at work again, there was no doubt the timing was suspicious. "What happened? What information do you have?"

"Well, as I said, it's just coming in now. What I can tell you is that based on the conversation over the police scanner, Lexi's mom went in to check her about an hour ago. She was gone. They'd put her in her bed, just like normal. The police are over there right now, searching the property."

"Did they call the FBI yet?"

Mike sighed, "I'm not sure."

Emily started to pace again, knowing she was asking Mike for answers he probably didn't have. If it was any normal case, the local police department would run point until they decided they couldn't handle it anymore, and then they'd call in the FBI. Whether that happened more quickly than normal with the history of killings in Tifton, Emily wasn't sure. What she did know was that her gut told her there was no coincidence here. The killer may not have ever grabbed a child before, but there was always a first.

12

The light was barely pushing up over the horizon when Cash Strickland's phone chirped. He'd been sitting on the edge of his bed, tying the laces of his shoes, getting ready for an early morning run. "Strickland," he said, answering the phone.

He heard Janet Crenshaw's voice on the other end of the line. "Morning, sunshine. The FBI is calling."

One of the things Cash appreciated about Janet was that her mood was always the same. It didn't matter if she had to come in on the weekend, the weather was bad, or the scene was gory. She was never moody and only vacillated between happy and content and focused on the job. Why he'd never been able to find a woman like that for himself, he wasn't sure. Unfortunately, Janet wasn't an option. She was married with two kids of her own. "Couldn't wait to see me at the office this morning? I was just about to go out for a run."

"The only place you are going to be running is to Tifton, Louisiana."

Cash's stomach sunk as soon as he heard the words. "What happened?"

"We just got a call from Tifton PD. A child is missing. Little girl. Lexi Cooper. Five years old, taken from her parent's house overnight."

Cash switched the phone to his other ear, "A child? Are they thinking this is the serial killer?"

"Well, that's where the fun begins. They don't know."

His plan for a morning run scrapped, Cash took a quick shower, packed an overnight bag with three days' worth of clothing, and headed into the office. By the time he got there, Janet and two other agents were already waiting for him. "The last two stragglers are just a couple minutes out," she said, handing him a cup of coffee.

"Anything new on the case?"

Janet spun her laptop towards Cash. On the screen was a picture of a young girl, blonde with a wide smile. "Meet Lexi Cooper. She's the one we're looking for. Five years old." Just as Janet finished her sentence, two more agents joined their group, only lifting their heads in greeting. Cash nodded and glanced around the room. Agents had different ways of coping with pressure. He noticed a couple of the agents staring directly at Janet, their faces pale, their eyes riveted on her. A couple of others were smiling and whispering. The jokesters. When Cash had first become a supervising field agent, he'd expected everyone to be as serious as he was about every case. He learned pretty quickly that some of his best agents were the ones that were the most lighthearted. They didn't let the job get to them and they were a lot more clearheaded about the details of the case, even in the heat of battle. After one particularly difficult case, one that involved rappeling into a ravine to retrieve a murder victim, Cash had an interesting interaction with the paramedics. With how physically exhausting the day had been, he'd asked to have each one of his agents checked.

The ones that worked and laughed were perfectly fine. The really serious ones didn't do as well. Two of them had to be transported to the hospital because their blood pressure was so high.

Cash's own personality put him somewhere in the middle, he reasoned. But this case brought out his serious side. He drummed his fingers on the table as Janet went through the basics of what they knew so far. It wasn't much. As soon as she finished speaking, Cash interrupted, "Janet, am I remembering wrong, or is this the first child that's been taken in Tifton?" Cash frowned as he waited for her to answer, trying to remember if they'd recovered any young bodies before. He didn't think so.

"No," Janet said, thumbing through the enormous stack of case files. "This is the first time that we know of. Could there be other bodies we don't know about? That's certainly a possibility with this guy." Janet looked at Cash, the FBI badge swinging around her neck from side to side as she stood up. "Okay, Cash. I'm done. You can take it from here."

Cash knew other supervising field agents would've been offended at the way that Janet spoke to him. Cash didn't care. As long as she did the job, that was what mattered. "All right. A few of you were with the same team six months ago when we went to Tifton, so you know the drill. A couple of you weren't, so talk to your colleagues or come and talk to either me or Janet with any questions." Cash glanced down at the time on his cell phone, "Let's be ready to roll in ten minutes. We'll meet downstairs in the garage. Don't forget your go-bags. We likely won't be coming back for several days." As the sound of chairs scraping on the floor echoed through the nearly empty room, Cash looked at Janet, "You bringing the binder?"

Janet nodded. "Wouldn't leave home without it," she said, picking it up.

The binder was the paper copy of every case the FBI had

connected to the Tifton torso killer. Although technology was nice, the agency had gotten themselves into more than one scrape where Wi-Fi or cell service wasn't available, and they needed details from the case file. That's how the binder was born. Not that they needed it every time they went out, or that it held every piece of information that Cash might need to make decisions, but it was a start in case of a tech failure.

Cash stopped in his office, flipping on the light to see if there was anything he forgot. He could still smell the remains of the sub sandwich from the night before, the odor of onions lingering in the air. From the hook on the back of his door, he picked up his FBI windbreaker. It was outrageously hot outside, but you never knew what kind of weather you might run into on the southeast coast. Something inside of Cash sunk. How could he be going back to Tifton again? What if they came back in a few days with nothing more to tell than they went and did an investigation, like with every other killing on this case? Butterflies formed in Cash's stomach. He couldn't come back without having found the little girl, no matter who had her. He needed a win, not just for his career, but for his confidence. No matter what it seemed like to the people of Tifton, he'd spend hours focused on their case. He just hoped he could solve it in time to save the girl. With another glance around, Cash shut off the light and locked the door, slinging his backpack over his shoulder and picking up his duffel bag from outside the door.

The ride in the elevator down to the parking garage was silent, Cash stepping in with two other agents, their backpacks and go-bags with them. Cash checked the time on his cell phone. It was just after seven-thirty in the morning. With any luck, they'd arrive in Tifton by nine. He'd send half the team directly over to Lexi Cooper's house and send another couple of people to go get rooms at the local bed-and-breakfast. At least it was a nice facility, he thought, sighing, as the elevator doors offered a quiet ping and then slid open.

Parked right in front of the doors were two matching black SUVs. How many the government bought every year, Cash wasn't sure, but it had to be a lot. The engines were running with the back doors open ready for bags and laptops. The motor pool was great about keeping the cars in good condition, fully gassed up and ready to go.

Cash walked to the lead vehicle, setting his backpack in the back and pushing his go-bag near it. He glanced over his shoulder at another agent who came up behind him, "Don't smash my backpack. It's got my laptop in it." The other agent nodded as Cash walked away.

Walking to the driver's side, Cash got in. Sometimes he liked to drive, other times he preferred to watch his cell phone as he got updates on the case while they traveled. If this case was anything like the other Tifton cases, they wouldn't have any more information until they got there. Thinking about the fact that they were going back to Tifton again sent a wave of nausea over him. Would this be the time they caught the killer?

Two minutes later, the last door on the SUVs closed with a thump and the driver behind Cash signaled they were ready to go. The two matching vehicles drove head-to-tail out of the parking garage, only slowing slightly for the speed bumps. As they approached the entrance, the gate automatically opened and Cash spun the SUV to the right, heading for the freeway entrance.

The drive to Tifton wasn't a difficult one. All Cash had to do was jump on freeway five twenty-four, and head west until they were far out in the country and then merge onto some rural roads to get into the city of Tifton. It wasn't really a city, though. Just a couple of neighborhood stores and a school that gave Tifton a location on a map. That was one of the things that was the most perplexing about the case, Cash thought, staring at the GPS for a moment. It wasn't like Tifton had a huge population where the killer could go around and have his choice of who he'd like to take. If he knew anything at all about Tifton, he knew it was a close-knit community. It surprised him that no one had any inkling of who was doing the killing. Or at least if they did know, they wouldn't say...

Janet, who was sitting next to him, broke the silence. "Penny for your thoughts?"

Cash glanced at her and mumbled, "What do you think?"

"Oh, I don't know. Maybe you're tossing around the new recruits LSU is going to put on the field this year? Maybe they might be able to win another national championship?"

Cash shook his head. Janet's sense of humor was well-placed, at least most of the time. "I'm not exactly thinking about football right now, Agent Crenshaw." He knew that calling her agent would sting, but he was trying to concentrate, trying to figure out why the killer had escalated to a child.

"Well, someone certainly needs their coffee this morning. How about if you tell me what's really on your mind?"

Cash could tell Janet wasn't going to take any notice of the barb he'd sent her way. "I'm just trying to wrap my brain around why a child got taken this time. Are you sure he's never taken a child before?"

Janet glanced down at the binder sitting on her lap. The navy-blue vinyl cover was emblazoned with large gold letters that read FBI, in the same design as their jackets, T-shirts, and other gear. "No, we don't know of any other children that have disappeared. Primarily, the killer targets only men. There's been a woman or two, but it's been mostly men."

That tracked with what Cash knew of the case. In his mind, and more importantly, based on what the profilers thought, the killer was most likely male. What the profilers weren't sure about was the motivation behind dismembering the bodies. Was it because the killer was simply trying to cover his tracks, or was it something more? For some reason, Cash's gut told him it had something to do with the rage inside of the perp. A rage that couldn't be contained.

13

T he news that another person had been taken in Tifton threw Emily into gear. She got dressed and grabbed her backpack, heading down a back flight of steps she'd found at the bed-and-breakfast. There was no time to stop for a meal now. Emily jumped in the truck, starting it up. She called Mike back. "Can you give me the address of where Lexi lives?"

There was a pause, "I don't think..."

Emily knew what Mike was going to say. It probably wasn't safe for her to get that close to local law enforcement. There was no telling if the FBI had been called or how quickly they might be on their way. But the fact that a child had been taken changed the game a little. Sure, Emily wanted to find the killer to get justice for Sean Barker and his family, but if the torso killer had the little girl, time was ticking.

A second later, her GPS beeped. Mike had inputted the new address. "Okay, you should see it now. You're only a couple of minutes out. But Emily..."

"...I know, be careful. Stay by your phone." Emily ended the call before Mike did. The last thing she needed him to do was babysit her. She knew the risks, even better than he did.

The drive over to Lexi's house seemed to take an excruciating amount of time, even though it was just a few minutes. It might be just the few minutes Emily needed to get information about the case before the FBI got there. She pressed the accelerator a little harder.

Turning down a side street, Emily slowed her truck. She passed by a small white house with black shutters, two Tifton parish police cars in the driveway and a third parked on the street. She pulled up ahead of the cars, seeing a couple of people outside of another house that was on a diagonal from where Lexi Cooper lived. Nosy neighbors. Getting out, Emily walked over to the cluster of people. "What's going on here?" Emily asked.

One of the people in the group, a man with an egg-shaped face, stared at her, "You haven't heard?"

Emily shook her head and made her eyes go wide, "No. I'm here visiting my cousin. That's a lot of police cars for such a small town, don't you think?"

The man looked down for a second and then glanced at another woman in the group. Must be his wife, Emily thought. He cleared his throat, "The little girl that lives over there — she's missing."

"Oh, that's terrible..." Emily said, looking toward the house. A single officer had come out of the garage, his arms tan and muscular underneath his short-sleeved shirt. He's got to be sweating something terrible, Emily thought, watching him key up the radio attached to his tactical vest. From where she was standing, she couldn't hear what he said. It didn't really matter. In a case like this, the FBI would be called. How long it would take them to arrive, she didn't know.

Emily didn't have to wait long for an answer. She only stood around for a few minutes listening to the neighbor's chat when she heard the rumble of engines in the distance. Two sleek black SUVs, blue and red lights flashing just under the roofline, pulled up in front of the house. Simultaneously, all of the doors opened, blue T-shirted FBI agents with badges dangling around their necks or posted on their hips stepping out of the vehicles. Emily watched for a second, stepping toward the back of the crowd, using the other bodies as cover.

"The FBI's back," one of the other women in the group said, mumbling. "Not that they ever do anything."

For a moment, Emily considered asking what the woman meant but decided against it. The less attention she drew to herself, the better. With the FBI arriving on the scene, Emily's heart started to beat a little faster. What she had come to Tifton to do had just become exponentially harder than before. It was one thing to get justice for a victim and their family years after the incident. It was something else to try to do it while law enforcement was hovering all over the case like bees on honey.

Emily stood for another second, staring. Her phone, stashed in her back pocket, vibrated. It was a text from Mike. "FBI has been notified."

"Yeah, I see that," Emily replied.

"They're there already?"

"Yep. I'm looking at them."

When Emily looked up, one of the women in the group was staring at her. Emily blinked, "Just my cousin texting me. Wondered where I was." Without saying anything else, Emily slid away from the group and walked to her truck. She didn't look behind her. Making eye contact could be dangerous. She knew if she went straight to her vehicle, no one in the FBI would give her a second look, at least not right now. If she stayed and watched, they would begin taking pictures and identifying the onlookers. Serial killers, for that matter, many criminals, oftentimes had an urge to go back to the scene. Law enforcement had gotten wise to the practice and had implemented taking pictures of whoever was standing around watching them work as part of their investigation. The last thing Emily needed was some junior agent finding out she was a disgraced detective from the Chicago PD. That would ring more than a few alarm bells.

Back at her truck, Emily started the engine and let out a long breath. She hadn't even realized she'd been holding the air in her lungs, but she had. Pulling away from the scene, Emily could see two of the FBI agents talking to the police officer that was standing in the driveway. As they drifted out of her view, Emily called Mike. "All right, I'm clear. The FBI just crashed the party."

"What are you going to do? That's going to make your job a lot harder."

"Well, we're both going to have to be on top of our game. Is there any more news?"

Emily continued down the street, away from Lexi Cooper's house, but unsure of where she was going. The streets in Tifton curved in strange directions. It wasn't as if the town was laid out on the north, south, east, west grid. Where the street headed, she didn't know. She just whispered a silent prayer that the road didn't loop back in front of Lexi's house. The last thing she wanted was to be spotted by the FBI.

"No, there's nothing else new, other than some chatter about the FBI arriving. One of the deputies just joked that they'd be taking over the bed-and-breakfast again."

Emily rolled her eyes. As if it wasn't hard enough to avoid them in a small town, now they'd be staying in the same place that she was. Emily made a mental note to try to figure out whether she should collect her belongings and check out and just sleep in her truck for the duration. She shook off the thought. There'd be time to figure that out later.

"Okay, I'll check in with you in a few hours."

Mike asked her, "Where you headed?"

"I have no idea."

14

The street Lexi Cooper's lived on dumped back out on the main road. Emily gave a sigh of relief at not having to go back past Lexi's house. Turning into the parking lot of an abandoned building, Emily pulled off to the side. Trying to figure out her next step now that the FBI was in town was giving her a headache. How was she going to operate with a bunch of federal agents sniffing around the town? Emily threw her truck into park and leaned back in the seat for a second, running through the options in her mind. She could just go home. That was always an option. She could go back to her life in Chicago, walking her dog and taking her boxing lessons. She could approach the case again once Lexi had been found or forget about it entirely. It was nice that Bradley had invested some time in her, but it didn't mean she owed him anything. Or she could stay. She didn't have to stay in Tifton. She knew she could drive a little further out, maybe find a hotel in a city nearby and stay there and wait for the FBI to get bored and leave. But, with a history of the serial killer in Tifton, that could take weeks. It was time she didn't want to spend in Louisiana, with its hot and horribly humid weather.

A second later, Emily threw the truck into reverse and pulled out of the parking lot. She knew what she needed to do. It was the reason she'd come down to Tifton in the first place — to help Bradley Barker get closure for his family. The memory of the haunted look on Bradley's face the day before popped up in Emily's memory. Those were the kind of people that deserved justice. That was the job she was in Tifton to do.

Twelve minutes later, she pulled into Bradley's driveway. It looked the same way as it did the day before, except for the fact that Emily didn't have to wait for Bradley to come out. He was standing in the driveway as if he was expecting her. As Emily slid down out of the pickup truck, she called to him, "Waiting for me?"

Bradley limped toward her, leaning on his cane, "Kinda wondered if you might stop by this morning."

"You heard?"

Bradley nodded. "Got a text from one of my neighbors just after it happened. She lives on the same street as Lexi Cooper. Thought I'd want to know."

Emily looked at Bradley. He had a strange expression on his face. It was like there was more to the story than he was saying. Or maybe it was just his old pain surfacing? Emily wasn't sure. "You mean, your friend wanted you to know because someone else was taken?"

"Well, that, and there's something else…"

By the way Bradley said it, Emily knew it wasn't good news. She frowned, knitting her brows together, suddenly feeling uneasy, "What is it?"

"Lexi Cooper is the granddaughter of one of the first victims."

Emily's mind began to spin. One of the relatives of an earlier victim had been taken by the same killer? In all of her years in law enforcement, Emily had never heard of anything like that. She sighed, staring down at her boots, kicking a little piece of gravel in Bradley's driveway. Before she could say anything else, Bradley said, the words coming out slowly, "Come back to the garage. Let me show you."

Emily followed him, adjusting the holster on her hip and pulling her T-shirt down over the butt of her gun. She had a sinking feeling in her gut that wasn't leaving her. Inside, Bradley flipped on the overhead lights, the bulbs buzzing. He walked over to the board where all the murder data was hung, his cane making a tapping noise on the concrete floor. "Here it is. See this man?" he said, pointing with his free hand as he leaned on the cane. "This is Junior Owen. He was body one-two. First-year, second body — at least the ones we know of — that's what the law enforcement people say. At the time, he had a daughter who was in high school, Keira. She's now married to a firefighter named Randy. They had a baby pretty much right away. That'd be Lexi. Lexi would've been Junior's grand-daughter."

Emily slumped down in the chair she sat in the day before. Bradley came and joined her, holding his cane between his knees, staring at the floor. They sat in silence for a couple of minutes. Emily kept glancing back and forth between all the pictures. "Are any of the other victims related?"

"Not that I know of," Bradley said. "Maybe the killer doesn't know she's related?"

"Anything is possible." The killer might know, or he might not. There was no way of knowing that, not yet. The details were still foggy. She turned and stared at Bradley, "Do you know anything else about what happened this morning?"

"Other than Lexi's missing?" Bradley shook his head, "Naw, not a thing."

Emily almost told him she'd driven by the scene on her way to his house, but decided against it, pressing her lips together.

The less information the people in town knew about her, the better. The more time she spent with Bradley, the less she saw him as any type of threat, but it paid to never be too careful. She'd been in situations in the past that had turned on a dime. One minute things were going fine, the next minute not so much. It was better to prevent those moments if she could.

Walking past all the information in Bradley's garage, she tried to absorb as much of it as she could. This was a much more complicated case than usual. For the most part, she dealt with one victim and one family at a time, not a whole town full of them. She needed to think. "I need to head out and handle a couple of things. I'll be in touch."

Saying nothing more, Emily walked back out to her truck. As she slid in, she saw the curtain in Bradley's front window flutter. Carla, Bradley's wife, must be inside. Why Carla hadn't come out to introduce herself yet, Emily wasn't sure, but it sent a shiver down her spine. She couldn't imagine what it was like for the two of them, the ghosts of the Tifton torso killer lurking in their garage. To some degree, Emily agreed with Carla — having all of the murder data constantly posted where it could be seen was a little bit creepy. Emily chewed her lip as she started the truck, hoping that Lexi Cooper's information wasn't added to that board anytime soon.

Pulling out of the driveway, Emily called Mike on the speakerphone as she headed into the center of Tifton. Even though it was pushing toward lunchtime, she needed coffee. "Anything new?" she asked, pulling into a parking lot where there was a small bakery that had its lights on with a neon sign in the window advertising hot coffee.

"Nothing yet. Flynn just got here, so we'll start seeing what we can find on our end. I've got a buddy that can help us with the FBI files."

How Mike knew someone that had access to classified

investigation files on an open case with the FBI, Emily didn't know. She didn't want to ask. "Think there's any way I can get in to talk to Lexi's family?" As soon as the words came out of her mouth, Emily knew that was impossible. Between the local police and the FBI, Lexi's parents wouldn't have a moment of peace until something got resolved.

Flynn's voice came over the phone, "I don't think so. The FBI has a pretty big black eye on this case, given how long it's gone on without them being able to solve it. It's not a good look if you know what I mean."

Emily knew exactly what he meant. That's why police departments and federal agencies had cold case divisions like the one she used to work in. Specialized agents could sometimes find evidence buried in a case that could solve it, even after decades. Emily leaned back in the seat, extending her arm straight, gripping the steering wheel as hard as she could. Nothing about this case is going the way it should, she realized. Instead of working on a cold case, she'd walked into an active investigation. She needed someone who could give her insight into the case and help her figure out who the actual killer was. "Is there anyone else that lives in town who's a relative of a victim from a while back? Not one of the newer cases, but one of the old cases?"

There was a pause. Emily could hear noise on the other end of the line; like someone was tapping on a keyboard and someone else was flipping through some papers. A second later, Flynn said, "There's one that might be worth talking to. Her name is Sierra Day. Her brother, Joe, was killed quite a few years ago — in year three. I saw information about him on the unsolved site, too. If I remember correctly there were two kids in the family, Sierra and Joe. Joe disappeared and they found his torso a few days later. Sierra is a pharmacist. Works at the local drugstore.

"You have any other information on her?"

"Based on what I'm seeing here," Mike said, "It looks like she's unmarried and has worked at the drugstore since she graduated from college. Looks like she lives on the outskirts of town. That's the address she pays utilities for."

"Her mom? Where is she?"

There was more typing at the other end of the line, "Dead. Committed suicide after Joe's death." Before Emily had a chance to say anything, she heard some mumbling on the other end of the line, "I've got the address for the house she lives in."

"Send me that," she said and hung up. Sliding out of the truck, Emily went into the bakery and came out a minute later with a bottle of water, a large coffee, and a ham and egg wrap sandwich. As she started up the truck, it beeped, a new location in her GPS. Sierra's house. Emily ate as she drove, her mind empty. She hoped that Sierra could give her something significant on the case. Without it, she'd be in the same position as the police and the FBI. She'd have nothing.

The drive to Sierra's house took a little longer than Emily expected, the GPS guiding her on roads that seem to twist and weave for no reason. Emily wondered why they weren't straighter, but looking at the dense foliage as she drove, she realized the first people that settled in the area probably built trails that avoided the largest of the trees and the swampiest parts of the land.

Following the road around a curve that skirted a bog, Emily saw knew that living with a loss like the families had suffered in Tifton was a nearly impossible proposition. Knowing that someone you loved could be at home one day and floating in the Little Bayou Pond the next seemed like a harsh reality against the gentle nature of the people she'd met so far. How they were surviving, she wasn't sure. From what she knew of the case, Sierra's brother had been a solid member of the community. Emily shifted in the seat of the truck, fighting off a cramp in her leg. From experience, Emily knew families did one of two things after a crime like the ones in Tifton – they banded together, or they broke apart. How Sierra's family was surviving, Emily would soon find out.

After a few minutes, the woods started to thin a little, the truck starting up a rise. Emily finished the sandwich she bought, balling up the paper and tossing it on the seat next to her. She took a long drink of water and then followed it with a couple of sips of hot coffee. In the heat, it seemed strange to want something hot to drink, but the cool air-conditioning pumping out of the vents in the truck made it pleasant. The caffeine wasn't a bad thing, either.

The road rose up one final hill and then plateaued, a small farmhouse off in the distance. Hearing the GPS beep, Emily turned right onto a driveway. The tires of her truck bumped onto the rough gravel as the big vehicle chugged up the hill. As she got closer, she could see the home, its wide porch spread out in front of her, the siding painted in pale yellow. Unlike some of the other homes she'd seen in the area, this one wasn't on stilts, but then again, it was at the top of the hill. If there was going to be torrential rain or flooding, the water would run right past the house and down onto the road Emily just drove over. Emily parked the truck in the front and sent a quick text to Mike, "Here," hoping there was enough cell signal for the text to deliver. At least if something happened, he'd know where to start looking for her.

As Emily slid out of the truck and slammed the door, the thick Louisiana heat covered her like a blanket. It made walking feel more like swimming, the humid air collecting on every surface, from her hair to her skin to her clothes. By the time she got to the front door, she was sweating again.

There was no doorbell on the front door of the farmhouse, so Emily knocked. A minute later, she heard locks clicking in the frame. The door opened. In front of Emily was a petite woman, not too much younger than she was. Sierra Day looked like the kind of person who spent hours running every week. She was fit and wiry, wearing a loose T-shirt and a pair of shorts, her feet bare. Her cropped hair was pulled into a short ponytail behind her neck. She wore no makeup. "Who are you?" Sierra said, staring at Emily.

"My name is Emily. I wanted to talk to you about your brother." As Emily said the words, she wondered how many times someone had shown up at Sierra's house saying the same thing. How many times had Sierra told the story of her brother's death, or what she knew of it?

"Are you with the police?" Sierra narrowed her eyes.

"No, I'm a private investigator. I'm working with the Barker family." It wasn't technically true that she'd been hired by the Barker's, but at least she could say honestly she was trying to help them. That was the best she could do.

"Bradley?"

Emily nodded. Sierra didn't invite her into the house. Instead, she motioned to a couple of chairs sitting on the front porch. "Okay, I have a couple of minutes. You can sit here. You want something to drink?"

"No, thank you. I won't be here long."

Though the South was famous for its hospitality, Sierra seemed uncomfortable, even awkward. Emily began to wonder if losing her brother had caused the sort of shift in her emotions that took away the warmth of so many of the people in the South. Emily pushed the thought away. It wasn't helpful, at least not at the moment.

"What do you want to know?"

"As I said, I'm here trying to help Bradley Barker get some closure about his brother's death. From what I understand, there's been a series of killings and your brother, Joe, was one of them. Is that true?"

Sierra nodded, looking down at her lap, picking at a cuticle.

"Yeah, that's right. Joe was victim three-one. His story isn't much different from any of the others. He left work one day, went out with some friends, and we never heard from him again. My dad called the local police, and they found his body a few days later — or at least what was left of it." Sierra looked at Emily, "He'd been chopped apart, like the others."

Unlike Bradley, Sierra's pain over losing her brother seemed fresher for some reason. Emily glanced at Sierra before asking her next question. She noticed that Sierra's fingernails were bitten down as far as they could go, her cuticles red and inflamed. Many victims developed nervous habits to try to cope with the loss. Some of them drank, some of them gambled, some of them bit their nails to the quick. There'd even been one family member Emily met years back who'd managed to pull most of the hair out of one side of her head. Grief was a strange business.

"You heard about Lexi Cooper?"

Sierra's head snapped up, her eyes wild, "No. Who's that?"

"A little girl. Five years old. Taken overnight out of her bedroom."

"Do you think it's him again?" Sierra said, standing up. She started to pace.

Emily watched her for a second, staying seated. As Sierra turned, Emily glanced at the waistband of her shorts making sure there were no weapons concealed there. Sierra had become agitated pretty quickly, enough to make Emily edgy. "I don't know. What I do know is there are a bunch of cold cases that local law enforcement and the FBI have ignored for a long time. That's why I'm here."

Sierra sat back down on the chair and looked at Emily, "So, you know Cash?"

Emily shook her head no, "Who's that?"

"He's with the FBI." Before Emily could respond, Sierra got up and darted into the house coming back a second later with a business card in her hand. "This guy," she pointed to the card, "This guy is in charge of the whole investigation. I just talked to him a couple of days ago. I think he's trying, maybe more than the last agent, but he doesn't have anything."

Emily pulled her phone out of her back pocket and took a picture of the business card, sending it off via a text to Mike. "Look into this guy for me?" she typed and then looked back at Sierra, handing the card back to her. "You said you just talked to him a couple of days ago?"

Sierra nodded. "I was worried this would happen. I called him to see if he found out anything else about the case, or if he had any new leads. He didn't. He seems to be a nice guy," she sighed, "but he's no different than any of the other investigators who've been on my brother's case since he died. They all say they're going to do something, but nothing happens."

Emily knew it was time to shift the conversation. If they got too far off on talking about the investigators, Emily might never get to the details she needed about the case. "If you don't mind, could you give me a little bit more information about what's been going on? Does anyone have any leads about who the killer could be?" Emily knew that asking Sierra if there were any leads in the case was likely a dead end, but she'd discovered early in her career that asking the obvious questions sometimes netted the best results.

Sierra shook her head. "That's the thing. No one seems to be able to get a handle on this case. We don't know if it's somebody who lives here in town or somebody who just passes through every six months — like a trucker. The idea that it's someone living here among us is just terrifying." Sierra shivered even though the heat of the day had settled on the front porch where they were sitting.

"What about the rest of your family? Do they have any theories about what happened?"

Sierra looked away for a second. When she glanced back,

her eyes were filled with tears, "A couple of years after Joe disappeared, my mom killed herself. Took a bunch of pills. Ironic, given the fact I'm a pharmacist." Sierra picked at her cuticles again. "My dad, he's not in good shape since Joe died. Joe was always the favorite if you know what I mean."

Emily understood that. Although parents were supposed to love their kids equally, they never did, at least not in Emily's estimation. Emily's younger sister, Angelica, was always the favorite, no matter how many rules she broke or how many times she disappointed their parents. "I know what you mean. My younger sister is the favorite, too." Offering little details about her own life, meaningless ones, helped to forge a bond between her and the person she was interviewing.

Sierra nodded, "So you understand."

"I do." Emily looked away for a moment, concerned she was offering too much information about herself. The goal was to be anonymous. But the more of these cases she worked, the harder it was to do that. Emily could have lied to Sierra, but if she played her cards right, no one would suspect she was doing anything other than helping Bradley. Mike had been wise to check her into the bed-and-breakfast without her real last name. Sure, someone could track her plates, but Emily suspected the FBI agents working the case were far too worried about Lexi to be concerned about what Emily was doing. That was good news, or at least she hoped it would be. With any luck, she could either resolve the situation on her own or at least send them in the right direction and get out of Tifton before she ended up in anyone's crosshairs. A shiver ran up her spine. Taking these cases was becoming riskier every single time. Working on cases on her own was the closest thing she had to police work, but it wasn't the same as when she was in the department. Emily made a mental note to do some thinking about her future when she got back to Chicago, but the time for that wasn't now. She was here to help the victims and do that to the best of her ability.

From behind her, Emily sensed movement. A cat appeared on the windowsill, orange and white. Sierra nodded, "That's Charlie. He keeps me company."

"Do you see your dad very often?"

"I stop over to see him every day or so. As I said, he's not doing well. I'm sure the news about the little girl won't help things. Seems like I just get him back on track and then another six months ticks by and there we go again."

Unsolved serial cases were some of the hardest on the victims. Every time someone else disappeared, the families were forced to think about the loss of their loved one again. "So, is there anything you can tell me about who you think the killer might be? No one has ever come up with a working theory?"

Sierra fidgeted in her seat, "As I said, the FBI doesn't seem to have anything. Why, I don't know. You'd think that after all these years, they'd have figured something out, but they haven't. They've left all of us hanging." Sierra stood up, crossing her arms. The conversation was making her uncomfortable. She looked back at Emily, "Listen, I've gotta go in and get ready for work. I'm working close today. The only other thing I would say is that I don't think it's somebody who knows much about this town. And the one thing I can't figure out is why this person kills. There has to be something to the six-month time-frame. It's like clockwork. I've always wondered if something happened to this person and he lives it again twice a year, punishing us all." Sierra dropped her hands down to her sides, "I don't know. The more I think about it, the more upsetting it becomes. I gotta go."

Sierra left Emily sitting on the front porch, the door banging closed behind her. For a second, Emily thought about pounding on the door again, but she didn't want to push her luck. She didn't need Sierra calling the local police on her. As

Emily got in her truck and pulled away, she looked in their rearview mirror. Charlie was still sitting there, Sierra's face looming above him. Did Sierra really have to go to work? Maybe she was just done talking about what had happened to her brother.

ash didn't waste too much time at the scene talking to the local police. They never knew anything anyway. He took a moment to introduce himself and then nodded towards the house, "The family inside?"

The officer standing in the driveway, whose name badge read Rogers, nodded. "Yeah, they are. It's not a good morning for them."

"That's the truth," Cash said, walking away.

Inside, the house wasn't what Cash expected. On the other trips he'd made to Tifton, he'd been inside many of the homes. Most of them were dated and worn. Not Lexi Cooper's house. It looked like whoever lived there spent every waking minute fixing it up. New floors, new paint, modern decorations. Not at all what you'd expect for a tiny rural town in the middle of nowhere, but then again, Cash realized you wouldn't expect it to be the target of a serial killer either. He heard the murmur of voices coming from the center of the house. Looking behind him, he saw Janet was in tow. He stopped for a minute and whispered, "Let's just assess this first. Maybe there is another explanation."

"Like what?" she frowned.

By the look on Janet's face, Cash could tell she'd already decided it was the serial killer again. "I don't know, maybe there is an ex-wife or ex-husband involved. Maybe an ex-boyfriend that could have taken Lexi. I don't want to assume it's our serial killer until we know something more, okay?"

Janet nodded.

Although Cash's gut told him the serial killer had escalated to nabbing children, he hoped it wasn't the case. How he and his team would respond would become clear in the next couple of minutes. He weighed the options in his head. Serial killer or domestic issue? Cash was betting on serial killer. Cash swallowed as he turned the corner into the kitchen, a bright space facing the backyard, a bank of windows staring out at the green grass. The kitchen was filled with white cabinets and hardwood floors. It looked like something from a magazine. Huddled around a table with four chairs on the opposite side of the kitchen island, a man and woman sat with a police officer. The noise of Cash and Janet coming into the kitchen alerted the officer. Standing up, he said, "Give me just a moment, okay? I'll be right back."

"Strickland, it's nice to see you again, I think," the man said, extending his hand.

"I feel the same way, Kevin. Wish it was under better circumstances." Two years before, Cash had met Kevin Barnfield after the last Tifton detective retired and moved out of the area. Kevin was a good guy but trying to deal with a serial killer on his own had proven to be too much. Cash was lucky, though. Kevin knew the resources needed to solve the case were far beyond what the parish could offer. He'd always welcomed Cash's help and never interfered. At least there was that to be grateful for. "Want to give me an idea of what's going on? We just got the basics this morning."

Kevin pulled a black-covered notebook out of his pocket,

checking his notes. "Wish I had more for you. Apparently, the mom, her name is Keira, went in to go and check on Lexi at about two o'clock in the morning on her way to the bathroom. Randy, Lexi's dad, was sound asleep. When Keira checked Lexi, she was tucked safely in her bed, from the way she tells it. When they got up this morning, she was gone. Dad found the room empty when he was getting ready for his shift at the firehouse. They searched the house and the yard but didn't find anything."

"Were the doors locked?" It was a basic question, but one that needed to be asked. Whether a five-year-old could unlock doors or not, Cash wasn't sure, since he didn't have any of his own children, but it was worth a shot.

Kevin nodded, "Yeah, unlike a lot of people in Tifton, Randy said they lock the doors every night." Kevin shook his head and leaned around the corner and pointed toward the front door, "Why more people don't lock up at night, I'll never understand, especially with the killer still running around." He pointed, "See that deadbolt there? Randy said it's too high for Lexi to open. She's just a little one."

Cash swallowed. He hated cases that involved kids. "Did I hear right she's five?"

"That's right." Kevin reached into his back pocket and pulled out a picture, handing it to Cash, "They gave me this. It was taken about a month ago."

Staring at it, Cash saw Lexi had long blonde hair and a wide smile. In the picture, she was wearing red shorts and a white top, her feet bare. It looked like a picture the family could have taken in the backyard while she was out playing. "Any chance this is a family abduction? Any exes in the picture we need to know about?"

"Doesn't seem like it," Kevin said, closing the cover to his notebook. "On background, Keira and Randy met in high school and got pregnant shortly thereafter, while he was at the

Fire Academy. Neither of them had any significant exes in their past." '

Cash frowned, "Neither of them was married before or had a lover that might be a problem?"

Kevin shook his head no, "Doesn't look that way. Wish that was the case, though. Might make the job easier."

Cash caught Keira looking at him. He turned away, not quite ready to talk to her yet. "Any chance Lexi just wandered off? Any idea about entry or exit points?" Cash knew he was prolonging the agony of having to talk to the parents, but at least if he could get some more details out of Kevin, he'd have a better place to start.

"The parents don't think she wandered off." Kevin pointed, "Let me show you her bedroom." Cash followed Kevin down the hallway, pictures of the family dotting the walls. A quick left turn and they were in Lexi's bedroom. It was on the first floor, at the back of the house.

It looked like what Cash imagined every little girl's bedroom did — pink everywhere cast against fresh white walls, a pink comforter on the bed. There was a patterned rug on the floor, and a dollhouse in the corner, a plastic one, like the one his niece had. She was only a bit older than Lexi. Cash swallowed. He couldn't imagine if his brother lost his daughter. Walking to the only window in the room, Cash looked out. It faced the backyard. There was a stretch of grass and then dense woods. Cash tilted his head and looked at the window. It was slightly ajar. "Anybody touch this?"

"Not that I know of. You see something?"

"It looks like the window isn't completely closed. You think Lexi would have done that?" Without saying anything, Cash looked over his shoulder at Janet, who gave him a nod. She pulled her phone out of her back pocket and sent a text. One of the agents they brought with them was a specialist in crime scene analysis. If anybody could find fingerprints on the window, it would be Jeremy. "Let's get Jeremy in here to take a look and see what he thinks. Maybe he can pull some prints for us."

Cash stayed by the window, wanting to make sure no one touched it until Jeremy came in. Jeremy was a thin man, the kind that could never eat enough food to fill out his frame. He had dark wavy hair and thick glasses. When Cash first met Jeremy, he assumed Jeremy couldn't see very well. On the contrary, Jeremy saw things that no one else did, solving more cases than he'd ever been given credit. Cash said a silent prayer that today would be one of those days.

A moment later, Jeremy came into the room, already wearing gloves and shoe covers, carrying what looked like a toolbox. Flipping it open, he looked at Cash, "What you got?"

"This window looks to be cracked open."

Jeremy leaned over and looked at it, "I agree. Want me to work it up?"

Cash nodded, "Yeah. Give me everything — fingerprints, fibers, hairs. And take a peek on the outside, too. No telling what might be out there."

"You got it."

Cash looked at Janet, "Let's get one of the other agents in here to stay with Jeremy while he does his thing. As far as I'm concerned, this entire room is now an active crime scene. Let's keep the parents out for the time being. And you and I, we're going to go see what they know."

Janet nodded, not looking up, still on her phone. The team came prepared with radios but didn't use them during the initial phases of the investigation. Texting was just as easy and was less disruptive to the victims. "Okay. All set."

"Good. Let's go," Cash said, leaving Jeremy behind.

Heading back down the hallway, Cash found Keira and Randy still sitting at the table. They were huddled over glasses of water and a box of tissues, some of them crumpled nearby.

As they got closer, Randy Cooper stood up, "Thanks for coming. I'm Randy," he motioned to Keira, "and this is my wife, Keira."

"Sorry to meet under these circumstances," Cash said. "Mind if I sit?"

"Not at all," Randy said.

As Cash sat down at the table, he heard Keira start to whimper again. "As I said, I'm sorry we're meeting under these circumstances, but I want to assure you that the entire weight of the FBI is behind figuring out what happened to Lexi. Can you walk me through it?" Cash knew that Kevin had likely given him all the information he needed to move forward but hearing it from the parents gave them something to focus on. It was also possible they hadn't given every detail to Kevin — it could be something they didn't remember or something they simply didn't want to tell someone who lived locally, especially in a town as small as Tifton. Word traveled fast.

Randy covered Keira's hand with his own and cleared his throat, "I'm sure the detective told you everything already, but it's pretty simple. We put Lexi to bed about eight o'clock last night. Keira checked on her at about two o'clock this morning on her way back from the bathroom. She was there. When I went in to check on her a couple of hours later, she wasn't there."

"About what time was that?"

"I don't know, maybe around four? I was supposed to be at the station by six a.m. We work twenty-four-hour shifts at the fire station. We've got twenty-four hours on duty and then forty-eight hours off. I was up early, getting my gear together to get to work."

"Thanks," Cash said, looking over his shoulder at Janet. She was leaning on the kitchen island, taking notes. They had worked enough cases together that he no longer had to ask her to do certain things. She just did them on her own. Case notes were one of them. "Any chance Lexi could have wandered off?"

Keira began to sob, "Wandered off? Why would my baby leave the house in the middle of the night? It just doesn't make any sense."

Cash hadn't looked closely at Keira until that moment. She looked like an older version of Lexi, the same long blonde hair and complexion. At the moment, her hair was pulled into a ponytail, her eyes red and puffy, a few stains on the front of her T-shirt. Cash guessed she slept in the same clothes the night before and hadn't bothered to change, not that he would have either.

"Ma'am, I'm not saying she did, but we have to look at all the possibilities so we know the best way to get Lexi back home. Does that make sense?" Cash said the words slowly hoping they could penetrate the grief written all over Keira's face. She nodded but said nothing.

Randy looked at Cash, "I don't think it's possible she got out of the house. Come over here, I'll show you."

As Cash got up, Janet moved to sit with Keira. At the front door, Randy said, "This deadbolt, here, we always keep it locked. Lexi isn't tall enough to get to it. I showed it to the detective, too."

"And you're sure it was locked last night?"

Randy shook his head, "At this moment I'm not sure about anything, but I'm more sure than not it was locked. We're in a pretty good habit of doing that."

As Cash stared at the door, Randy's voice interrupted his thoughts, "I didn't need to bring you over here to show you the lock. You could've seen that from over there." Randy glanced toward the kitchen where Keira was still seated at the table, "I just want to ask you about this, man-to-man, away from my wife. She's awfully upset. You think it's the serial killer?"

Cash's stomach clenched. The idea that the Tifton killer

had a little girl was almost more than he could bear, but he needed to stay professional, no matter what, "Honestly, it's too soon to tell. We found Lexi's window cracked open. It could be as simple as she decided she wanted to go outside in the middle of the night and didn't want to wake you and got herself turned around in the woods."

The muscles in Randy's jaw flickered, "Do you think that's a possibility, what, with the timing? It can't be a coincidence that we're at the six-month mark."

Cash paused. There was a point in every investigation when the people involved, whether they were the family or the investigators, had to face reality. Whether that time was now or not, Cash wasn't sure. He didn't want to say anything that would upset the Coopers more, but he had to balance that with the fact that Tifton had an active serial killer that hadn't been caught. Randy was right, the timing was coincidental at best, suspect at worst. "I understand where you're going, Mr. Cooper," Cash said, "but my job is to make sure that the team keeps every option open so that we can get the best result. In other words, we don't know. I wish I could be more specific, but I've been here for precisely fifteen minutes and this might take a little bit of time. Can you be patient with me?"

Randy nodded. "I get it. When I get on the scene of an accident, people are cryin' and yellin'. It's not easy." He reached out and put a hand on Cash's arm, "You'll do whatever you can to save my baby, right?"

"Absolutely."

16

Emily stopped back at the bed-and-breakfast after meeting with Sierra. The day had started in such a hurry she hadn't even taken a shower, and in the summer heat of Louisiana, she needed one.

After getting cleaned up, she used the back staircase to get to her truck. She found a little restaurant on the outskirts of town and grabbed a bite to eat, waiting to hear from Mike and Flynn.

As Emily was finishing her sandwich, she glanced up and saw an FBI agent standing in line at the cashier. The woman behind the counter was stacking up white bags, filled with Styrofoam containers. A takeout order, probably for the team at Lexi's house, Emily thought. That didn't bode well. They were probably hunkering down if they were ordering dinner for the team. Emily wiped her mouth and left enough money on the table to cover the check and a generous tip for the waitress. Part of her wanted to go right out to her truck and drive away, but another part of her was curious. Was this the same agent Sierra had told her about? Emily walked up and stood in line behind him. He had FBI written all over him, from the yellow lettering on the back of his T-shirt to the oversized holster and gun on his hip. Emily leaned around toward him and said, "Excuse me? Are you with the FBI?" It had to sound like the dumbest question in the world given how much lettering was all over his body.

The man turned. He was blonde, with cropped hair and narrow eyes offset by a square jaw. The front of his T-shirt had the round emblem of the FBI and on the other side it said "Strickland." Bingo, Emily thought.

He nodded. "Yes. You need something?"

"Well, I'm a researcher. I'm in town looking into the serial killer that supposedly is here in Tifton. Is that why you're here?" Emily tried to make herself sound naïve. It was a huge risk talking to the investigator of the case, but she had to know what he was like. Knowing his personality could be the difference between her leaving Tifton in handcuffs for interfering in an investigation, or something worse, or finding an ally. Which one he was, she didn't know. Not yet.

Cash's eyes narrowed, "What kind of researcher?"

Emily's heart started to beat a little faster in her chest, wondering how long she could prolong the lie, "I'm getting a degree in criminal justice and I'm working on a paper. You know, that kind of research."

"I can't talk about an ongoing investigation. You should know that." Cash turned back around, watching the waitress as she assembled the bags of food.

"Oh, I know," Emily said to his back. "I was just hoping you could maybe send me in the right direction?"

"Exactly what are you trying to find out?" Cash said, spinning around.

By the way he said it, Emily knew she was in his crosshairs. She could tell he was taking a mental picture of her, noticing the details of her face and what she was wearing. Hopefully, her gun was concealed well enough underneath her shirt that he wouldn't notice. "I don't know, I'm just trying to figure out the motivation behind the killings. Serial killers are all different, right? Would you agree with that? It seems like they all carry psychological scars, don't you think?"

Cash turned away from Emily, handing the woman behind the counter a credit card. FBI issued, Emily was sure. A moment later, Cash jammed the card back in his pocket and picked up the orders, turning towards her, "Listen, I don't know who you are. Maybe you're doing research, maybe you aren't. What I will tell you is if you're sniffing around for a story, you're sniffing in the wrong direction. As I said, I can't talk about an ongoing investigation. Now, if you'll excuse me, I have work to do."

Emily watched him walk out the door, calling behind him as he left, "Okay, thank you!

Have a nice dinner!" She hoped it wasn't too much, but it probably was. So much for staying anonymous, she thought, mad at herself. What was wrong with her on this case?

At the counter, she bought a brownie from the woman and walked out to her truck. She chewed it, the air-conditioner pouring cool air over her as she thought about Cash Strickland. Emily wiped her fingers on a napkin and pulled out her phone, looking at the picture of the business card she'd taken at Sierra's house. Yup, it was the same person. She didn't expect him to be quite so harsh, but then it would be hard to blame him for his lack of public relations skills with the pressure he was under. Just as she put her phone down, it rang.

"You have news for me?" Emily said.

"Well, sorta. How are things down there?" Mike asked.

"Getting a little tense, if you know what I mean. I just bumped into the lead investigator for the FBI."

"What? How did that happen?"

"There's only one restaurant here in Tifton. I stopped to get a bite to eat. He was there picking up food. I went up behind him and pretended I was a criminal justice student and asked him some questions. Not receptive. Very by the book."

"Why did you do that?? Did you tell him your name?"

"I don't know. It seemed like a good idea at the moment, you know, get a read on him. And no, I didn't tell him my name. He didn't ask. I would've lied anyway." For a second, it bothered Emily that she was able to spread so much untruth around her, but it was the only way for her to do her job without getting caught. Not that there was anything wrong with investigating, but there were consequences for offering the kind of justice she provided for her clients. "He just gave me the typical 'it's an ongoing investigation' commentary and walked away. Definitely need some lessons in PR, if you know what I mean."

"That was part of the reason I was calling. Flynn and I just got done digging through Strickland's FBI files."

"Your buddy got you access?"

"And then some. I've got files on the whole team, just in case. The FBI sent their heavy hitters down to Tifton. Strickland's been on the job for eleven years. From the personnel file, it looks like they gave him this particular team to try to solve the issue in Tifton. There's a lot of pressure on him. I don't know if he knows that, but he's met with the FBI's top profilers and forensic scientists over the last three months."

Emily heard another voice on the phone. Flynn. "Just like any organization, the FBI has different levels of experts. The ones that Strickland has been meeting with are top-notch, the best the agency has to offer."

Mike continued, "Not that they're as good as those of us on the outside if you know what I mean."

Emily smiled. She knew Mike preferred people who were experts in their field outside of culture. Based on his bring up, she couldn't blame him. Mike didn't have the personality to fit in in any normal organization. She sighed, "Okay, give me an overview of what I'm dealing with when it comes to Strickland. I'd like to talk to Lexi's parents if I can."

Flynn's voice interrupted, "I don't think that's a good idea. I'd stay well away from Lexi's house. Strickland is tough. He's closed some big cases. That's how he got the gig to go to Tifton. Their house is going to be crawling with the FBI and law enforcement. If you want to try to get in and out of Tifton without being detected, going over there isn't the way to do it." There was a pause, "In fact, with how much law enforcement is hanging around, you might want to just come home..."

Emily frowned, taking another bite of the brownie. "How am I going to leave this case sitting when there is a five-year-old girl that is missing, not to mention the slew of bodies this person has left behind? You two are the ones that convinced me to take the case, and now you want me to just turn tail and run?"

Mike came back on the phone, "That's not exactly what we're suggesting, Emily. Just be careful around Strickland and his team. They want to get this guy as bad as you do, maybe even more so. Strickland's not the kind that will stop at anything to meet his goal."

"All right. I gotta go." Emily hung up on them. They weren't helping.

Emily started the truck and pulled out of the parking lot, not sure where to go next. She could go back to the bed-and-breakfast and regroup, waiting until the morning, but she wasn't ready to quit for the night yet. She pulled the truck out into the little traffic that was trickling along the road and she turned the wheel, not knowing exactly where she wanted to go. The image of Lexi Cooper's face was burned in her mind. Where was she? As Emily drove out of town, she started to think about Bradley and Sierra. Emily hadn't even met the rest of the families and yet the burden of their grief was almost overwhelming.

There'd only been one other time in her career that Emily had dealt with a serial killer. It was in her second year in the cold case division. A couple of homicide detectives had shown up at the office first thing in the morning, huddled with Detective Aldo. A few minutes later, the detective waved Emily into her office. "These guys have some questions about some of the cases you're working. Can you help them out?"

Helping them with a few case files turned into weeks of work, connecting the dots between victims that seemed to not be related at all. Three months later and with two more dead bodies in the ground, Emily and a couple of other detectives arrested a small man that ran a dry-cleaning shop. Over the time he'd owned his store, he managed to kill twenty-five people, dissolving their bodies in dry cleaning solvent and dumping what was left in a field outside the city after they complained about his service.

Driving through Tifton, what Emily remembered most about that case was the press conference after. All of Chicago PD's brass had shown up in their dress uniforms, a wooden podium set up in the lobby. The police chief, the mayor, and a couple of other senior staff members, including Detective Aldo were lined up behind him, the bright lights and the chatter of camera lenses taking thousands of pictures making it difficult to concentrate. Emily remembered standing in the back with her partner, Lou Gonzales. They were both tired. Neither of them had slept much in the few weeks before. Emily remembered scanning the crowd, seeing the faces of people she and Lou had interviewed, sitting in their houses, drinking cup after cup of lukewarm, weak coffee, watching the pallid sadness on each of their faces. Their grief was a weight she couldn't shed.

After the press conference, Detective Aldo had called Emily and Lou to her office. She gave them each a week off, paid, without using their vacation time. "Lord knows you've spent enough time working on this case over the last few months. I tried to get you two weeks, but the chief would only approve a week." Emily remembered objecting, telling Detective Aldo that she was fine to go right back to work. Detective Aldo shook her head. "Nope. This is not a discussion. Both of you need to go home, spend time with your loved ones, eat some good food, sleep and watch a bunch of trashy movies. I don't want to see you or hear from you for a week. That's an order. Now go."

Emily still remembered the restless feeling she had all that week, as though there was unfinished business when there wasn't. What was unfinished was the fact that yes, they had solved the case, but they weren't able to resolve the grief the families lived with every day. Sure, there were no more questions, but that didn't mean it was the end. The families would have to face the killer again in court, for what could be weeks and months, and even years of trials and appeals.

It would be the same for the families in Tifton, no matter what she was able to do.

As Emily turned into the bed-and-breakfast, she felt the same restlessness as when she worked the serial killer case in Chicago. She sat in the truck for a minute, taking a sip from a water bottle she'd had from earlier that morning. She couldn't just go up to her room, watch television and go to sleep. Somewhere out there was Lexi Cooper, and the person that had her was likely the same person that killed Sean Parker and Joe Day and Corey Hawkins, not to mention all the other names in the file.

Emily put the car in reverse and drove back out of the parking lot. Sleep could wait. As she drove back out of the center of town, Emily's mind drifted to her dad. They'd never been close. He was a quiet man and hardly ever said a word. People like that were hard to get to know. As Emily passed the drugstore where Sierra Day worked, the lights just flickering on with the sunset drooping over the horizon, Emily wondered if Sierra felt a strain around her dad the same way she did around her own. Emily wasn't sure if she and her dad could ever repair their relationship. She swallowed, pressing the accelerator a little harder, a knot forming in her stomach. So many of the things that life promised — a husband, a family, a good job, friends — all those had been stripped away from her. What did she have? Her dog, a guy that taught her boxing, and a few acquaintances here and there. Even Angelica, her sister, was hard to connect with since she lived overseas. At that moment, Emily thought that maybe she would just pack everything up, figure out a way to get Miner on a plane, and move to Europe to be near Angelica.

But, for the moment, she was still in Tifton, chasing a serial killer.

A few minutes later, Emily came to the turnoff for Bradley Barker's street. Without thinking, she turned her truck onto the street and then up his driveway. There were a few lights on in the house and a couple more on in the garage. She threw the truck into park, getting out. The heat hadn't abated at all. Emily started to sweat before she ever got to the garage, not bothering to go to the house. As she pushed the door open, she saw Bradley, leaning on his cane in front of the whiteboard, a roll of tape in his hand. He was staring at something. "You're back? Didn't expect to see you again today."

Emily stared at the spot where Bradley was standing. There was now a picture of Lexi Cooper attached to the wall, a blank spot below her. "Can't manage to stay away. Had a run-in with the FBI agent that's in charge."

"Strickland?"

Emily nodded. For a second, she thought it was strange that everyone knew exactly who he was but given the fact the FBI seemed to show up every six months, maybe it wasn't. "Yes. Not exactly friendly."

"He's not. I've talked to him or tried to. What did you tell him?"

"I more or less tried to ask him a couple of questions. He blew me off." Emily nodded toward the whiteboard. "What's going on here?"

Bradley sat down in the chair and motioned for Emily to join him, "Just added Lexi Cooper to the board. I hope I can take her down in a day or two, but I'm not thinking it's gonna work out that way. Looks like she might be victim fourteen."

For a minute, Emily thought it was strange the way the words came out; as if he knew something. "How can you be so sure she's not just lost in the woods or something?"

Bradley tilted his head to the side, "I don't know. Maybe it's just a gut feeling, but something tells me the killer has her now."

Emily glanced around the garage as Bradley spoke, noticing the number of tools hanging on the walls. She stood up and walked over to them, looking at his workbench. Saws, drills, sets of screwdrivers, and wrenches — they were all clean and well-maintained. "What's all this for?" she said, a tingle running up her spine.

Bradley shifted in his seat, "Oh, you know. I have a project here and there that I have to take care of. Tractors don't run forever on their own."

Emily squinted, looking back at Bradley and the murder boards and then at the tools. His yard wasn't big enough to need a tractor. Something didn't seem quite right. "Okay. I think I'm gonna head back and do more research. I'll let you know if I find anything," she said, walking for the door, a sick feeling lingering in her stomach.

17

The day spent at the Cooper's house had largely been a waste, Cash realized, sitting in the SUV, finishing the sandwich he got from the restaurant up the road. It didn't take long for Jeremy to process the window, both on the inside and the outside. There was nothing there. Not a hair, not a fiber, not a fingerprint. "That's not all the bad news I have," Jeremy had said, stripping off his gloves just a couple of hours earlier. "I checked in the yard to see if I could find any footprints, you know, places where the grass had been crushed. When the parents ran outside in the middle of the night looking for Lexi, they made a mess of the yard. I've got no way of telling if that was the entry and exit point or not."

"What does your gut say?"

Jeremy raised his eyebrows and tilted his head, "I can't find any other way she could have gotten out of the house. The fact that the window was only slightly open doesn't give us much, but it's better than nothing. If I had to guess, someone got the window open, stepped inside of her room, and pulled her out of the house. That's the risk with a first-floor bedroom."

Sitting in the SUV, Cash replayed the conversation they'd

had in his head. Jeremy was probably right, he thought. Cash had gone over the house with a fine-toothed comb. The only thing that seemed out of place at all was the fact that Lexi's bedroom window was cracked open. He sent agents to talk to all the neighbors. No one had seen anything, no strange vehicles or anything else. It was a small town, so there wasn't much traffic. If anyone had parked on the street, someone would've noticed something.

Cash slipped the last potato chip in his mouth before crumpling up the bag and putting it in the trash and pushing it back inside one of the white plastic bags the food had come in. He wiped his hands on his pants and got out of the SUV, slamming the door. Randy and Keira said the agents were welcome to sit inside to cool off in the air conditioning, but Cash couldn't eat while they were looking at him, their watery eyes begging him for answers he just didn't have.

Walking into the backyard, Cash fought off a wave of frustration. There had to be something they were missing in Lexi's room. He and Jeremy had done a walk-through of every inch of her bedroom but found nothing. How was that possible? Criminals never got in and out without leaving something behind, even a trace. That's all they needed. Just one, small mistake. Rounding the back corner of the yard, Cash stared out, a wave of green grass in front of him, dense woods in the distance.

Cash took a deep breath and thought he could hear the sound of bullfrogs somewhere in the woods. Must be water or at least a few puddles nearby, he realized. The wind was moving in the trees, a few of the branches near the house rubbing together. The breeze did nothing for the humidity.

He walked over to the window of Lexi's room and looked at it again from the outside, wondering what they missed. Figuring out these cases was like trying to do a jigsaw puzzle with half the pieces and no picture of what the end result was

supposed to be. It was hard work — mentally and physically --
in a way most people couldn't understand.

Cash sucked in a deep breath of the humid air, praying it
would cool down, even just a couple of degrees. Staring at the
windowsill, he didn't see anything, not even a chip of paint.
How the perpetrator had been able to wedge Lexi's window
open without chipping the molding, he wasn't sure. Cash shook
his head, turning and staring out in the yard. He felt the
tension in his jaw that was threatening a major headache. They
needed a break and needed one badly. Maybe Lexi got out of
the house another way? To his left, a couple of agents were
standing at the back corner of the driveway, talking to each
other and playing on their phones. Janet was one of them,
nodding and smiling. Cash turned back and looked out across
the backyard, his mind searching. If he was going to kidnap a
little girl out of the house like this, how would he do it? The
thought rattled in his head for a moment as he glanced back at
the window. He looked down at the ground thinking about the
entry points of the house. The front door had too many locks
on it. If what Randy said was true, Lexi wouldn't have been able
to reach the top one to get the door open. Could she have gone
out through the garage? It was possible, but it was likely one of
the parents would've heard the rattle of the garage door
opening in the middle of the night. Her bedroom window was
the best entry and exit point, but how?

Cash walked back over to the window putting his fingers on
the sill, staring at it. In the lower right-hand corner, there was a
slight dent, almost imperceptible. No paint had chipped off. By
looking at it, it was hard to determine if it was a manufacturing
defect or the spot where something small, like maybe a screwdriver, had been pushed in to wedge the window open. "Janet?"
Cash called.

Within a couple of seconds, Janet was by his side. Cash
pointed, "See that dent there? What does that look like to you?"

Janet bent over and stared at it, then frowned, "I dunno. What are you thinking?"

Cash raised his eyebrows, "Well, either it was a goof during manufacturing or that's how somebody wedged a tool in and got this window open. Get Jeremy over here to look at this. I want to know which one it is."

Over his shoulder, Cash saw Janet walk purposefully around the back of the house, disappearing around the corner. Cash walked out into the middle of the backyard, about halfway between the house and the edge of the woods. If the perpetrator had taken Lexi out through the window, then what? Cash looked left and right. To his right, there were more woods, to his left, there was another backyard a way's off. Weighing the options in his mind, Cash realized if someone had grabbed Lexi, they would've had to park a vehicle on the street to move her, or maybe the person disappeared another way.

By the time Cash turned around, Janet and Jeremy were staring at the windowsill. Jeremy had on optics over his glasses that looked like the same kind surgeons used during delicate procedures in the operating room. Cash shook his head. Every time they went on a case, Jeremy had some new gadget he was testing out. "Janet?"

"Yeah?" she said, walking over.

"Do we know what's behind the stand of woods over here?"

She nodded, "The local guys said there's something like a park on the other side. I'm not sure, though."

"Well, let's find out."

18

By the time Emily got back to the hotel, it was nearly dark, the sun sinking low over the horizon, casting an orange and pink glow over Tifton. It was the kind of sunset that photographers loved to take pictures of, but even with its beauty, Emily couldn't shake the fact that there was some sort of pall hanging over Tifton.

Using the back entrance to the bed-and-breakfast, Emily went straight to her room, not wanting to risk bumping into any of the FBI agents that were staying there, not that they'd be back yet. Emily suspected the team would stay at the Cooper's house for most of the night — or at least the majority of the team would, agents cycling in and out to make sure there was a presence at Lexi's house at all hours of the day and night until the case was resolved on the off chance there was a ransom demand or some other contact from the kidnapper. Emily's gut told her no contact was coming.

Slumping down on the bed, Emily pulled off her work boots, her feet hot and sticky from moving around in the Louisiana heat all day. After a quick shower and a clean set of clothes, Emily felt better, ditching her jeans for a pair of leggings. She sat down on the bed, crossing them, leaning against the headboard, her laptop in tow. She pulled her long hair around her shoulder, the damp strands leaving wet streaks on her T-shirt. She had to decide what to do next. Thinking about the last interaction she had with Bradley, Emily weighed whether he could be the killer. Could he? It was something worth thinking about. She picked up her phone and texted Mike. A second later, the videoconferencing software on her computer let her know he was initiating a call. She accepted and within seconds his smiling face was on the screen, along with Miner's. "Well, this is a nice surprise!" she said, looking at her dog, who seemed confused to see Emily on a computer screen, "Hi, boy," she said, her heart sinking in her chest. She swallowed, knowing she needed to stay focused on the case. In her mind, the image of Miner was quickly replaced with that of Lexi Cooper and her blonde hair, wherever she was.

"How are things going down there?" Mike said, Miner disappearing from the screen.

"Okay, if you count avoiding the FBI for a full day and coming back with no leads as a success." Emily's stomach soured as soon as the words came out. That was the truth, wasn't it? She'd been in Tifton for a couple of days and had achieved not much more than avoiding local law enforcement, except for Agent Strickland, and talking to a couple of the families. Pick up the pace, Tizzano, she mumbled to herself, not loud enough for Mike to hear.

"What did you say?" Mike asked, looking confused.

"Nothing. Any news on your end?"

"Yeah. I was just about to call you when you texted."

From the expression on Mike's face, Emily could tell it wasn't necessarily good news. "Spill it. What's the problem?"

"That agent you talked to earlier today?"

Emily's mind flashed back to the interaction she had with Cash Strickland at the restaurant. "Yeah? What about it?"

"Well, apparently he didn't buy your story. The FBI is looking into your background."

Emily's heart started to race. "How's that possible? I didn't even give him my name!" Emily searched her memory for any possible way he could track her, "The truck."

Mike nodded. "That's my guess. You know how I always suggest getting a rental car? That's why."

Emily scowled, "They could search the records of the rental agency and figure out who got it."

"I can hide that a lot better than I can your big blue truck, that's for sure."

Emily shook her head. She'd never had a problem taking the truck on cases before, but nothing about this case was going to plan. No leads. The FBI swarming all over the city. She shook off the thought. "How do you know?"

"A couple of hours ago, my buddy who has access to the FBI files, let me know there was some strange activity. Turns out, after you bumped into Cash at the restaurant, he got your plate number and ran it. He asked the Baton Rouge office to do a full background check on you. Probably because you're asking questions."

"Me and my big mouth," Emily said, half-joking, but half not. It wasn't like her to be impulsive. Maybe the stress of the case was getting to her already.

Mike turned serious, "Emily, this is nothing to joke about. This Strickland, he's got a reputation for being like a dog with a bone. That's the reason the agency gave him the Tifton case in the first place. He doesn't give up. Not ever. At least, that's his reputation within the agency."

As Emily heard the words, the danger in front of her settled on her shoulders. Not only was there the ongoing grief of families who lost loved ones to deal with, but now the very present grief of the Cooper family. On top of that, she was in the crosshairs of the FBI. She swallowed. "Thoughts?" Emily almost didn't want to ask Mike for advice, but she felt paralyzed. It wasn't a feeling she was used to.

"I thought you might ask me that, so my best suggestion would be that we figure out what he knows about you in case you need to slip away before something happens."

"And how do you propose doing that?" Emily said, recrossing her legs on the comforter and staring at the screen.

"The best way? I think you should clone his phone."

The way Mike said it, it came out as plain and as easy as asking her to make pancakes on a Saturday morning. Somehow, Emily didn't think it was going to be that easy or without risk. It was the going to federal prison kind of risk. But Mike was right, knowing what the FBI knew could give her a significant advantage, one that might just be worth it. "How exactly would I do that?"

"Well, actually, I'll do it for you. The thing is, you gotta get close enough to him for your phone and his to connect. Once that happens, I'll be able to see everything he sends out and receives on his phone."

"How close?"

"Six feet. It'll go quicker if you're closer to three. Takes about a minute."

What Mike was talking about was close to professional suicide, not to mention breaking at least a dozen cybersecurity laws. It was one thing to get close to Cash Strickland one time, but to attempt it a second time? That sounded crazy. "There has to be another way. How am I going to get that close to him?"

"I knew you were going to say that. The problem is my buddy with access to the FBI files can only get into them here and there. They keep changing the firewall on him, so Strickland could get information on you and try to make a move and we'd never know. Cloning his phone is the best way to figure out not only what's going on with you, but with the case in general. His information will come right to my laptop. He'll never know. You'd have the same information he does." Flynn's face emerged in the background. He waved but didn't say anything.

Although Emily didn't like the sound of having to get close to Cash to clone his phone, she did like the idea of being able to access the same information he had. That might give her the edge she needed to get justice for some of the other victims.

"Okay, let's table that for a second. Listen, I ran back over to Bradley Barker's house right before I got back to the B&B. There's something about him that I'm not sure about. Any chance he's the killer? He's got a bunch of tools in his garage. Said he needs them for fixing tractors, or something, but I'm not sure I believe him."

Mike got a faraway look on his face as he started typing on his computer. "Let's take a look. Flynn and I did a quick search on him before you went down there, just making sure he was who he was, but I don't remember all the details." There was silence for just a second, Mike's eyes darting back and forth across the screen. "Okay, here it is. Yeah, he was injured in a tractor accident a while back. Broke his leg. He's been married to the same woman, Carla, for about thirty years. He worked as a farm equipment repair guy for his career, that was until he broke his leg. Took disability after that."

Flynn's face emerged on the screen, "What exactly are you looking for?"

"I don't know. Something seems strange." Emily got up off the bed, turning her laptop toward her, pacing, "This case, it's got more twists and turns than I can keep track of. There's just something about Bradley that's a little creepy, you know? I mean, he has a murder board set up in his garage."

"He does?" Flynn's eyes got wide.

"Yeah, didn't I tell you that? He's got more information than we do about the case, I think."

"And you think he could be the killer?" Mike said, his face emerging on the screen.

Emily stopped for just a moment, staring back, "Well, if he was, he'd be awfully clever. He would've had to kill his brother, though. Other than that, it would be like hiding in plain sight." Emily shook off the thought. The more she ran the scenario in her head, the less plausible it seemed. "Let's go back to talking about cloning the phone. Exactly how do I do that?"

Ten minutes later, Emily hung up with Mike and Flynn, understanding what she needed to do. The more Mike talked about it, the more Emily knew he was right. They needed to know what Cash was up to on a moment-by-moment basis. That was the only way Emily would have any freedom to work the case at all. Otherwise, she might as well just get back in her truck and go home. The minute she thought about that as an option, the image of Lexi Cooper's smile popped up in her mind, the stream of her long blonde hair behind her back, and the haunted look in Sierra Day's eyes. Whether Emily figured out who was doing the killing or the FBI did, someone needed to stop the murderer. Someone needed to stop whoever was terrorizing Tifton.

19

While Jeremy was looking at the indentation on the windowsill, Janet came up behind Cash. "I've got the information you wanted," she said. She pointed just beyond the backyard from where they were standing behind the Cooper's house, holding a tablet out to Cash. "Just on the other side of the wood line is a small park. From the information on the plat and a map from the local park service, it looks like just a single loop. I just sent one of the Tifton officers to go drive it for us. One of the locals said there's not much more than a couple of picnic tables there that no one uses. Probably some sort of conservancy land that was deeded to the county at one time or another.

Cash nodded. They worked with plats a lot on their cases, the sizes and outlines of pieces of land and who they were owned by, usually kept by the local county recorder. "Any reports of something strange happening over there last night?"

"The guy I talked to said he was on duty. Apparently, he rolled through the park at about the same time Lexi disappeared. Said he saw a van parked there with some sort of writing on the back – like a work van — but took a look at it and there was no one in it. He didn't make anything of it. Said when he rolled back through it was gone. Figured it broke down and whoever owned it came to get it."

Cash raised his eyebrows, "And that didn't seem suspicious to anyone?" His stomach churned.

Janet took a step back from him, holding up her hands, "Now, before you get all hot and bothered about this, I asked him the same question. He said they have a lot of people that go to the park and hunt for a little while in the middle of the night. Small game, that's all. So, seeing a van there wouldn't have raised any eyebrows, though maybe it should have. But, then again, no one knew Lexi was missing when the guy saw it."

Cash shook his head. "Still, that could very well have been the escape route for our kidnapper." He stared off at the woods, "Let's take a walk."

As Cash moved toward the woods, he noticed Janet was lagging behind. She was on her phone, probably letting the rest of the team know they were headed off into the woods. By the time he reached the first line of trees, Janet had caught up, her blonde ponytail bouncing behind her. Cash glanced down at the ground and held up his hand, "Stop," he said, bending down. Covered by a few leaves, he saw a partial footprint, heading away from the house. Cash stood up and glanced over his shoulder. He could still see the outline of the Cooper's white house behind him. "There's a boot print. Let's get a couple more agents back here. Watch where you step, we don't want to tread on top of them."

Cash felt his chest tighten a little, the first glimmer of hope he'd felt since arriving in Tifton. Could this be the first actual lead they had on the case? Cash stood and stared at the ground for a moment, glancing from side to side. They didn't have a lot of time. The sun was dropping in the sky. He looked at Janet. "Better get some portable work lights out here," he said.

As Janet turned away, Cash stayed where he was standing until a few more agents arrived to mark the spot. With dusk approaching, the last thing he wanted to do was lose the one actual new lead they had in the case. It was the first in the couple of years since he'd taken over. Could this be the break they needed? Looking from left to right, scanning the ground, Cash looked for more footprints but didn't see any. He tried to stay calm. That didn't mean they weren't there, it just meant he couldn't see them. Finding them was Jeremy's job. Luckily, it was something he was very good at.

It was going to be a long night.

20

E mily slept fitfully, waking every few hours, wondering what was going on with the case. Every time she did, she rolled over to look at her phone, but there was no news from Mike or Flynn. It wouldn't have surprised her if Mike was up all night long, trying to dig for more information, but on the off chance he was trying to get a few hours of sleep, she decided not to bother him.

By about six o'clock in the morning, Emily couldn't sleep anymore. She had a project to do, a project that might not only save her life but Lexi Cooper's. After taking a quick shower, Emily pulled on a pair of running shorts, running shoes, a tank top, and a baseball cap. She pulled a light windbreaker over her shoulders and zipped it up halfway. After her call with Mike and Flynn the night before, she had to try to intercept Cash in town somewhere. It was a risk, but one that might pay off, getting them information on the case. It could also pay off in a bad way, though, with her sitting in a set of handcuffs in the back of an FBI car. Emily rubbed her wrist absentmindedly remembering the last time she'd been in cuffs. It wasn't something she wanted to experience again.

Was the risk worth it? Emily stopped for a moment, thinking, running through Mike's reasoning again. He'd have moment-by-moment information he could share with her, plus give her a heads up if Cash decided Emily was the real target. Setting her jaw, she decided it was worth it.

The most likely place to bump into Cash again would be at the same little restaurant she found him the day before. No matter whether the agents were up all night or not, they would need food at some point during the day. It might be a long stakeout, but she had to get it done.

Emily swallowed. What Mike and Flynn asked her to do, getting close enough to Cash to clone his phone, felt a lot like walking right into a lion's den. Trying to stay anonymous was the part that made her job work. Without it, she had no cover — no way to protect herself — and the peace she'd found after being fired from the Chicago Police Department could evaporate at any moment, shattering the little life she'd managed to put together after she lost her job and her husband.

Emily walked into the bathroom after getting dressed, staring at the mirror. Not sleeping well was taking a toll on her, black circles under her eyes. She smeared some balm on her lips, wondering if she should just go home. But as soon as she thought about the idea of getting in her truck and driving away to avoid Cash and his FBI cronies, the image of Lexi Cooper surfaced in her mind. How could Emily leave the little girl behind, not knowing what happened to her? That might be something the FBI was okay with, but Emily wasn't. She looked in the mirror, pulled the brim of her hat down low, and headed out of the bathroom, grabbing her cell phone and her truck keys, sending Mike a text before she left the room, "On my way. I'll text you when I see him."

Outside, the heavy heat of Louisiana had already started to descend, even though it was still early. She had no idea when or if Cash would show up at the restaurant. He could just as easily send one of the other agents to go get coffee for the crew since they likely wouldn't take the time for the elaborate breakfast at the Tifton bed and breakfast, but for some reason, Emily doubted that. Cash seemed to be the kind of guy who liked to be in charge, in control. Not to mention he might want to get away from the Cooper's house for a little while. Emily knew how hard it was to sit with the victim's family for hours at a time. Unless the FBI had active leads, there would be nothing much for them to do until there was a ransom demand or a break in the case. As Emily pulled out of the parking lot of the bed-and-breakfast, she frowned. If there was an active lead in the case, she was sure that Mike would've texted her to let her know. A second later, her phone chirped. It was Mike. "I'm ready when you are," the text read.

Out on the road, there was little traffic around Tifton. Emily passed a few cars and a couple of trucks headed to work. Passing the restaurant, Emily saw there were only a couple of cars in the parking lot, none of them long black SUVs like the FBI drove. She chewed her lip for a second, and then spun the wheel, pulling the truck into an abandoned office building that was two doors down. She drove around the back, angling to see if there was a good view of the restaurant parking lot. There was. She pulled the truck in, hoping Cash or any of the other FBI agents wouldn't notice her out-of-state plates if she parked two doors away. Sitting back in her seat, Emily rolled down the window and shut the engine off. It was time to wait.

About a half-hour later, Emily saw what she was looking for, a long black SUV pulling into the restaurant. "Time to feed the agents," she muttered to herself. Emily leaned forward in the seat, wondering who would get out. From the distance, Emily could see two people, but she couldn't tell exactly who they were. If it was Cash, she only had a couple of minutes during which he'd be in the restaurant. She picked up her phone, "Heading in."

Her phone chirped back, "He's there?"

"Don't know," Emily wrote, shoving the phone in her pocket. She pulled a pair of sunglasses from the visor in the truck, rolled up the window, and locked the doors.

Emily walked down the sidewalk, approaching the bakery from the front. At the last second, she decided to use the side entrance, hoping that Cash was standing somewhere near the front of the building. As she walked in, she immediately looked down, pretending to check her phone. She hoped that with the change in clothes and the baseball cap, he wouldn't notice her. She stayed by the door for a second, pretending to look at something, and then glanced up. He was there. She saw his broad back at the register, in almost the same position he'd been in the day before. Cash was standing next to another agent, one with a long blonde ponytail piled on the top of her head. They were talking in low, hushed voices. Emily sent a quick text to Mike, "Game time," she wrote, setting her phone to vibrate.

Trying to look as casual as possible, Emily walked up behind the agents. There was a man in between them, wearing jeans and a rumpled plaid shirt. Emily tried to judge the distance between her and Cash. She texted Mike again, "Now!"

Another text came back a second later, "I don't see his number. You're not close enough."

Emily took a couple of steps to the side, coming out from behind the cover of the man with a plaid shirt a bit, her heart pounding. She turned away from the people in line, focusing on her phone. "Now?"

"Got him. Stay in that position. I need about a minute."

Based on the conversation she'd had with Mike and Flynn the night before, she knew that cloning Cash's phone required the two phones to connect. She breathed a silent prayer, hoping nothing would appear on his phone letting him know what was happening. Mike had assured her it wouldn't, but he wasn't the one standing in the restaurant. From the corner of her eye, she saw the line inch forward. Cash and the woman he was with were now at the register, paying for their orders. If Mike didn't complete the connection now, she wasn't sure when he would be able to. Her heart started to beat faster in her chest. They had to know what Cash knew. They had to know if he had any leads on the case. Emily swallowed. She tried not to look up and stare at him. People somehow always knew when that was happening. Another text came from Mike, "Hang on. Almost there."

From ahead of her, Emily could hear Cash's voice telling the cashier thank you. She glanced up for a second, seeing Cash and the other agent gather up a tray of coffee and white bags filled with food, his handcuffs shiny and silver attached to the belt at his back. Just the sight of them nearly made her freeze, the memories flooding back over her of the night she was arrested. Time was running out. There was no way Emily could follow them out the door and hope not to be detected. She moved to the side, a little closer to the man in the plaid shirt. His height was a godsend. It helped to block her from his line of sight. Emily stood still, half staring and half glaring at her phone. She hoped Cash and the other agent were so preoccupied with their conversation he didn't notice her.

As they walked away, Emily's thoughts started to race. Did Mike get the clone done in time? What kind of leads did they have on the case, if any? Where were they going? The questions came fast and furious in Emily's mind while she tried to steady her body. The last thing she wanted to do was look fidgety and nervous as the agents were making their way past her and out the door. Emily pivoted towards the man in the plaid shirt as they passed by, holding her breath. If Cash saw she was in line again, she wasn't sure it would raise a lot of suspicions, but any attention thrown her way could prove to be disastrous to the case.

The man in front of Emily stepped forward. From behind her, Emily could hear the little bell on the front door of the restaurant ring as Cash and the other agent walked out. She glanced up, seeing them pass by the big glass window in the front of the building. Cash never looked back. Emily stared at her phone, "Did you get it?"

Mike didn't answer. The line moved up again, the man with the plaid shirt stepping off to the side. Emily took her turn at the counter, "I like to order takeout, please." As she gave the waitress her order, a large black coffee and a blueberry muffin, Emily waited, staring at her phone. She kept her head down. A second later, just as she moved away, she saw the door open again. It was Cash. He'd come back into the restaurant. Emily's heart raced, but he beelined for the counter, standing not more than ten feet from her. Using as much self-control as she had, Emily turned away, walking toward the bathroom, never looking back.

Inside the bathroom, the smell of fake floral deodorizer hung in the air, the bright fluorescent overhead lights casting shadows on everything. Emily took a minute, splashed some water on her face and waited. She flushed the toilet and ran water in the sink, although she hadn't used the bathroom just in case someone was listening outside. Who would care, she wasn't sure, but there was no reason to arouse any suspicion. Emily stood at the door for a second, closing her eyes, taking a deep breath. Please be gone, she thought as she turned the knob.

Pretending to stare at her phone again, Emily walked out of the bathroom and paused for a second. Having the baseball cap so low on her forehead gave her good cover. No one could see her face unless she looked up. And, with her shorts and wind-breaker on, she looked like someone who just finished their run, a local, not someone who'd come in from Chicago to interfere in a serial killer case.

Before going back to the counter, Emily turned on the camera feature on her phone, changing the angle so it would capture the counter. In the viewfinder, she could tell that Cash had left. Why he'd come back into the restaurant, she had no idea. Maybe they forgot napkins or plastic utensils, or something? It didn't matter. He was gone.

Emily walked back to the counter. The waitress nodded at her, "Your order's right there, honey."

Emily waved without saying anything, picked up the paper bag and the coffee, and used the side entrance to head out to her truck. In the parking lot, there were no black SUVs. That was good. Emily let out a long sigh. It felt like she'd been holding her breath for hours when it had only been a few minutes. Getting back in the truck, she started the engine, turning on the air conditioning. Her forehead was drenched with sweat, the tension of trying not to get caught pouring out of her. She stared at her phone again. Still nothing from Mike.

A wave of frustration passed over her. How long could it take to figure out if he got the clone or not? She took a bite of the blueberry muffin, breaking off part of the top and then called him. "What's taking so long?"

"Nothing, I mean, I got it. I was just trying to configure it when you texted me. What happened?"

"Other than I almost got caught? Nothing. Would've been nice to know if you got it."

"Yeah, sorry about that. You know me, I got caught up in the tech stuff. Anyway, I'm just starting to go through his texts now. Give me a couple of hours and I'll get back to you. Flynn and Alice are gonna give me a hand."

Emily nodded, "Okay." The fact that Flynn and Alice were helping was good news in Emily's mind. More brilliant eyes on what little information they did have. If Alice did nothing else than keep Mike focused and calm that would be a start.

21

C ash was sitting in the truck in front of the Cooper's house, finishing what was left of a mediocre, watery omelet from the local restaurant when Jeremy walked up to the car. No one on the team had gotten much sleep after finding the footprints on the ground.

"Good omelet?" Jeremy said, leaning against the side of the car.

"Not really," Cash said, wiping his face. "Any news?"

"Not a lot. We followed those footprints you found, and I've sent the data back to headquarters. They're trying to run it for the type of boot, but best we can tell it's a size twelve men's utility boot. That brand's pretty common on the market."

"Anything else?"

"Well," Jeremy said, using the back of his hand to wipe his forehead, "based on the directionality of the footprints, I'd say they belong to our killer or at least someone who had approached the back of the Cooper's house and then turned around and went back the way they came. If it was a hunter, there would be no reason for them to go directly to the Cooper's house and then directly back."

Cash slid out of the car, "So, what you're saying is that the path of the footprints looks intentional enough that you think whoever has Lexi is the person wearing those boots?"

"Can't say for sure," Jeremy said, tilting his head to the side, "but what I can say is it doesn't seem all that logical for a hunter to walk directly towards the Cooper's house and then turn around and go back the way they came, unless they were tracking something that was in their backyard. That said, if I'm a hunter, I'm not shooting something so close to someone's house, unless I'm using a crossbow. A loud rifle blast isn't exactly what a homeowner wants to wake up to in the middle of the night, if you know what I mean." Jeremy squinted his eyes, "Man, it is hot out here already."

Cash nodded, "It is. Did you get any sleep last night?"

Jeremy shook his head, "Nope, been up all night."

"Why don't you head back to the bed-and-breakfast, get some food and a few hours of sleep." Cash checked his cell phone. It was just after seven o'clock in the morning. "How about if you get back here around noon? I'll text you if we need anything sooner."

Jeremy nodded, "Thanks. My eyes could use a rest, that's for sure."

"I'll bet. See you in a little while."

Knowing that the boot prints approached the Cooper's house and then went back the way they came was a small lead, but it was a lead, nonetheless. The problem was Jeremy was right — it certainly could have been a hunter who was tracking something through the Cooper's backyard, but it could also be the person that abducted Lexi. There was no way to know.

The frustration of having only a tiny bit of information made Cash want to pound his fist into the hood of the SUV but losing control and damaging FBI equipment wasn't a good look for a senior agent. Cash stared down the street as a black sedan pulled out of one of the driveways a couple doors down from Lexi's house. There'd been no ransom demand, no sighting of Lexi and other than the boot prints, they had no information. If this was the torso killer, they were running out of time.

22

By the time Ollie unlocked the basement door and went downstairs, Lexi was awake, but just barely. She seemed to be drifting in and out of consciousness. Ollie realized he might have hit her too hard, but the crying was no good. That wouldn't help anyone, even her. Staring at her, the smell of urine filled his nose. She had wet herself. He could've been mad, but he wasn't. She couldn't be blamed. After all, she was strapped to the chair with no way to get up and no way to call for him. Even if she could call for help, he was the only one around. He sat on the step in front of her and stared at her. She looked so much like Sage it made his heart hurt.

He watched her for a moment, thinking about touching her hair, but he didn't, keeping his hands balled up at his side. Glancing up, he saw the calendar and noted the date. It was almost time. Almost.

23

Her part of the cloning job complete, Emily decided to drive back to the bed-and-breakfast to change. There wasn't much she could do until Mike got more information. Heading up the back steps of the bed-and-breakfast, Emily felt a little stronger, knowing that Mike, Flynn, and Alice were figuring out exactly what Cash knew. She hoped it would make her job a little easier or at least keep her out of jail.

Pushing the key card into the slot and hearing a quiet beep, Emily went into her room. She quickly changed out of the running gear she had on during her morning trip to the restaurant, sliding back into a pair of jeans and her boots. Just as she was fastening her pistol on her hip, her phone chirped, "We need to talk." It was Mike.

Her stomach clenched. "That fast?" she muttered, as she dialed his number.

"Houston, we've got a problem," Mike said before Emily even had a chance to say hello.

Emily started to pace. "What is it? Did you find something already?"

"Unfortunately, yes. I've been scrolling through Cash's texts over the last twenty-four hours since he got to Tifton. When he bumped into you yesterday, we know he ran your plates. What I didn't know was that he asked for a full background check on you. Not a partial."

"A full background check? Why?" Emily's heart started to flutter in her chest.

"I guess your story about being a criminal justice student didn't ring true to him."

Most of the time, Emily could get away with her lies. Apparently, not this time. She shook off the thought. "Did the information come back yet?"

"Not that I can tell." There was a pause, "When it does, he's going to see everything."

The words hung in the air. Mike didn't need to tell her that Cash would know she was a disgraced Chicago police officer who'd been handcuffed and humiliated in front of her peers. Anger rose in her chest. "What is it to him if I'm here? What does he care?"

"I don't know. Maybe he's just doing his job trying to see who's in the city? You know, cases like these tend to attract all sorts of people."

Emily didn't answer for a minute, hoping the anger would subside. It didn't. Regardless of what had happened to her in Chicago, she knew she was a good cop, probably better than Cash, even though he'd earned an FBI badge. The fact that he was interested in her enough to pull a background check told her more about him than she needed to know. He was paranoid and suspicious. Maybe he had every right to be, Emily thought. Working a case like the Tifton killer could make anyone second-guess their career direction. "How long until he gets the information back?" she asked.

"Probably sometime today."

"So, we have a little time."

"Not much. What are you thinking?"

Emily continued pacing back and forth in her room at the bed-and-breakfast, next to the side of the bed. "Well, there are a couple of options. Number one, I can pack up my roadshow and head back. If I'm not here, the worse he can accuse me of is lying to him about who I am. The FBI has better things to do than worry about me in that context, though. The second option is that I stay."

"But he's going to know exactly who you are in the next few hours," Mike stammered. "He's going to be watching for you."

"I'm not sure he's going to be watching so much for me or my truck." An idea popped into Emily's head as the words came out of her mouth. "I gotta go. Keep me updated about things." She hung up on Mike before he had a chance to respond.

Emily grabbed her truck keys and the key card to the room and ran down the back steps of the bed-and-breakfast, heading out the same way she'd come in just a few minutes before. She took a deep breath of the hot humid air and checked left and right. No FBI agents anywhere in sight. They were probably still at the Cooper's house. In reality, Emily didn't care who caught the killer, but something had to be done. She was of more use to Cash chasing down leads than running scared away from the city. That wasn't her style anyway.

Getting in her truck, Emily headed back out to Bradley Barker's house. It was early, but not too early for a visit. On the way, she weighed in her mind what she'd seen the day before, the tools and the murder boards. Based on what Mike and Flynn had found, there was nothing in Bradley's background that made him a suspect, other than Emily's gut. Usually, her gut was right, but she wasn't so sure it was right this time. This case had her out of sorts. Emily fiddled with the radio, finding a station where they were talking about sports, the upcoming football season for the New Orleans Saints, the start just over a month away. Her thoughts drifted. She forced them to refocus on Bradley Barker. She needed to know if he was a legitimate suspect before she turned in his driveway. By the looks of where she was on the road, she had about five minutes to figure that out. What did she really know about him? She ticked off the information in her mind — he was married to Carla and had been for thirty years, he had a significant, documented injury from falling off a tractor that gave him a pronounced limp, and most importantly, he had murder boards and tools in his garage. Emily also knew that he posted on the unsolved forum which was where Flynn had found him. So, based on the information she had, Emily wondered why she thought he could be the killer. It was the tools. She picked up her phone and called Mike, "Quick question," she asked as soon as he picked up, "Did you run financials on Bradley Barker?"

"Of course. That's standard."

The way Mike said it almost made Emily laugh. Nothing was standard about the work they did. "Okay, what did you find in terms of income?"

Mike sighed, "Well, he gets disability because of the injury to his leg."

"Anything else?" The answer to the second part of the question was what Emily needed to know to decide on Bradley.

"It looks like he has some sorta little side business where he does tool repair. He files it as an LLC. Hold on for a sec, pulling up the tax records."

Emily was quickly approaching Bradley's house. She pulled off the side of the road, the truck dipping to the right a little bit as she did. She waited, resting the palms of her hands on the steering wheel, feeling calmer and more focused than she had since she got to Tifton. Something had shifted, she just didn't know what.

"Here we go," Mike muttered. "Yeah, I remembered

correctly. He has a little side business. Only makes about twenty thousand a year doing it, but it looks like he fixes tractors and other machinery for the locals. The company is called Barker Fixes. Not that original of a name, I'd say."

"Can you take a look and see who paid him? Does it look legit?"

There was more typing on the other end of the line while Emily waited. "Yeah, there are a bunch of deposits from companies in agriculture, like Tifton Agricultural, Louisiana Ag, Clement County Tool Works. They look legit. They all have EIN's to them."

Emily knew an EIN was an employer identification number, the social security number for businesses given by the IRS. "Anything else in Bradley's financials that looks sketchy?"

"Nothing that I can see. Doesn't look like he travels. There's more money in his bank account than just from the disability and the Bradley Fixes business, but I'd guess he gets paid on the side to do some cash jobs. There is little additional spending around Christmas every year, but that seems normal to me."

Emily nodded and put the truck back into gear. That's what she needed to know. "Thanks. I'm headed over there now. I'll be in touch."

Pulling into Bradley's driveway, the tires of the big truck thumping on the uneven ground, Emily took a deep breath. She'd gotten spooked the night before. It happened to everyone, even trained police officers, she told herself, trying to stay calm. Knowing that Bradley had a business made her feel a little better about the shiny tools hanging in his garage.

As she expected, Bradley was outside when she arrived, the big garage door open. Bradley was huddled on a little stool, leaning over a push mower. He barely looked up when she arrived, "Morning," he said.

"What you doin' there?" Emily said, putting her hands on her hips.

"Neighbor busted his mower. Asked me if I could take a look at it." Without looking up, Bradley pointed, "Mind handing me that set of pliers over there?"

Emily bent over, pulling a pair of black-handled pliers out of Bradley's toolbox. She passed them to him. "Here you go. You do repairs for a lot of your neighbors?"

"Yeah. When they have a machine that breaks, they come running." Bradley stood up, wiping his hands on a dirty rag. "Any news on Lexi?"

"No, nothing new." Emily stared at Bradley for a moment, catching a look at the murder boards in the garage. They'd been pushed off to the side. Emily guessed Bradley had tools he needed to access that were stored behind them. Emily sat down on the driveway, looking at the mower. It'd seen better days, rusted and dented from years of use. She traced her finger along the top of it, cleaning some of the grime off the cherry red paint on the housing. Her finger came away black. She wiped it on her jeans. "There is one development, though."

Bradley leaned on his cane. "What's that?"

"Agent Strickland is doing a background check on me." Emily scrambled to her feet and stood on the opposite side of the mower from Bradley, feeling a little uncomfortable that he was standing over her with a cane in his hand. Anything could be used as a weapon. She swallowed, hard. Chasing back the thought that he was the killer, she said, "Before we get to that, let me ask you a question."

"Sure." The words came out of Bradley's mouth slowly with his southern accent.

"These tools you have in your garage, those are for your business, correct? Nothing more?" As the words came out of her mouth, Emily thought they sounded preposterous. Taking such a direct approach to questioning Bradley was one that could easily backfire, but Emily had to try. She had to be certain she knew what she was dealing with. Nothing in Tifton was as it appeared.

"Yeah, of course." Brandley glanced over his shoulder and then looked back at Emily, "You don't think..." he said, his eyebrows furrowed.

Emily didn't give him a chance to finish his sentence, "I just have to ask. I mean, look at all those tools."

Bradley shook his head in disbelief, "I don't know whether to laugh or to yell," he said. "I mean, I lost my brother."

Emily sighed. These kinds of conversations were never easy. "I'm sorry, I don't mean to offend you, but it would be clever to hide in plain sight as one of the victims, right?"

Bradley leaned heavily on his cane, staring at the ground. He looked up, "I'm going to say this one time and one time only. I am not the killer. Now, why are you here?"

Bradley's tone had changed. He sounded angry. Emily couldn't blame him. Being accused of being a serial killer wasn't exactly something that happened every single day. And accusing one of the victim's family members of it was offensive. "Let me get back to what I started by saying — Strickland is on my tail."

"What does that mean?"

Bradley stood stock-still. Emily wasn't sure what would happen next. "Well, I found out a little while ago that he's requested a full background check on me. I don't have to tell you who I am, you know that. Now, I know who you are. But Strickland, he could make my life difficult, if not impossible."

"So, you came here to ask me if I was the killer and then say goodbye?"

"Not exactly. At least, not the second part. I want to stay. I want to find out who took Lexi and more importantly who killed everyone else in the last seven years, including Sean."

Emily hoped that by mentioning Bradley's brother, it would soften him a little bit.

"But you need something?" Bradley's eyes narrowed, "That's why you're here."

Emily looked at him. "The problem is Strickland is tracking me in my truck. That's how he figured out who I was. Out-of-state plates. It won't take him long for him to figure out I'm not the criminal justice student I told him I was."

Bradley whistled, "You lied to Strickland?"

Emily shook her head, "Yeah, probably not my smartest move, but that's what I'm working with. Any ideas?"

Bradley nodded and lifted the cane, pointing inside the garage. "I've got an old Jeep in there that runs like a top. She'll get you through anything. Why don't we put your truck in my garage and you can drive the Jeep around town? It's so old, nobody will give it a second glance. Even has historical plates, so you'll be legal on the road."

Emily raised her eyebrows in surprise. "You want to help me?"

"Well, for a minute, I almost didn't. It's kind of early in the day to accuse someone of being a serial killer, but I forgive you," he chuckled. A seriousness settled over his face, "Miss Emily, you are the only person who has shown any interest in my brother Sean in the last few years. A man's gotta take what he can get, you know what I mean?"

Emily nodded. She knew exactly what he was talking about. Even when she was with the Chicago Police Department, just having a detective show interest in a case brought the family comfort. When cases went cold, it could be years before someone from any law enforcement agency showed up to check on the family. In a way, it broke Emily's heart that Bradley felt like no one was caring for his brother's memory. Her chest tightened. It showed how little progress the FBI had made on the case, no matter how many man-hours they had put in it.

"Are you sure? You're okay with me borrowing your Jeep?"

"She hasn't been driven in a while. Not good for the engine. If you wouldn't mind putting some fresh gas in her, I'd appreciate it. High-test, please. That's all I ask."

Emily followed Bradley as he went into the dark of the garage. He flipped on a light, illuminating a car covered with the brown tarp. "Here she is," he said, tugging on the tarp.

As he pulled it off, Emily saw a forest green Jeep, probably from the late 1970s. The paint was dull, but the tires looked new. There was a coat of dust on the hood, but that was it. "And you said she runs?"

Bradley raised his head in a little bit of a challenge, "Go start her up and see what you think."

Emily opened the door and slid in, pushing the key into the ignition. Giving the engine a little gas, she turned the key. It fired right up. "She sounds good," Emily said, getting out, letting the engine warm up a little. "Anything else I should know about her?"

Bradley had a towel in his hand and was wiping some of the dust off of the hood. "Naw, just drive her and go figure out what happened to my brother, will you?"

Emily nodded and then stopped where she was standing. She looked at Bradley, realizing how sad he looked, the years of grief piled on top of the injury he sustained. It was a miracle he had as good of an attitude as he did. Something inside of her broke. She took a couple of steps forward and gave him a quick hug. "I'll do my best," she whispered.

Bradley didn't say anything, turning his face away from her as she stepped back and got in the Jeep. As Emily pulled out of the garage, she handed the keys for her truck through the window. "Here you go. In case you need to use my truck."

Bradley shoved the keys in his pocket. "I'll pull your truck in the garage so that snake Strickland doesn't see it's here. Keep me posted on what you find out, okay?"

As she pulled the Jeep out into the driveway, Emily stopped, an idea forming in her mind. Leaning out the window, she called to Bradley, "Want to go for a drive?"

"Where to?" Bradley asked.

"Little Bayou Pond."

24

B radley and Emily didn't say much as they drove out of town, Bradley just pointing occasionally where Emily needed to take a turn. Emily made a mental note to let Mike know she'd swapped cars. The Jeep was fun to drive, but Emily was already missing the air-conditioning and the GPS.

As they got close to the site where the killer had dropped the bodies for the last seven years, Emily's stomach started to clench, wondering what they would find. "It's just around the corner," Bradley said.

Bradley pointed again and Emily took a sharp turn onto what looked like a dirt road, the woods crowding in on either side of the Jeep. This was clearly not a county or state-maintained park, Emily thought, slowing down to avoid hitting a rut in the road.

The sun had come up over the ridge, sending streams of light down into the woods. Long shadows darted across the dirt road, the trunks of the trees projected as black marks. The Jeep cut through the rough road with no trouble, the sunlight blinking on and off of the windshield as the light filtered through the trees. "Up there," Bradley said, pointing. "Just a little further," he whispered, barely loud enough for her to hear over the engine.

Emily downshifted the Jeep, slowing. She pulled it off to the side and turned off the engine. There wasn't a parking area, just a little clearing. Getting out, her boots hit the clay with a thud. She took a minute to look around. The area around the pond was silent, eerily so. She scanned, seeing the stretch of the pond in front of her. On any other day, she'd expect to see a photographer taking pictures of the area. It was beautiful, even with the history it had absorbed.

A rickety wooden dock was at the end nearest to her. She walked through some tall grasses to get close enough to see what it looked like. The wood had buckled and rotted so badly, Emily was unsure the dock was even usable. A breath caught in her throat as she imagined the killer dropping a torso into the water. Did it make any noise? Did he throw it in, like bait? Or maybe he set it in the water like a child with a paper sailboat, watching it float away. Thinking about it made the hair on the back of her neck stand up.

Looking back at the Jeep, she saw Bradley. He was standing at the front bumper, half leaning on his cane and half leaning on the car. She wondered what was going through his mind. How many times had he visited this site before? She walked back over to him, "You okay?"

He nodded, "Okay enough."

Emily walked in the opposite direction from the dock, her back turned to Bradley. The pond itself was fairly large. Near the shore on the far side, there was algae and some sort of vegetation growing up out of the water. She didn't know what it was. On the near side, where they'd parked the Jeep, there was an easy entrance to the water, the lip of the water touching the edge of the clearing. Someone could push a raft or rowboat into the water with no problem. For a minute, she wondered if the killer used some sort of boat to drop the bodies off, or if he just submerged them on the edge of the water, watching them float away.

In the background, Emily could hear the rustle of small animals and the buzz of bugs, but the foliage was so thick it was almost impossible to see exactly what was happening. For all she knew, it could be anything from a squirrel to something larger, like a deer. She stood for a moment, staring at the water, wondering why the killer chose this particular pond. Why was this location important to him? Every single body had been found at the Little Bayou Pond. There was something about it, something that attracted the killer every single time. It was almost ritualistic. Emily imagined the killer coming to the edge of the water and letting the bodies go, watching them disappear under the surface. She shook off the thought, knowing that anyone who would do such a thing had to be stopped. Emily swallowed hard and then gritted her teeth. That's why she was in Tifton — to stop the killings from ever happening again.

Walking back to the Jeep, she looked at Bradley. He was staring off in the distance as though he was trying to imagine something. Maybe he was seeing the ghost of his brother? "Are there any other roads that lead in and out of here?"

Bradley blinked for a minute and then turned his head to look at her, "Not that I know of. But this is Louisiana. There's always a little bit of voodoo on the land."

Emily frowned. Voodoo? "What do you mean?"

"People who've lived out here for generations will tell you that strange stuff happens, and we don't know why. No explanation for a lot of it. Can't even come up with an example at the moment, but what I can tell you is there could be one hundred ways to get to this pond. We've only traveled on the most obvious one."

Emily looked back at him and nodded. Some things just couldn't be explained. "You okay if I leave you here for a minute? I wanted to take a walk back past the dock to see if I can spot other trails."

"That's fine. I'll be here."

As Emily walked away, she wondered if asking Bradley to bring her to the pond was the right move. He had a distant look in his eyes she hadn't seen before. Not that she knew him well, but the last thing she wanted to do was traumatize him more. Make it quick, Tizzano, she thought to herself, not wanting to force Bradley to stay at the pond any longer than he needed to. Not that she wanted to stay there either. Though it was beautiful, the whole place was pretty creepy.

Passing the dock, Emily walked close to the waterline, glancing occasionally toward the woods to see if she could spot any other trails. There weren't any she could see. Stepping on a rotted branch hidden in the grass, she nearly turned her ankle and then heard a hiss. Emily shrieked, jumping to the side. It was a snake. That was enough to get her to go right back to the Jeep.

Bradley called her, "You okay?"

"Yeah. Nearly stepped on a snake."

"We have those here. Most of them aren't poisonous, just a nuisance." He looked away for a second, "Find anything?"

"No. You were right, I didn't see any other trails. But the pond is big enough that if someone wanted to sneak in and put something in the water under the cover of night, it wouldn't be hard to do it, even if someone else was here."

Bradley nodded, "That's what I've always thought. I think that the police or the FBI have tried staking out the pond, but they've never found anything. The killer is able to slither in and slither out just like that snake, with no one the wiser."

The image of the killer as the snake sent a shiver up Emily's spine, "All right, I've seen enough. Let's go."

The old Jeep started up without any hesitation. Emily pulled it forward and back a few times, careful to avoid the edge of the water. The last thing she wanted to do was drop Bradley's Jeep into the pond.

Back on the road, Bradley fussed with the radio. "You can just drop me off at the house if you don't mind. I gotta finish fixing that mower for my neighbor. Said his grass is getting too long."

Emily nodded, "Sure thing."

An announcement on the radio interrupted their silence. "For those of you in Clement County, including Tifton, be advised, the National Weather Service has just issued a tropical storm warning. The information is just coming out right now, but you can expect the storm to arrive sometime within the next twenty-four to forty-eight hours, coming in over the Gulf. Batten down the hatches, folks. It's comin'."

25

A t some point during the night, Ollie had moved over to the old green chair in the basement from where he'd been sitting on the step. What time that happened, he didn't know. He'd ended up sleeping there the entire night. When he woke, he checked on Lexi. She was still unconscious, but every few minutes she'd move, as though she was trying to wake up.

Heading upstairs, Ollie retrieved a bottle of water from the kitchen and took it downstairs. By the time he got back downstairs, Lexi's eyes were open, wide and afraid. He stared at her and then pulled the tape off of her mouth. "Don't cry," he said, holding the bottle of water up to her lips. "I hate crying. No need for it."

After she took a couple of sips, Ollie went back upstairs and got a few crackers, taking them back downstairs and feeding her small bites.

"Please don't hurt me," Lexi mumbled, her eyes searching his face.

He looked away. The last thing he wanted to do was hurt

her, but he didn't have a choice. "I have to go to work. I'll be back later. No one else is in the house, so there's no point in screaming and crying." He left without saying anything else, leaving Lexi in the murky darkness of the cellar, one bulb casting a dull glow.

26

Elliott Day hadn't slept in almost thirty-six hours, the thirty-six hours since he'd heard that Lexi Cooper was abducted. His mind wouldn't rest, darting between the face of the son he lost and the little girl who was missing.

As Elliott got up from his chair, the television playing in the background with the morning news, he walked past the pictures of his family hung on the walls. He stopped at one of them, seeing the wedding picture of him and his wife. The grief of losing Joe had been too much for her. Pills had been her way out when she'd been unable to overcome the grief. He stood for a moment, staring, seeing the pictures of Joe and Sierra when they were little, pictures taken on a summer vacation they'd had in Florida. There was another set of pictures from one summer when they'd escaped the Louisiana heat and driven the entire way to Maine, the kids standing on huge boulders on the Atlantic shore at a park they found just by happenstance. Those were happy days.

Today was not.

Elliot stared at a picture of Sierra for a minute. He loved her and knew she was doing everything she could to help him, but he knew that underneath it all he was holding her back. He rubbed his fingers together. Elliot stared at the kitchen table. It was covered with bottles of pills — antidepressants, anti-anxiety medication, medicine to make him sleep, medicine to wake him up. It was all too much. His heart told him that Sierra didn't need the hassle anymore. She'd never even gotten married, much less had a serious boyfriend, because she was so busy taking care of him. A wave of sadness covered Elliott. He turned back, looking at the little house where he and his wife had raised their kids, staring at the pictures and their old furniture.

From the kitchen counter, he picked up the set of keys to his old Buick. Walking out into the garage, he left the overhead door closed but firmly pulled the house door shut behind him. He felt empty inside. He stopped for a minute, staring at the walls, Sierra and Joe's bikes still hanging from the ceiling, Sierra's pink handlebars, and Joe's black ones. "Pink is for girls," he remembered Joe saying the day they bought him his bicycle. "I want the black one."

Elliott shook his head as if trying to dislodge the thought. They should have been good memories, but they weren't. He sat down on the step for a second, all the strength in his body seemingly gone. His mind replayed over and over again the faces of the police officers who came to his door to tell him that Joe's body had been found in the Little Bayou Pond, or at least what was left of it. It was bad enough trying to bury your son but burying part of the mangled body didn't soothe their grief at all. His wife had never been the same, constantly walking around the house with a haunted look on her face, until one day, she could take it no more. Elliott found her, cold on Joe's bed. She hadn't left a note. She didn't need to. Elliott knew why she'd taken so many pills. He thought back to what the paramedics said, "I know it's no consolation," one of them said, putting his hand on Elliott's arm, "but the pills she took would've put her to sleep first. She wouldn't feel any pain."

Elliott stood up brushing his hands off on his pants. He walked over to the side door of the Buick and slid in, closing the car door behind him. He started the engine but didn't raise the garage door. He rolled down the window and leaned the seat back, taking deep breaths of the sweet fumes from the engine. His mind flashed the pictures he'd seen on the news of Lexi Cooper, Joe, and Sierra over and over again. Life was no good anymore, he thought, as he drifted away.

27

J ust after dropping off Bradley at his house, Emily's phone rang. It was a number she didn't recognize. Answering, she heard a female voice, "Emily?"

"Yes?"

"This is Sierra. Remember? You came to my house and asked me about my brother?"

"Sure. What can I do for you?"

"I was just wondering if you had any new leads on the case?" There was silence for a second, then a sob, "I'm at the hospital. My dad, he tried to kill himself this morning."

Emily swallowed. "I'm so sorry. What happened?"

"I went over to his house to take him some breakfast. He's been despondent the last couple of days. Seems only to mumble about Joe and Lexi — you know, the little girl that was taken?"

Emily nodded, "Yes."

"Well, when I got there, he wasn't in the house. I thought maybe he was in the garage getting something. When I opened the door, the entire garage was filled with fumes. I shut the car off and opened the garage door and got him out into some fresh air. He's alive, but just barely." Sierra sighed. "I think they're going to admit him to the psych unit if he survives."

"That's terrible, Sierra. I'm so sorry."

"Emily, someone has to stop this guy. This has destroyed my family. It's like he kills my dad over and over again every single day. I don't know what to do. Even if I try to get my dad more help, there's no telling if he'll try to kill himself again. Do you understand what I'm saying?"

Emily weighed the situation in her mind, realizing that Sierra was on the verge of losing everything. First, Sierra lost her brother, then her mom, and now her father had decided that life wasn't worth living anymore. Emily couldn't imagine the weight on Sierra's shoulders, just knowing that at any moment, she could lose what was left of her very small family. "I'm working on it," she swallowed. "Keep me posted on your dad, all right?"

"I will."

28

Cash checked his cell phone for what seemed like the thousandth time that morning. There were no new leads in the Lexi Cooper case. The only thing they'd managed to find in the two days they'd been at the Cooper's house was a small dent that looked like someone might've jimmied the window open and a few sparse footprints in the woods. Nothing conclusive. Nothing they could use to identify who had her. To top it all off, there hadn't been any ransom demand and no sighting of her either. It was looking more and more like the torso killer.

"Can I get you more coffee?" the waitress said, passing by his table again.

Cash shook his head no, "Thanks, I'm okay." As the waitress walked away, he watched her as she bounced from table to table, offering hot coffee to whoever might want it. Cash had been sitting in the restaurant for more than an hour, what was left of his breakfast growing cold. He'd left two agents at the Cooper's house and told the rest of them to go get some sleep. But he couldn't. This case is going to kill me, he thought, wrapping his fingers around the cup of coffee and taking a sip. It was lukewarm. He should've asked the waitress to heat it up when she passed by.

Cash stared at his phone. He'd made calls to his boss and the profilers, trying to find a new angle they hadn't already worked, but there was nothing to go on. The profiler he spoke to said, "I'm sorry, Cash. I can't imagine how hard this is, but I don't have anything for you. To save that little girl, you gotta have a lead, and we don't have any."

In his gut, he knew what the profiler said was true. FBI profilers, their team of specialized psychologists, could only draw him a basic picture of who the killer might be. It wasn't the same as forensic evidence — like fingerprints, or fibers or DNA — that could help them get closer to whoever did it.

Cash fiddled with the coffee cup, turning it around in a circle and then setting it on top of his napkin. He needed a break in the case, that was a fact. How he was going to get it, he wasn't sure.

Without warning, Cash's cell phone beeped. His phone wasn't the only one. He glanced up, to see everyone in the restaurant huddled over their phones. He looked down, seeing an automatic alert from the National Weather Service, "Tropical storm warning issued for Clement County, including Tifton. Tune into your local news station for evacuation orders and more information."

Cash pounded his hand on the table. Seriously? A tropical storm. How was he supposed to conduct an investigation with howling winds coming up out of the Gulf? He quickly pulled up a weather app and checked the forecast. The first bands of rain would probably be arriving in the next few hours, followed by the swirl of the storm coming up out of the Gulf later on. Things were going to get nasty, and fast.

Standing up from where he'd parked himself in the booth at the restaurant, he pulled a few dollars for a tip out of his wallet and took a last sip of the cold coffee before paying his check at the counter and heading out. It was hard enough to find a little girl in good weather, let alone the howling storm raging up out from over the ocean.

Cash quickly sent a text to his team telling them to assemble at the bed-and-breakfast. It was time to meet and go over what they knew. Or, in this case, what they didn't know.

29

S taring at the screen, Mike felt a little uneasy, his stomach twitching. It wasn't as though he hadn't looked at private information before. It was just that Cash's texts were private. Mike knew he'd be furious if someone had cloned his phone, but this was for a good cause. At least he thought it was. Mike swallowed and licked his lips, taking a sip of coffee as he sat at Emily's kitchen table. He reached down underneath the table and stroked Miner's fur. It was warm and soft against his fingers. They'd gotten back from a walk a half-hour before, and the dog was now collapsed under the table, his head on Mike's bare feet.

Frowning, Mike stared at the texts that were popping up on his screen. The cloning program gave him access to every text that went in and out of Cash's phone, though it didn't tell him who the numbers belonged to. Following all of the conversations was tricky. Mike knitted his brow, trying to guess who some of the people were that Cash was texting. There seemed to be one conversation with a lead agent, probably someone female by the way Cash talked to her. There were a couple of texts from the FBI's home office in Baton Rouge, and a couple of personal ones — maybe a girlfriend, something about missing him and wishing they were together. Mike sighed. The whole process of reading Cash's texts made him feel like nothing more than a peeping Tom.

Halfway down the list, Mike saw what he was looking for. It was the original text where Cash mentioned Emily. "Track these plates for me?" The plates were Emily's. Mike recognized them from seeing the truck in the driveway as many times as he had.

The timestamp on the next text came back just a few minutes later, "Emily Tizzano of Chicago. FYI, she's a former Chicago police detective. Why are you asking?"

Cash hadn't bothered to reply.

Mike made his way through a few more texts before he heard a knock on the door. Miner jumped up, growling. As Mike walked to the door, his phone beeped, "I'm here," Flynn wrote.

Putting his hand on the doorknob, Mike looked down at Miner, "It's okay, boy. It's just Uncle Flynn."

Flynn and Mike had been spending a lot of time at Emily's house while she was gone, trying to piece together any other information they could find about the case. They'd come up short. There were plenty of news reports about what happened in Tifton, but little detail other than the fact that the bodies had been dismembered. "Any news?" Flynn said, dropping his backpack on the floor and stopping for a second to kneel and scratch Miner behind his ears after shutting the door.

"I was just going through some of Agent Strickland's texts," Mike said, slumping back down into the chair in front of his laptop.

"Anything interesting?" Flynn said, sitting down next to him.

"I was just getting to that part, I think." Mike turned his computer towards Flynn so they could both look at the screen together. Mike pointed, "See here? That's where Cash makes the initial request to run Emily's plates. I want to look down further and see when he requested the background check."

Flynn nodded, "Yeah, my buddy said the request came in not too long after the FBI got to Tifton."

Mike frowned and rubbed his eyes. It seemed like it was taking a long time to get the background check on Emily back to Cash. That could be a good thing or a bad thing. He didn't know which. Unless, of course, Agent Strickland already had it, and they just didn't know.

Scrolling down, Mike found the rest of the thread where Cash was talking to the person who ran the plates, "Chicago police detective? What's she doing in Tifton?"

Whoever Cash was texting with, replied, "I have no idea. Maybe family?"

"She told me she was a criminal justice student. Get me a full package on her, will you?"

Mike looked At Flynn, "Think he's suspicious?"

"Might be almost as suspicious as you, Mike," Flynn said, smiling. "Keep looking. There has to be something on the background check."

Mike scrolled down the page, squinting, trying to find where the rest of the information might be. One of the problems with the software used for the cloning program was that it pulled up all the texts chronologically, without organizing them by phone number. That meant a lot of digging. Another two pages of texts down, there was another text from the same person who ran the plates for Cash, "I requested the background check on the person of interest you mentioned," the text read. "You should have that later on."

Agent Strickland replied, "Okay. Hurry it up, will you?"

Mike's heart started beating faster in his chest. By the time stamp on the text he was reading, Agent Strickland should already have the background check. The question was, what did it include? How much of Emily's life would be exposed? Mike got up and walked over to the sink, pouring out the coffee from his cup, rinsing it, and putting it in the dishwasher. The least he could do for Emily would be to keep her house nice for when she came back... if she came back. Mike sighed, thinking about the situation. No one had ever positively identified Emily on a case before. At the same time, Emily had never jumped headlong into an investigation with as much active law enforcement on it as this one. "It's our fault if she gets caught, Flynn. We're the ones who told her to take the case." Mike watched for a second as the color drained from his friend's face.

"Then we better get her all the information we can so she can protect herself and come home," Flynn said, reaching for his laptop.

D riving Bradley's Jeep made Emily feel instantly more comfortable. He was right, no one would suspect that the disgraced cop from Chicago had switched cars. The only people interested in taking a look at her might be someone who had a fascination with vintage Jeeps. In Tifton, she wasn't sure how many people that might be.

After leaving Bradley's house, Emily decided to take a cruise by the Cooper's. At least in the Jeep, she thought she'd have a shot of not being spotted by Cash or any of his FBI crew. If she was careful with her body language, she wouldn't look like anything more than someone passing by. As she got closer, Emily swallowed, feeling the worn spots on the steering wheel where drivers before her had gripped it. The windows were down, the hot afternoon air blowing through the Jeep. With her baseball cap and sunglasses on, Emily thought she hardly looked like the woman that Cash had run into just a few days before.

Turning down the street, Emily gripped the wheel a little harder. As she rounded the curve before the Cooper's house, she leaned to her left a little, peering forward, wondering how many FBI-owned SUVs there might be parked on the street. As the house came into view, she realized there were none. Not one. Emily chewed her lip and then pulled to the side of the road, stopping the Jeep. Where had they gone? Her heart beat a little faster. Was it possible they had a lead they were chasing, something Emily didn't know about? Excitement and fear surged through her. If the FBI had found something, then maybe they were getting close to solving the case. In her mind, it didn't really matter who solved it, just that it got solved and she got home safe.

Emily checked her rearview mirror and saw movement from the house. A man and a woman pulled down the driveway and drove right past her. Emily caught a glimpse of Keira and Randy Cooper as they drove by, the woman dabbing at her eyes as she passed, her long blonde ponytail, a match for Lexi's, pulled up behind her head, her husband gripping the wheel with both hands. Where they were going, Emily didn't know. She started the Jeep and pulled out slowly behind them, keeping her distance. The last thing she wanted was for them to be spooked by a strange Jeep tailing them.

The road widened as Emily followed them. It seemed the Coopers were headed into town. The fact they left the house was strange, Emily thought. She furrowed her brow, wondering where they were going. If the FBI had an actual lead Emily thought Randy and Keira would've stayed home, waiting for news. But maybe not. Now in the center of town, the Coopers pulled into the only drugstore Emily had seen since she arrived, the Sunrise Pharmacy, the same one where Sierra Day worked.

Emily was two cars behind Randy and Keira. She pulled into the pharmacy just in time to see them walk into the store., Selecting a spot on the other side from the Coopers, Emily threw the Jeep into park. She walked quickly towards the door, hoping they were still inside, her hands clammy even in the heat.

The Sunrise Pharmacy looked the same as the drugstores Emily frequented in Chicago — bright lights, rows and rows of everything from makeup to cleaning supplies to milk — flanked by a long pharmacy counter in the back. Though the building on the outside looked old, Emily could tell someone had put a lot of money into rehabbing it.

Taking off her sunglasses, Emily walked down an aisle with notebooks and pencils and circled back towards the pharmacy. Though she didn't know why the Coopers had gone in, it made sense to search the building from back to front. Emily swallowed again, realizing she didn't have much of a plan.

At the pharmacy counter, Emily caught a glimpse of the Coopers. Sierra was talking to them, wearing the white lab coat of a pharmacist, their voices just above a murmur. Emily stayed by the magazine rack nearby, trying to listen, pretending to stare at an issue of a decorating magazine. "This might make you a little bit sleepy, but you probably need some sleep. It will help you to think clearer when you wake up. Just call me if you have any questions, okay?" Emily heard the creak of the half door that blocked the pharmacy from the customers as it opened. Sierra reached for Keira. "I'm so sorry for what you're going through," Sierra said, hugging the grieving woman as she handed her the prescription.

"I just can't believe Lexi's gone," Keira said, looking down.

"And they haven't given you any information at all? The FBI hasn't made any progress?"

Randy shook his head, "Nothing. They seem to think that someone jimmied her window open in the middle of the night and pulled her out, but we didn't hear anything. Nothing at all!"

"And that's the only information they've been able to give you? There's been no ransom demand, nothing?" Sierra said.

Emily picked up another magazine and turned her back to

the three of them, listening. Eavesdropping on their conversation was giving her more information than she'd had in the last couple of days. Her mind was racing. The FBI had nothing if they only said the window had been jimmied. In her mind, that was less than nothing. Emily heard their voices above the flutter of the pages of the magazine, "There's been no ransom demand. That's why the doctor said I should take these," Keira said.

"There's no shame in taking a little anxiety medication, Keira," Sierra said. "This whole situation, it's been hard on all of us. My dad..."

Emily turned just in time to see Randy reach his hand out to Sierra, resting it on her arm, "I'm so sorry to hear about him. Some guys at the station told me what happened. How's he doing?"

Out of the corner of her eye, Emily saw Sierra tilt her head, "He's okay. I mean, he's still in the hospital. They're trying to rebalance his medications — get them off of some and start him on some new ones." There was a pause, "I just never thought he'd try to kill himself. I knew things were bad, but to find him like that..." Sierra paused, "I'm not sure I'm ever going to get the image out of my mind."

It was time to leave. As Emily went to put the magazine back on the shelf, a cheap novel fell and hit the floor with a thud. Bending over, she picked it up, trying to replace it on the shelf, without being noticed. It didn't work. Before Emily could walk away, Sierra was standing next to her. "Emily? What are you doing here?"

Emily held her breath, her heart pounding in her chest. She didn't want to get caught this way. Eavesdropping wasn't a good look. By the time she started to answer, the Coopers were looking at her, too. "I trailed you from your house."

Emily saw Randy move in front of his wife, their eyes wide.

Sierra held her hand up, "It's not like that. Emily's a friend. She's here to help. Tell them."

Emily walked a little closer to them. As she did, she could see the dark circles under their eyes, the blotchy redness of their skin from the stress of the last few days. She swallowed, not knowing exactly what to say. Emily never had kids of her own, so was hard to relate, or at least it felt that way. "I'm a private investigator, you could say. I'm working with Bradley Barker to help him find out what happened to his brother." Emily glanced at Sierra and then back at the Coopers, who were still staring at her. "I met with Sierra the other day just to get a little of background on what happened to her brother Joe."

Randy looked at Emily, his eyebrows knitted together, "Why were you following us?"

"Honestly? I couldn't exactly walk up to the door and ask you questions while the FBI was hovering."

"You think our daughter's kidnapping is somehow linked to what happened to Joe and Sean?" Keira asked.

Emily shook her head. "At this point, it's hard to know. I'd be lying if I told you the timing wasn't suspect, but taking a child doesn't exactly fit the torso killer's profile."

As soon as the words torso killer came out of Emily's mouth, Keira began to sob again. "I'm sorry," she said. "It's just the idea that our little girl is out there somewhere where we can't be with her, scared to death, at the hands of some madman, is driving me insane."

The last thing Emily wanted to do was get caught up in the hysteria. She understood that Keira was hurting, but her pain wouldn't help Emily do her job. Emily needed to stay clear-headed and calm. She held her breath for a second, and then let it out, "I can't imagine, really I can't. Is there anything else you can tell me about what happened to Lexi?"

Randy stared at Emily for a second and then at Sierra.

When he looked back, he said, "Are you going to help us, too? Is that why you're asking?"

The way he said it made it clear he was suspicious of Emily. Emily didn't blame him. "If there's an intersection between your daughter's case and the other cases, then I'm going to end up in the middle of this any way I look at it." The reality that Emily could be bumping into Cash Strickland and his cadre of FBI agents at any moment sent her stomach fluttering. Where was Mike with the information that Strickland had requested? She refocused on Randy. "Listen, I can't promise you anything, but neither can the FBI. All I can tell you is I'm going to be down here for the next couple of days trying to figure out what's going on." Emily glanced toward the door. It was time to leave. "The only thing I ask is that you don't talk to Agent Strickland or any of his other agents about me. The FBI doesn't like it when there are other investigators involved in the mix. I'll keep a low profile and give information to Sierra if I get anything, but I need you to keep quiet about what I'm doing." Emily swallowed hard, knowing that her future might rest on whether the people of Tifton could keep her out of the view of the FBI. As the words came out of her mouth, her phone buzzed. It was Mike. "Listen, I gotta go. Like I said, I'll get information to Sierra if I find anything. I'm hoping the FBI can find your daughter, but please know I'm going to be looking, too."

Emily walked out of the drugstore without saying goodbye and without any assurances from Keira and Randy they wouldn't say anything to the FBI. The only thing Emily could hope for is that Sierra would talk to them and tell them that exposing Emily would do nothing to bring Lexi home. Emily made her way out to the Jeep, started it up and pulled away, heading out of town. She pulled down a side street on the far end of town and found an empty parking lot. Dialing Mike, she leaned back in the seat, trying to take a couple of deep breaths.

Spending time with Randy and Keira had drained her. "What's going on?"

"Have you been parked at Bradley Barker's house all day? The truck hasn't moved." Mike said.

"Yeah, about that. I ditched the truck. Bradley's letting me drive around in his Jeep."

"Does it have GPS in it? If so, I can hack it so I can locate you."

Emily shook her head, "Naw. It's vintage. Isn't even an automatic. No air conditioning either."

"No air conditioning in the Louisiana summer? That's not good."

"Tell me about it. What's going on?" Emily knew she could banter with Mike for the next half hour, but there was a reason he called. She wanted to know what it was.

"Well, Strickland is on your case. Have you seen him around?"

Emily shook her head. "I haven't. I have no idea where he is."

31

As Cash pulled into the bed-and-breakfast, he noticed the other SUV was already parked there. The other agents must've all piled in together for the meeting. He walked in the front door, seeing his agents milling around, waiting for him, all dressed in the same, identical black work pants and navy-blue T-shirts with yellow FBI lettering. All of them had guns on their hips and handcuffs attached to the back of their belts, all of them except for Jeremy, who focused on forensics. There was no one left at the Cooper's house for the moment. He needed them all together out of earshot of the family.

Cash motioned to his team, waving them into the breakfast area, which was abandoned, the early morning breakfast service long over, "Let's go in here," he said. As they filed in, Cash shut the doors behind them, hoping for some privacy. The last thing he needed was the locals listening in on their investigative progress.

As they got settled, Cash looked at Janet and then at the rest of the group, "What do we know?"

Silence settled over the room. Finally, Jeremy spoke up,

"Well, from a forensic perspective, the only thing I have that's solid is that little, tiny mark on the windowsill outside of Lexi's bedroom. By the time we arrived at the scene, any footprints left behind were gone. The only other forensic evidence we have is a set of footprints leading through the woods. Unfortunately, the kind of boot print we found is very common. Based on my research, almost a million pairs of those same work boots sold this past year at many of the national chain discount stores. That's particularly true because it's a size twelve. That's one of the most common shoe sizes for men."

Cash fought the urge to stare at Jeremy and yell, "Thanks for nothing!" as frustration crept up in his chest. He clenched his fists, "Anyone else?"

Janet cleared her throat, "I've done a little background research on the Coopers. As all of you know, Randy is a firefighter/paramedic with the local department. He's been there for ten years. Keira is a stay-at-home mom. The cost of living isn't super high here in Tifton, so it's not too hard for them to make it on one salary. Based on their financials, they live a pretty normal life. In the last few years, they've taken only one vacation and there are no interesting deposits or withdrawals in their accounts. They have just the one daughter, Lexi, who you all know about."

Although Cash was grateful that Janet spoke up — someone had to — what she said didn't exactly offer earth-shaking news. Just like every other one of the Tifton torso killer cases, the person who was missing lived a relatively normal life. Cash started to pace, "Unfortunately, like the other cases in Tifton we've run across, there's very little evidence and nearly nothing we can build a case on." Cash stared at the group, searching their faces, hoping that someone had noticed something that hadn't been brought up yet. It didn't look like there was. "So, what we have is a missing five-year-old girl who possibly was taken directly out of her bedroom and carried through the woods. We do know a van was spotted at the park behind the Cooper's house that night, though it looked abandoned to local law enforcement. There were some markings on it, but the officer didn't note them. And, we have little or no forensic evidence," Cash said, giving a nod to Jeremy, "Is there anything else we haven't talked about?"

One of the agents from the back of the room, Dan McClellan, cleared his throat and looked at Cash, "Are we sure this isn't a domestic situation? Some grandparent that hasn't been able to see the little girl in a long time? Are we sure she just didn't run outside and get lost in the woods? I mean, look at this place. It's covered with hundreds of acres of woods. If she got outside, there's no telling how far she could have gotten by now."

Cash continued pacing, looking down at the toes of his boots, thinking. "Is it a possibility somehow Lexi got out of the house and got lost in the woods in the middle of the night? Maybe. But why would she go out there?" Cash stared at McClellan, who didn't have an answer. "Could it be a grieved relative, someone who wants access to Lexi but doesn't have it? Grandparent? Aunt or uncle? According to the family, that's not a possibility."

McClellan spoke up, "Maybe they're lying?"

"That's certainly an option, but usually people that are desperate to get their child back will tell you everything about themselves including how many pennies they have in their bank account and how many affairs they've had while they've been married. Desperate people will do desperate things to get what they love back. You learned that on the first day of Quantico."

Cash started to pace again, feeling frustrated with his team, but mostly himself. By now they should have something, and they didn't.

32

Though Emily hadn't planned on talking with Randy and Keira directly with the FBI hanging around, there was a part of her that was glad it happened. At least she got to size them up. They certainly didn't seem like the kind of people who'd do something drastic to their own child and then try to pretend they didn't. Emily started up the Jeep and headed back to the bed-and-breakfast, needing a little time to regroup. The radio started at the same time as the engine, offering another repetitive announcement about the tropical storm coming into the area. Just as the announcements stopped, a few heavy droplets of rain hit Emily's windshield. At the next stoplight, she rolled up the windows, trying to protect the interior of the Jeep for Bradley. It wasn't as easy as in her truck since they were hand-crank windows. Instantly, she felt the hover of humidity coating the inside the Jeep. She turned on the fan system, hoping the windshield wouldn't fog too badly. She cracked the driver's side window, just trying to get some fresh air in the Jeep. Emily frowned. Horrible timing for a storm.

A couple of minutes later, Emily pulled into the bed-and-breakfast, seeing the two black SUVs parked out front. Her heart skipped a beat. The last thing she wanted to do was run into Cash Strickland in one of the hallways of the building. If they bumped into each other one-on-one, the odds of him not recognizing her were slim. Emily felt a tingling in her spine. She needed to talk to Mike about what he'd found, not get caught by Cash.

Parking the Jeep in the back lot, Emily jumped out and ran to the back door, pulling the baseball cap down low on her face to keep the rain off of it. As she slipped her key card into the slot, she stepped inside, the darkness covering her. She took the steps two at a time, running upstairs to the second floor as quickly and quietly as possible. As she cracked the door to the second-floor open, she glanced down the hall, seeing two FBI agents opening the door to their room and disappearing inside. They are right on my floor, she thought, swallowing. Her own door was just across the hall. She took two steps, stuffing the key card in the reader, hoping it would click open quickly. It did. Emily lunged inside, pushing the door closed behind her.

Inside of her room, Emily pulled off the baseball cap and shook out her long hair, slipping out of her work boots. The air-conditioning cooling her room felt almost cold as it touched her skin. She texted Mike before she sat down, "I'm back in my room. Call me?"

"Let's do a video call. Give me two minutes."

Emily pulled her computer off the charger and sat down on the bed, resting her back against the headboard. Her stomach clenched. What had Mike found?

A moment later, Mike's face appeared on the screen of her computer. Emily frowned, "What's going on?"

Mike cocked his head to the side, "Well, Flynn and I spent the last couple hours digging through Agent Strickland's financials and taxes to figure out what makes him tick. To be honest with you, he doesn't have much of a life."

"As much as I'd like to hear about that part, let's focus on the background check." For a second, Emily felt like Mike might be trying to soft-pedal the start to the conversation. Her stomach clenched. How much information had Cash Strickland managed to get on her?

Mike cleared his throat and moved a little bit to the side, as Flynn adjusted his face on the screen. "Well, it looks like he has it all. The jacket was just delivered to him about a half-hour ago."

Emily didn't say anything for a second. It seemed like it had taken a long time for the FBI to pull together her information. "That's strange? What's up with the delay?"

Flynn leaned forward toward the camera, his face growing large on Emily's screen, "We had the same question. In a way, I guess the answer is good news — they've never pulled a background on you before, so they had to start from scratch."

Emily raised her eyebrows, "And the bad news?"

"Like I said, they have it all."

Emily swallowed. She knew what that meant. It meant that Cash Strickland, at this very moment, had her entire history at his fingertips. Everything from where she was born and where she went to school to her career information — even her arrest and termination from the Chicago Police Department. If the FBI truly did their job, he'd also be able to see that her case was dismissed, she got a large settlement, and she'd been married to one of Chicago's most notorious crime bosses' son, Luca Tizzano, before he left her and overdosed.

Before Emily could say anything, Mike interjected, "Emily, we don't think this is necessarily a bad thing," he said, biting his lip. "I mean, to the degree you told him you're a criminal justice student, that might be a problem, but there's nothing really in your file that would suggest you're there to hamper his investigation, so hopefully, he'll just leave you alone."

Emily shook her head a little, "I appreciate what you're

trying to do, Mike, but the reality is that now Cash Strickland has his crosshairs on me as well as the torso killer."

Flynn leaned forward, "But don't you think he'll be more worried about the torso killer than you? I mean, he's gotta try to find Lexi Cooper before something happens to her."

Emily didn't want to talk about herself anymore. She felt her face go hot. Ever since her arrest, her privacy had become one of the most important things in her life. Knowing that there was someone out there that had all of her information, every bit of it, sent a wave of uneasiness over her. "Listen, I gotta go. Reach out if you find anything else, okay?"

Emily ended the call, slammed the lid on her laptop closed, and tossed it to the other end of the bed. She got up pacing. Why did Cash Strickland care who she was? What was it to him? Emily clenched her jaw as she paced back and forth, wondering what exactly was in the file. Mike should get that for me, she thought, then pushed the idea aside. She had to stay focused on trying to find Lexi Cooper and whoever had killed Sean Barker, Joe Day, and the rest of the victims. She stopped at the window, just in time to see a flood of agents go back to their black SUVs and leave. For a second, she thought she caught a glimpse of Cash's hair, but she wasn't sure. They were just a little too far away. Within a second or two, the black SUVs left, probably heading back to the Cooper's house. Emily said a silent prayer hoping Randy and Keira wouldn't tell Cash they'd run into Emily at the drugstore. If they told him, she could be getting a knock on her room door at any time.

She stopped in her tracks, biting her lip. Why hadn't Cash come up to her room to question her? That didn't make any sense. He had to know she was staying there. Unless... unless they only pulled her history, not her financials. Mike did register her under a flimsy fake name, but it was fake anyway. Emily started pacing again, her anger over Cash's intrusion into her privacy changing into curiosity. Had he even looked at her background yet? A glimmer of hope lit in her chest. It was possible that he had requested the background information and then decided it wasn't important or had even forgotten about it. There was no telling. It was possible, though, if there was some development in the case that took his attention away from her. Was that the reason the SUVs had so abruptly left the bed-and-breakfast? Emily had more questions than answers. It was the answers she needed before it was too late for Lexi Cooper.

33

R ight in the middle of Cash's meeting, he got a call from Kevin Barnfield, the detective working the case from the local law enforcement side. "We've got a body. Can you meet me?"

Cash looked at his team and said, "Let's roll. We've got something new to look at."

Running out to the SUV, he jumped in the passenger side of the lead vehicle, his jaw clenched. Was it Lexi Cooper? Most of the agents had grabbed their windbreakers before the meeting, the threat of rain already arriving in Tifton. The timing couldn't be worse. Tropical storms brought sheets of wind and water that made traveling and moving around impossible, not to mention the inevitable power outages and flooding. Listening to the wipers swipe back and forth on the windshield, Cash yelled, "The timing for this blasted storm couldn't be worse!" The agent driving nodded.

Cash programmed the address into the SUV's GPS and texted it to Janet Crenshaw in the vehicle behind them. Not that the second vehicle needed it. They were trained to follow bumper-to-bumper with lights blazing on their way to a scene. But at least she'd have it for the record.

By the time they got out to the address, the rain was coming down in a steady tempo, soaking everything in sight. Cash felt calmer, but only slightly, as he got out of the SUV, wondering where they were. Up ahead, he spotted a single Tifton Police Department cruiser and what he thought was Detective Kevin Barnfield's car. Before walking over, Cash went to the back of the SUV and grabbed a long rain slicker and a baseball cap. Putting it on, he glanced around the area. It looked like an open field. There were no homes in sight and no other structures, even a barn or garage. The dense woods of southern Louisiana were off in the distance. It looked as though the field he was standing on was used for farming, or at least had been at some point, the native weeds having grown up and curling over the remnants of any former crops.

Zipping his raincoat, Cash pulled the hood up over his head and the bill of his baseball cap down low over his face. He trudged over to where Kevin Barnfield was waiting, standing in the open as if it was a beautiful day. It wasn't. "Thanks for coming. Hope I didn't interrupt anything, but I thought you should see this."

Cash nodded and swallowed. Going to a crime scene was something he'd never gotten completely used to. He developed the habit of mentally bracing himself, putting up a filter in his mind so he didn't absorb too many of the images he saw, but it was hard. It was hard to protect himself from what he saw. There were times he wondered if long after he retired, he'd still see the line of bodies, or in this case, bodies cut up into parts, while he was relaxing on some beach drinking a beer. It would be nice if he had a family with him, but at the rate he was going, he'd be alone. He shook the thought out of his head. Focus, Strickland, he reminded himself. "What you got?"

"A couple of kids riding some ATVs called us when they

found this." Kevin leaned over and pulled up the edge of a yellow tarp that had been sprawled on the ground. Cash knelt down, staring. From what he could tell, it was a skeleton, or at least part of it. He could make out what was part of the spine and rib cage in the mud. Cash stood up, tilting his head to the side, "Human? You think?" His breath caught in his throat. Was this the torso killer again?

Kevin cocked his head to the side, "I guess, but your forensics guy would probably have a better time with this than I would."

Cash turned around, looking back at the SUVs, and waved the rest of the team over, yelling for Jeremy. Nearly swamped by the long slicker, Jeremy wandered over, tripping on a rock as he got near the skeleton, "Easy there," Cash said, extending a hand to catch him. "Careful."

Jeremy pulled off his glasses, frowning. "When it rains, I can't see a darned thing."

Cash stood watching Jeremy for a moment as he tugged the bottom hem of his T-shirt out from under his slicker, trying to wipe the raindrops off of his glasses. It was hard to be patient with Jeremy sometimes, Cash thought, staring at the ground, chewing the inside of his lip. The science guys were a different breed.

A moment later, Jeremy knelt down next to the skeleton. Cash waited, wondering what exactly Jeremy could see from the remains that were left behind. "Anything?"

"Well, I'm no medical examiner, but obviously, this is part of what looks to be a human skeleton." Without touching anything, Jeremy pointed, "See these grooves on the edge of the bone?" Cash knelt next to him, trying not to end up flat on his face in the mud. "Those don't look natural to me," Jeremy said to Cash through fogged-up glasses. "I'd suggest we get a tent put up over this thing and call the County Medical Examiner.

That's all Cash needed to know. Within a minute, the team

had erected a portable tent they carried with them in the SUVs. Though the rain wasn't letting up, at least it prevented the spot where the bones had been found to become a mudhole.

Kevin Barnfield came into the tent and motioned to Cash, "Dr. Wiley's on his way. There's some flooding already on some of the side roads. He said to give them a couple of extra minutes."

Cash nodded, stuffing his hands in his pockets, gripping them into tight fists. He didn't want his team to see how frustrated he was, but nothing about this case was moving quickly enough. He knew they were on the clock with Lexi Cooper. Whether this skeleton they found in the field would contribute to their case or distract them, Cash didn't know. He stood back for a second, watching Jeremy take initial pictures of what was left of the body from what seemed to be a million different angles. Cash knew Jeremy wouldn't make the mistake of touching the body until the medical examiner arrived. Bodies were county jurisdiction, not the FBI's, but there was no harm in taking pictures as long as it didn't disturb the scene.

There was a lull in the action while they waited for the medical examiner to arrive. Cash kept checking his phone, hoping for an update, but none came. All he could do was wait.

Stepping under the tent, Janet Crenshaw pulled the hood down off of her head. "Man, that's a lot of rain. Seems like it started out of nowhere."

"You've lived in Louisiana long enough to know how these storms show up," Cash said. Glancing at her, he asked, "Any news on the ME?"

She nodded, "I was just sitting with Detective Barnfield in his car. He's just a couple of minutes out."

"That's good news."

There was silence for a minute. Cash felt Janet looking at him, "What is it?"

She narrowed her eyes a little bit, "You okay? You don't seem like yourself."

"I'm okay. Just trying to get the job done." Cash walked away, pretending to look at the skeleton, moving to the other side of the tent, and kneeling down. After a minute or so, he glanced up at Janet, who was still staring at him. He could tell by the look on her face that she knew he didn't want to talk about what was eating at him. Lexi Cooper. It was bad enough to have a trail of bodies unaccounted for, but a missing child left a very bad feeling in the pit of his stomach he'd been unable to get rid of for the last few days. Before he had a chance to think much more about it, an older man trudged up to the tent and ducked under the edge with Detective Barnfield and a young man in tow, "Cash, you remember Dr. Wiley, the Clement County Medical Examiner?" Kevin said.

Cash looked at Dr. Wiley. He was a big man, broad-shoul-dered with gray hair. The bulk of his body was covered with the slicker, not unlike the ones that Cash and his team wore. Thick glasses sat on top of his nose. "Doc," Cash said with a nod. They'd seen each other every six months for the last couple of years, every time a body was found. It wasn't the kind of friend-ship Cash wanted.

Dr. Wiley nodded, taking his glasses off and wiping the lenses. "Gettin' a bit of rain, huh?" he said. Dr. Wiley gave a little nod toward the bones on the ground, "What did you manage to get yourself into this time, Kevin?"

Kevin cleared his throat, "Sir, a couple of ATV riders found these remains about an hour ago. Thought you should prob-ably take a look at them."

"You'd be right about that," Dr. Wiley said, bending over the skeleton, his hands on his knees.

Silence dropped over the people in the tent as they waited for the verdict from Dr. Wiley. Questions ran through Cash's mind. Was it human? A part of an animal? His gut told him that the bones left behind were human, but all of it had to be confirmed through the local medical examiner. This wasn't a decision he had the authority to make on his own. And if they were human, what did that mean? Were the other bones just dragged off by wild animals? How long had the skeleton been out in the field? Cash tried to calm himself knowing that within a couple of minutes, he'd at least get some cursory information from Dr. Wiley if Cash could only be patient.

Dr. Wiley stood up, glancing at Cash, "Well, I'd like to look at this back at the office, but my initial assessment is these are human remains." He pointed towards the hip joints of the skeleton, "See those striations there? If I had to guess, I'd say those are cut marks. I'll need to take a look at them under the microscope to be sure, but that's what I'm thinking for the moment." Dr. Wiley turned his bulk towards Cash, "I'm thinking we've just found another addition to the torso killer's resume, Agent Strickland," he said.

"I'm sorry to hear that," Cash said, shifting his weight from one leg to the other, "Any idea if this skeleton is earlier than any of the other bodies? Any way to know how long it's been out here in the field?" Cash had a feeling the medical examiner would avoid telling him anything until he had time to do a more thorough examination back at the office, but Cash did know him a bit from his other trips to Tifton. Sometimes, Dr. Wiley would at least give him a trickle of conjecture on what he saw.

The big man tilted his head to the side, "You probably know what I'm gonna say about that, don't you?"

Cash nodded, "Yes, sir. You'd like to look at it back in the office. But if you had to offer a guess?"

"That I will not be held to?"

Cash nodded.

"Based on the color of the skeleton, I'd guess this one has been out in the elements for a while — probably several years at the least." Dr. Wiley raised his eyebrows, "You could be looking at one of the original bodies, which would explain why everything else has been found in Little Bayou Pond. The killer may have changed his drop location when this one wasn't found."

The idea the bones in front of him could be some of the very first from the killer sunk in as Cash thought about what Dr. Wiley said. Dr. Wiley gave a quick nod to his assistant, who pulled a camera out of his equipment bag and started taking another set of pictures. Jeremy stood politely off to the side, watching the medical examiner work. Kneeling down again, Dr. Wiley looked at Cash, "Any of your team bother to look for the rest of this body out here in this field?"

"No, sir. We were waiting to talk to you."

"Well, it's time for your team to start getting their boots muddy. Go have a look, will you? If there were appendages attached to this one and they were left behind, they wouldn't be too far off. Animals don't drag them that far. I'll be here packaging this up. Let me know if you find anything else."

As much as Cash didn't want to muck around in a muddy, rain-soaked field, it was better than standing and staring at Dr. Wiley and his assistant while they poked and prodded at the skeleton. "Okay, let's do what Dr. Wiley asked. Fan out in all directions," he said to his agents. "Let's see if there are any other remains we haven't seen yet."

Cash stepped out into the rain, pulling his hood up over his head. He started walking slowly away from the tent, Janet off to his right and Dan McClelland off to his left. All the agents had the same hunched-over posture, staring at the ground for any evidence of bones left behind.

From underneath the hood of his coat, Cash could hear the patter of raindrops hitting his shoulders, back, and head. Though the weather was terrible, at least the FBI's investment in good quality rain gear made it tolerable. Cash took a couple of steps forward staring at the ground, his boots squishing in the mud. He shook his head a little bit, not taking his gaze off the ground. If the rain kept up like it was, the entirety of Tifton would be nothing more than a mud hole within the next couple of days. The only saving grace was the heat, Cash realized. The minute the sun came back out, at least it would dry up pretty quickly.

Cash looked up for a moment turning around to see where his team was. He and Janet and Dan were working on one side of the tent. The other agents had fanned out taking the other three sides. A few of the agents had walked into the distance and had turned around already. Cash lifted his hands, his palms open, silently asking them if they'd found anything. Everyone's head shook no. A knot formed in the pit of his stomach. Could what Dr. Wiley said be true? Could they have stumbled upon one of the earliest bodies of the torso killer? If so, why did the torso killer change locations for his drops? Was it that he was frustrated that no one found the bodies? Cash stared at the ground again, chewing his lip. The case was like Pandora's box, he thought. Every time he felt like they were getting a handle on it, something else came up, another question they couldn't answer.

34

Before Emily had a chance to catch her breath wrestling with the realization that Cash Strickland had her entire life at his fingertips, her phone rang again. Mike. "Emily, something's come up."

"What is it?" The words came out more impatiently than they should have. Mike was just trying to help. Don't shoot the messenger, she told herself.

"That FBI agent, he's getting texts about some sort of body they found in a field."

Emily's heart stopped for a second. "Is it Lexi?"

"I don't know. The only information I have is a text he sent back to the Baton Rouge office."

"Read it to me."

"Body found in field. Only bones. Will send more information as soon as I get it."

Emily raised her eyebrows and paced next to the bed in her room. What exactly did that mean? If it was only bones, could the torso killer have stripped the flesh off of that poor little girl in the last day or two? A shiver ran through Emily's body. The idea of mutilating someone after they were dead was not something she wanted to think about. "Any idea where this field is?"

"No. I can keep watching Cash's texts, but there's nothing in here about that."

"Okay," Emily said, holding the phone to her ear using her shoulder as she rummaged through her bag. "Ping his phone and let me know if you hear anything."

"Where are you headed?"

"Bradley's."

EMILY SHRUGGED on her raincoat and put a pair of dry socks on her feet before sliding her feet back into her boots. She grabbed her baseball cap from the end of the bed and headed downstairs, getting into the Jeep. She wasn't worried about seeing any of the FBI agents now — they were all likely at the scene, looking for evidence. Or, at least, that's where they should be.

Emily ran to the Jeep as fast as she could. The rain was coming down in sheets, the gray clouds thick and low in the sky. The wind had picked up and nearly blew the cap off of her head as she jumped in the Jeep. Slamming the door, she started it up, setting her phone off to the side.

The drive to Bradley's was a little slower than before, water running off the side of the roads and filling the drainage ditches almost full. "If this rain keeps up, we're going to be dealing with a flood," Emily murmured to herself. She reached for the knob that controlled the fan system on the Jeep, adjusting it so it pumped out every last bit of air at the windshield to keep it from fogging. The dark clouds had made it hard enough to see. With the end of the day coming up, it was only going to get worse.

Pulling into Bradley's driveway, she noticed the lights in the garage were off. Without thinking, she ran to the front door and pounded on it with her fist, "Bradley!" Emily yelled, trying to get underneath the overhang enough that she was out of the rain. "Are you in there?"

A short woman cracked the door open, her stubby fingers gripping the edge of the door. It had to be Carla, Bradley's wife. "Who are you?"

"Emily."

"Hold on. I'll get him."

A second later, the door pulled the whole way open, "What's all the hubbub about?" Bradley appeared at the door, squinting.

"A body. A body's been found," Emily said, trying to catch her breath.

The surprised look on Bradley's face melted into one of seriousness, "Meet me in the garage. I'll be out in just a minute. The side door's unlocked."

Emily didn't wait or take the time to chat with Carla. Running from the porch, Emily darted across the driveway, and nearly pushed the side door off its hinges, stepping in and out of the rain. She found the switch for one of the banks of lights in the garage and stood, shaking the water off her slicker when Bradley walked in, his cane wet from the downpour, "A body's been found?"

Emily nodded, "My tech was able to intercept some information from the FBI."

Bradley raised his eyebrows above the thick frames of his glasses, "What do you mean by that?"

Emily closed her eyes for a second and shook her head, "Don't ask. You don't want to know. Anyway, they just found the body out in a field. Who do you know that can get us information on this?"

"Well, I do have one in," Bradley said, a grin spreading on his face.

Bradley's smile confused Emily, "What are you smiling about? Who do you know?"

"The medical examiner, Dr. Wiley? He's one of my best customers. Our families have been friends for generations. If anyone knows what's going on, he will. If you'd like, we could head over there now. If there's a body coming in, he's either out in the field or he's on his way back to the office."

"For sure. Let's go!"

Emily ran back out in the rain to the Jeep, getting it started while Bradley joined her. As soon as he got in, he looked at her, "We can go over there, but are you sure your FBI buddies aren't going to be hanging out with Dr. Wiley? I mean, wouldn't they do that?"

Emily's stomach sank. Bradley was right. Sure, she and Bradley could go to the Medical Examiner's Office, but what if Cash Strickland was standing in the lobby? Emily paused, blinking, "Well, that's a chance we might just have to take." She swallowed hard, chasing bile back down her throat.

35

After about twenty minutes of searching out in the mud, Cash turned around and waved his team back in. Dr. Wiley was waiting under the tent, the skeleton carried to their van by his assistant. "Anything?" he said as Cash ducked under the edge of the canvas.

Cash shook his head, "Nope. I didn't find anything within about five hundred yards of the tent." Cash almost referred to the skeleton as "the chunk of body," but stopped himself. The stress of the case is getting to me, he thought. "What now?"

"Well, we'll get the skeleton back to the office and take a look at it in the morning."

Raising his eyebrows, Cash said, "Any chance you might be able to look at it tonight?"

Dr. Wiley shook his head no, "I gotta get back to my farm, make sure all my animals are okay. We get some flooding out there. Gotta keep the living alive if you know what I mean."

As Dr. Wiley picked up the last equipment bag and walked out into the rain, his head uncovered, his shoulders hunched against the wind, making his way back to his van, Cash groaned out loud. Janet Crenshaw ducked under the tent, "What's going on?"

Cash shook his head, "Dr. Wiley isn't available to take a look at our skeleton until the morning. He's got livestock to tend to."

Janet cocked her head to the side and raised her eyebrows, "Even with Lexi missing?"

Cash shrugged, closing his eyes for a second. Nothing about this case was ever easy.

Janet blinked, "Well, he's in charge. He gets to set his own hours. It's not like the skeleton's having a heart attack or anything." She unzipped her jacket and then looked at Cash, "What do we do now?"

"We wait."

36

"I have an idea," Bradley said, pulling an old flip phone out of his pocket. "Gimme a minute."

Emily pulled the Jeep up at a red light in the center of town still worried about running into the FBI at Dr. Wiley's office. She pulled out her phone and sent a text to Mike, "How's that location on Strickland coming?"

By the time Mike texted back, Bradley was on the phone with who Emily guessed was Dr. Wiley. "James? How are you on this fine evening?"

Bradley pointed down the road as the light turned green, still talking to Dr. Wiley. "Listen, I heard you might've found something out in a field. You know how I feel about this stuff. Any chance I could stop by the office and hear more about what you've got going?"

Emily gripped the wheel a little harder. If she could manage to talk to the medical examiner, or better yet, see what they'd brought in, it would give her a leg up on the case. Some real information. But all of that would go away if the FBI was there.

"Yeah, that'll work," Bradley said. "Thanks, buddy. I'll see you in a few."

"Good news?" Emily asked.

"Yep. He said we can come to the office. We're just around the corner now."

Emily sucked in a breath. The fact they could see the medical examiner was great, but where were Cash Strickland and his team of agents? And where was Mike? What was taking him so long to get a location? Mike must have read Emily's mind because a second later, her phone beeped. "His phone is pinging that they are on the road. Don't know the destination. No info on that."

A tightness passed over Emily's chest. The next few minutes could determine whether she'd have to face down Cash.

37

Leaving the field where they'd found the skeleton, Cash and his team pulled their SUVs behind Dr. Wiley's van on the way to his office. Although the medical examiner said he wasn't going to work on the skeleton until the morning, the least they could do was make sure he got back to the office in one piece with the evidence. Although it wasn't technically a chain of custody issue, since Dr. Wiley had ownership of the body, Cash knew he'd feel better if he knew everything got to Dr. Wiley's office in one piece, especially with the weather howling overhead.

Cash leaned forward, squinting at the windshield, "Can't remember when I've seen this much rain. Almost seems more like a hurricane than a tropical storm, don't you think?" he said to Janet, who was sitting on the passenger side. She pulled off her rain slicker and stuffed it down near the side of her seat.

Janet reached over and pressed the button for the seat heater. "I know. Haven't seen weather like this in quite a while. Gave me a chill."

"In eighty-degree weather?"

"Don't ask. You're not a woman. We are much more sensitive to temperature."

Cash shook his head. "I'm a little aggravated that Dr. Wiley doesn't want to take a look at the skeleton until the morning. This is the first real lead we've had and with Lexi missing... I just don't understand it."

Janet shrugged, "I know. I don't get it, but he's probably thinking the bones have been out in the weather for a while. I guess it's okay. What's one more night?"

Cash pursed his lips. That very attitude was the one that might not let Janet ever move forward in her career, he thought. He shook his head a little, realizing that most of the agents on his team were as far ahead in the FBI as they were going to get. They didn't have the urgency, the drive they needed to get promoted. But he didn't want to be the one to tell Janet that. He liked her. "I guess you're right. Just be nice to know if the skeleton we found is the work of the torso killer or not."

The two of them said nothing more until they got to Dr. Wiley's office. It was a one-story building with a garage door on the side. Cash pulled in right behind Dr. Wiley and his assistant, watching the garage door go up. As the van pulled inside, Cash watched. Dr. Wiley's big, lumbering frame could be seen getting out of the van in the murky darkness of the garage.

Without thinking, Cash darted out of the SUV, running for the cover of the garage. "You need anything else? You want us to stay?"

Dr. Wiley shook his head a little bit, "Up to you, but all I'm gonna do is log the body in and head home."

Cash nodded, his stomach tightening. It was going to be a long night of waiting.

38

As Emily and Bradley rounded the corner, she spotted the sign for the Clement County Medical Examiner's Office. It was a low building, squat to the ground as if it was perched on the soil rather than towering over it. Made of block and brick, it was dark against the dusk and the driving rain.

Pulling into the parking lot, Emily was nearly on top of the FBI SUVs before she realized it, "No!" she whispered, driving slowly past them and around the back of the building.

"What's the matter?" Bradley asked.

"You know as well as I do. That's the FBI! I don't want to get tangled up with them." Emily gritted her teeth. He knew she was working on his brother's case as an off-the-books pursuit. Getting involved with the FBI would be a mistake, one she wasn't sure she'd ever recover from.

"Hang on there, Emily," Bradley said, pointing around the back of the building. "Pull the Jeep in over there. It's so dark that none of them can see us." Bradley picked up his phone again and dialed.

Emily picked a spot in the back corner of the lot, her heart pounding in her chest. Had Bradley done this on purpose, trying to get her in the hot seat with the FBI? Hopefully, that wasn't the case. She chewed the inside of her lip, waiting.

Next to her, Bradley had the phone up to his ear. He didn't say anything for a minute, and then he glanced at Emily, whispering, "Hold on for a sec. Let me see what I can do here."

Emily stared off into the darkness, trying to stay calm. She knew she hadn't done anything wrong. She hadn't broken the law while she was in Tifton. Why was she so paranoid? Knowing that Cash had all of her information at his fingertips resurfaced in her mind. It was nearly impossible to make any moves without running into these people, she thought. A tightness traveled across her chest. What had started off to be a major breakthrough in the case was rapidly turning into another dead end, especially if the evidence she needed to see was just a few steps from the Jeep, but she was unable to see it. She continued to stare off at the darkness letting her eyes remain unfocused, trying to relax, taking a few deep breaths.

A moment later, Bradley was off the phone. "Doc said to give him ten minutes and then hopefully the FBI guys will disappear. He said we can use the back entrance once everything is clear."

Emily looked down for a second, just in time to hear her phone ping, it was Mike. "You are practically on top of Cash. Do you know that?!"

Emily texted back, "Yes. I'm aware. Thanks for the heads up." At least she'd managed not to be short with Mike. After all, he and Flynn were just trying to help.

Bradley and Emily sat in the car in silence, the Jeep dim. To anyone who drove by without paying attention, they might not even notice the two people sitting in the front seat. The rain was working to her advantage, Emily thought, the mist and humidity and large droplets shielding the Jeep from prying eyes. Emily took a couple of deep breaths, glancing over her left shoulder when she saw the wash of headlights. "Get down," she hissed, putting a hand on Bradley's shoulder.

The two of them slid down, avoiding the headlights from the black SUVs as they passed by. Emily didn't dare look until the darkness had covered the Jeep again. "Did two of them pass?"

Bradley nodded, his eyes wide.

"Are you sure?" Emily said, staring at him.

Bradley nodded again. "I think we're good. Let's go in and see Doc before he leaves. He's waiting for us."

Emily swallowed and hesitated. Having the FBI lurking around every corner had her off her game. Could this be a setup? Could Bradley be working with the FBI? Maybe the SUVs just pretended to leave, and they circled around the front of the building, the agents taking up positions inside as she sat in the Jeep. Emily swallowed again, realizing she had a decision to make. Could Bradley be trusted or not? She'd bumped up against the question a couple of times since she got into Tifton. It was time to decide. "Let's go," she said.

Emily slid out of the Jeep into the darkness, following Bradley. He was surprisingly fast, even with his limp. At the back door, Bradley put his hand on the knob and turned it, light from the inside of the building pouring out, welcoming them in. Emily stood in the doorway for a moment, taking in her surroundings, waiting to hear the voices of FBI agents yell at her, "Stop!"

They never came.

Water dropped off the back and sides of Emily's rain slicker, leaving a puddle of the tropical storm on the floor. Emily stood there for a moment, listening, ready to run right back out to the Jeep if she needed to. She felt every muscle in her body ready to spring into action. Bradley's voice broke through the noise in her mind, "Come on. His office is down the hall."

In the back of the medical examiner's building, there wasn't a lot to see. Her heart starting to slow down, Emily was able to absorb more of the details of the space. There was a long hallway that ran parallel to the back wall of the building. The door they'd come in was a double door, one that could be open wide to allow for larger deliveries in and out of the building. Deliveries of bodies, Emily was sure. Directly across from the set of double doors was another set of matching doors, protected by a keypad. She followed Bradley down the hallway, the two of them leaving little drips of rainwater as they walked. The hallway itself was plain and looked much like a hospital — dull gray linoleum floors and vanilla painted walls, the harsh fluorescent light softened by some sort of filters in the ceiling. At the end of the hallway, there was a set of double doors that were open. Emily could feel the wind from the storm blowing outside swirling around. She glanced to her right to see a two-bay garage with an extra high ceiling. Dr. Wiley's van was parked inside. As she turned the corner, Emily saw someone pushing a cart down the hallway ahead of them. He disappeared around the corner.

Bradley stopped at a door on his left and pushed it open, going inside. It was a brightly lit examination room, but not the kind that Emily had seen when she visited the doctor. There was a bank of steel doors against the wall opposite her. Cold storage for bodies. In the center of the room there were two stainless steel examination tables. To her right, there was a long table filled with scientific equipment — microscopes, an autoclave, and some other specialized equipment Emily didn't recognize. In the corner of the room, she heard a grunt, "Over here, Bradley. Yeah, Buster, just leave it here. I'll take care of it. Thanks. You can go home."

The man pushing the cart walked right past Emily and Bradley, giving Bradley a tiny nod. "Have a good night, Buster. Be safe out there," Bradley said as the young man walked by.

Rising from behind one of the examination tables which

had blocked her view, Emily saw a large man with rounded, sloping shoulders stand up. He had on a one-piece jumpsuit, much like the one she'd seen veterinarian's wear. As he turned, he looked at her and then Bradley and said, "I didn't know you were bringing a friend. Who's this?"

The way he said the words didn't stir up any alarm inside of Emily. It was as simple as if he'd asked about the weather outside. A sense of calm began to settle over her. Emily sighed as she listened to Bradley. "Doc, this is Emily. She's giving me a hand trying to figure out what happened to my brother. We heard through the grapevine you might've found something tonight. I was wondering if you'd do me the favor of sharing what you know with Emily so maybe she can put the pieces together for us."

Dr. Wiley came out from behind the examination table and leaned his back on it, crossing his legs at the ankles and his arms over his chest, "You're interested in the torso killer case?"

Emily cleared her throat, "That'd be right."

"Are you some sort of private investigator?"

"You could say that, too."

Dr. Wiley stared at Emily for a second and then at Bradley, a broad smile covering his face that pushed his cheeks up underneath his glasses, "I like this one, Bradley. Doesn't waste time with chit-chat."

Before she could say anything else, Dr. Wiley walked past her to the long steel table and opened a file drawer underneath, pulling out a thick manila folder. He laid it out on the steel examining table, sorting the papers into different stacks. He glanced over his shoulder and looked at Emily and Bradley, "Here's some basic information on the torso killer." As Dr. Wiley straightened up, he looked at Bradley, "You think she can do a better job than the FBI?"

"Well, you know what the FBI has done for us..."

The words hung in the air for a moment, the reality that

even though seven years of bodies had accumulated, and now another, the FBI had been unable to solve the case. They hadn't made much progress even though they'd been coming to Tifton twice a year for almost a decade. Emily wondered why they hadn't narrowed down at least a suspect list. Or maybe they had, and they were running through the list at that very moment. That was something to try to remember to ask Mike about.

Dr. Wiley's voice interrupted Emily's thoughts, "That's true. What did you say your name was?" he said, looking at her.

"Emily."

"You don't sound like you're from around here."

"I'm not." Emily glanced at the stack of papers and then back at Dr. Wiley. She wasn't about to get into a discussion about where she was from. "Can I ask you a few questions, especially about what you found today?"

Dr. Wiley went back to leaning on the edge of the metal examining table, re-crossing his ankles and his arms over his chest, "Shoot," he nodded.

"I heard that you found something today out in the field. What was it?"

"Yes, that." Dr. Wiley pointed over to a cart sitting in the corner of the room. It was covered with an off-white sheet. "That over there is a pile of bones that some kids found in a field not too far from here. Local detective said they were riding ATVs around there — some of those fields used to be planted up with corn, but it's been going fallow for a long time now — and they ran across what looks like a rib cage and spine from a human body."

"Human?" Emily said, walking over to the cart, "Mind if I take a look?"

Dr. Wiley shook his head, "If you're a friend of Bradley's, you're a friend of mine."

Emily walked behind the stainless-steel examining table

and lifted the edge of the sheet. Laying on a metal tray was exactly what Dr. Wiley had described – what looked like a complete rib cage still attached to the sternum, a line of vertebrae and pelvic bone. The bones were off-white. Emily bent over, looking more closely at the pelvis and the top of the spine, squinting, careful not to touch anything. "These marks on the edge of the bone, Doc, what are those?"

Dr. Wiley walked up behind her and then stepped to the side, pointing with a pen he pulled out of his chest pocket, "The ones right there?" he said.

Emily nodded.

"I think those are cut marks."

The reality that the skeleton found out in the field was likely part of the torso killer case made Emily swallow, the bile rising in the back of her throat. She pressed her lips together and sucked in a breath. Looking at Dr. Wiley, she said, "Anything else you can tell me about the skeleton?"

Dr. Wiley straightened up, cocking his head to the side, "Well, I can tell you these bones have been out in that field for quite a while, probably years by their color. The rain and sun kind of bleaches them and causes them to dull at the same time, just like what you'd see with animal bones. If you're asking me directly whether I think these marks are the same as the Tifton torso killer, let me show you."

Dr. Wiley lumbered over to the piles of papers spread out on the stainless-steel tables. Emily glanced behind her to see Bradley had pulled up a chair and was sitting down, probably resting his leg, she thought.

Flipping through the pages with his thick fingers, Dr. Wiley pulled up a couple of different examples from earlier bodies, lifting the photographs to the top of the stack, "See this here?" he pointed, leaning over the table. "They look pretty much like the same marks we see on that skeleton over there." Emily moved out of the way as Dr. Wiley slid down the line and pulled out a few more photographs for her to look at, "We see the same thing here, only this time it's on the spot where the humerus would have fit into the shoulder joint." Dr. Wiley stood up, towering over Emily. She knew she wasn't a petite woman, but Dr. Wiley took being large to a whole new level. He was the size of a modern-day offensive lineman on a football team. "Tools on bones make specific marks. Almost like fingerprints. I've shown all of this to the FBI, but they have not been able to make any sense out of it, at least not in a way that leads to a suspect." Dr. Wiley paused for a second, "But, I'd have no trouble sitting in a court of law saying that the same saw that cut up the remains we just brought in tonight is the same saw that cut up these other people."

There was something about the situation that didn't make any sense, Emily thought. "Why isn't the FBI here right now? Why are you telling me all this and not them?"

Dr. Wiley raised his eyebrows and looked at Bradley and then he looked back at her, "The FBI? If you know anything about this case, then you know the FBI has done little or nothing to help the citizens of Tifton except show up, drive around our city at breakneck speed in those fancy SUVs they have, and make a mess over at the local bed-and-breakfast. They might be working the case, but I haven't seen any results." Dr. Wiley pulled out a squat metal stool from underneath one of the examining tables and lowered himself. It was like watching a tree fall, Emily thought. Dr. Wiley continued, "Realistically, they make a good show of it, but they haven't gotten anywhere. I was hoping maybe this new agent — what's his name?" Dr. Wiley frowned, looking at Bradley.

Emily interrupted, "Cash Strickland?"

Dr. Wiley nodded, "Yeah, Strickland. I thought he might make some progress on the case, but I haven't seen anything that tells me he's been able to. Every time I see him, he tells me he's met with some sort of special expert in something or another, but it never leads anywhere. At this point, when they find something, me and Buster go out and pick up the body, bring it back, and write the report. There's not a lot more I can do."

"Is that why you're letting me look at this information? I mean, isn't all of this usually confidential?" Emily asked, leaning against the examination table where Dr. Wiley stood a few minutes before.

Dr. Wiley nodded, leaning his forearms over on his thighs, "That's right. Bradley's a smart guy. Doesn't let many people see it, but if he's found you and he says he thinks you can help, well, that's good enough for me. What other questions do you have? I gotta get back to my farm and go make sure my livestock hasn't floated away."

Over the next few minutes, Emily took pictures of the skeletal remains that Dr. Wiley and Buster had brought back in from the field as well as pictures of the reports and images Dr. Wiley laid out on the table. The medical examiner hadn't moved, staying in the same bent-over position on the stool while she worked. Emily didn't have the feeling he was being impatient, just waiting. For a moment, she wondered how hard it must've been for him over the last seven years, going out to pick up abandoned torsos from the pond, bringing them back to his examination room, trying to give what was left of the body as much dignity as possible. Emily felt a weight descend on her chest, the same weight she realized must have been sitting over Tifton for the last seven years. She realized, shoving her phone into her back pocket, it made sense why Dr. Wiley gave her access to all of the records. They had no hope in the FBI. They had no hope at all.

BACK OUT IN THE JEEP, the rain rattled on the roof. Emily had more than enough information for Mike. Before driving

Bradley home, Emily attached all the images into one large file, running the encryption program Mike had given her and then emailing it to his fake account, one that couldn't be connected to either his name or Emily's. Attaching a note asking him to see what he and his tech friends could figure out with the evidence she'd sent, she hoped maybe they would see something that everyone else had missed. Setting her phone down, she looked at Bradley, "Ready?"

"Yup. I'd be grateful for a ride home in this monsoon."

Neither Emily nor Bradley said much in the car on the way back to his house. Emily glanced over at him a few times while she was driving. He seemed quiet, lost in his thoughts. Maybe he was just tired, Emily realized. It'd been a long day. It couldn't have been easy for him to be in the medical examiner's office, knowing that it was the last stop his brother made before he was buried. As she drove, Emily drummed her fingers on the steering wheel, wondering if what Dr. Wiley said was right — had the town lost faith in the FBI? Did it appear to be just some sort of good faith effort by the government to send a herd of agents, make a lot of noise and then leave again, forcing the people of the town to suffer through another six months of agony? Emily chewed her lip. If there was one thing she knew about criminals, it was that they made mistakes. No one, not even Cash Strickland or any of his experts, could convince her that whoever was doing the killing hadn't made a mistake. They just hadn't found it yet. Emily swallowed, a calm settling over her. She would find this guy, hopefully in time to rescue Lexi.

39

Ollie had stopped at the bar on the way home from work. There wasn't any rush to get home now that Lexi was secured in the basement. He knew she'd be waiting for him when he arrived. She couldn't have gone anywhere at all. He pictured her face in his mind, her wrists bound to the chair, her long hair streaming behind her. It was a comforting thought. Getting in his truck, a little woozy from a couple of shots he'd drunk right before leaving, Ollie wondered if maybe he should have smacked the little girl in the head again, putting her to sleep before he left. Starting up the van, he realized there'd be time for that later.

The weather had worsened while he was in the bar, the now constant rain coming in sheets that thrummed over the hood and windshield as the van pushed forward into the night. At least it was a good distraction from the tension in his chest he couldn't seem to get rid of. Sage. That was nearly all he'd been able to think about over the last few weeks. His little girl.

From a front pocket of his shirt, he pulled out his phone, dialing his ex-wife. It was late in Tifton, but the spot Libby had taken the girls to in Canada was a couple of hours behind them. He waited for the call to connect, trying to hear the phone over the pounding of the rain. Ollie slowed down, hoping she would pick up. A second later, Ollie heard a voice on the other end of the line, "Ollie? Why are you calling?"

"I want to talk to the girls, Libby. You never let me talk to the girls."

"Are you drunk again?"

"It's not your business what I'm doing, Libby. We're divorced, remember?" he hissed.

"And it's my job to protect the girls, remember?"

"I need to talk to them, Libby. You can't keep me from my girls forever. I have half a mind to drive right on up there and come and see them myself. The judge said I was allowed to." Ollie's chest tightened, a wave of fury rising over him. He swerved, not seeing the edge of the road, but managed to get the van back on the pavement in the rain. It was hard enough to see in the storm. Arguing with Libby at the same time didn't help.

"Well, maybe if you'd been a better father then they'd want to talk to you."

"What are you saying? They don't want to talk to me?"

There was a pause. Ollie knew things had not been going well between him and Libby. It had been a long, long time since he'd been able to talk to the girls. They were teenagers now. Sure, it was late in Canada, probably ten o'clock, Ollie figured, but teenage girls were usually up late. Wouldn't they want to talk to him? To tell him about their day and what they'd been up to?

Libby interrupted his thoughts, "That's exactly what they're saying to me. Sage said to me just yesterday that she doesn't even know you. Doesn't remember you, either."

The barb hurt. Ollie pressed his lips together, tightening his jaw, "This is all your fault, Libby. You gave me those kids and then stole them away to live with that other man. You should be ashamed of yourself. You wait, things like this, they come back to people. You'll get yours." Ollie ended the call, throwing his phone down onto the floor of the passenger's side of the van. His body was hot, rage filling him. Libby had destroyed their family. If it weren't for her, he would be sitting at home right now, thinking about his girls, worrying about them, and planning for their future, not alone thousands of miles away, drunk, driving through a rainstorm.

Sage. That was all he could think about. The shape of her face, her wide eyes, the pink roller skates she loved so much, the noise of the wheels rattling up and down the driveway as she rolled back and forth, the only interruption when she fell, her giggles lifting over the yard. This was all Libby's fault. For a second, Ollie thought about going home, getting his bag, and driving straight to Canada. He'd never been there. Maybe it was time for a visit. But then his mind floated back to the basement and Lexi Cooper. She was there, waiting for him. She was probably one of the few things that would help heal the hurt in him, the hurt that seemed to surface every six months, at the beginning of the year for Willow and six months later for Sage.

Thinking about Lexi changed things. Ollie started to feel calm and focused. He imagined gripping Lexi's arm and setting his saw to her shoulder, seeing the flesh pull away from the bone. He thought about carrying her small torso and laying it gently in the pond, saying goodbye once again to the family he wanted but didn't have.

Lexi. He needed to get home.

40

B y the time Emily got back to the bed-and-breakfast, nearly all the lights were off in the rooms, at least the ones she could see from the outside. The black SUVs were sitting in the parking lot, parked side-by-side in the shadows and the pouring down rain. Emily darted from the Jeep into the back door of the bed-and-breakfast, pulling her cap down low over her face. There was no reason to think any of the FBI agents would be roaming around the building, but just knowing they were that close made her skin tingle.

As soon as she got in her room, she pulled off her slicker and baseball cap, shaking the coat out, leaving little rain droplets all over the carpet. Standing in the doorway, the power went out and then back on again. "I hope this place has a generator," she mumbled, heading for the bathroom. After a quick shower, Emily felt better, the sweat of the day rinsed off of her. She sat down on the edge of her bed, pressing her bare feet into the carpet. She called Mike. "Sorry to call so late," she said.

"No worries," Mike said. "I got the files you sent. That's a lot of information."

"Yeah, it was."

"How did you manage to snag all that?"

"Well, it turns out Bradley Barker is good friends with the county medical examiner. He let me take a look at the files and the remains they just brought back in."

"I wondered how that happened. How was he?"

Emily frowned for a second, "Honestly? He seems frustrated by the lack of progress the FBI is making. I think that's why he let me look at all the files. He said they come down, hang around for a couple of weeks, and then head home with the promise they'll figure something out, but they never do."

"So, you're their next best hope?"

"I guess."

"And they're gonna keep your presence quiet?"

That was the question Emily wrestled with after dropping Bradley off. Would Dr. Wiley slip up and somehow mentioned to Cash that she'd seen the remains? If Cash found out she'd seen the case files he'd probably slap her within an obstruction of justice charge or an interfering in an investigation charge. Emily swallowed, "I hope so." Shifting on the bed, Emily changed the subject, "Can you get your people together and take a look at those files I sent over? I'll take any sets of eyes I can get on this case."

"Yeah, of course. Flynn is already here, and Alice is on her way over. Any news about Lexi?"

"None."

With the promise to touch base in the morning, Emily ended her call with Mike. At least Alice was in the mix, she thought. Alice's background might not be the same as Dr. Wiley's medical degree, but she'd bet any money that Alice would be able to sort through a lot of the scientific data, probably better than Mike and Flynn. It would be a long night for all of them.

Emily pulled her laptop and the charging cable out of her

backpack and sat on the bed, turning on the television low in the background. After midnight, there wasn't a lot of programming, just constant weather coverage with the tropical storm blowing into Louisiana. Emily turned on her computer and sent the files from her phone to her laptop, so she could see everything on a larger screen. Was there anything to find? She wasn't sure. She hoped there was. Lexi's life depended on it.

41

Randy Cooper had grudgingly gone into work. He wasn't sure about leaving Keira at home by herself, but she had insisted. "I know they will let you stay home, but I don't want you to burn up all of your family time. There's nothing going on here. As soon as I hear anything, I'll let you know. I'd rather have you home when Lexi gets back." The way Keira said it, Randy wasn't sure if he should believe her. She looked like a ghost a little more every day that Lexi was gone. But maybe she was right. Maybe keeping themselves busy was the best thing for them to do while the FBI tried to figure out what happened to Lexi. Just thinking about it left a knot in his stomach. He swallowed, "Okay, but I'm going to call your sister and have her come sit here with you while I'm at work. And, if you need anything, I'm going to come right home."

Looking off in the distance, Keira didn't argue, "Okay."

Driving to the station in his truck, Randy started to think, watching the rain pound on his windshield. During a tropical storm, Randy never knew what to expect on his shift. Scratching his head, he remembered there'd only been once during his time with the Tifton Fire Department that the chief sent everyone home to wait out the storm. That had been years ago. For the people in the area, a tropical storm wasn't much of anything, not much more than just a big hassle that slowed things down a bit.

Walking into the station, Randy took his overnight bag into the bunk room. It wasn't much, just two lines of twin-size beds pushed against the wall on either side of a narrow room, a few nightstands and lamps scattered between them, the block walls of the firehouse painted a dull gray. He sat down on the end of one of the beds, bent over, tightening the laces of his boots when Bill Kinzer walked in. He sat down on the bunk next to Randy, his eyes protruding from his head, staring, "I'm surprised you're here," he said. "Everything going okay?"

Randy looked at Bill and blinked. The two of them had gone through the fire academy together, spending months scrambling up and down ladders and in and out of smoke-filled buildings to prove they could handle the pressure of the job. Bill had dragged Randy out of one of those buildings while they were training, the seal on his mask breaking in the middle of a test. Randy remembered not being able to see anything, not even the fingers in front of his face. He kind of felt the same way now; lost without Lexi at home. It was as though someone had taken his entire life, lifted it up, and dropped him and Keira in a place they were completely unfamiliar with — life without Lexi. "Keira made me come in. Didn't want me to burn any more of my family leave time."

Bill shook his head a little bit, "It's gotta be so hard, man. I don't even know what to say. Does the FBI have anything? Any ideas at all?"

Randy stood up and stared at the wall as a wave of anger passed over him, "As a matter of fact, they've got nothing. The only thing they've been able to tell me and Keira is that it looks like somebody might have stuck a screwdriver or something in the window of Lexi's room to get to her. Might. They aren't even sure about that." He felt a wave of emotion rush over him. Without thinking, a yell came out of him as he ran to the wall on the far side of the room, slapped it with both of his hands, and punched it with his right fist. When he turned back to Bill, the anger was starting to subside, but there was blood on his knuckles. "Sorry about that," Randy said, panting. "I've been trying to hold it together for Keira, but it's so horrible. I can't begin to tell you what the last few days have been like."

Bill stared at Randy for a second, blinking, fish-like eyes jutting out from his head. Without saying anything, he got up and walked over to the doorway, opening a first aid kit that was bolted to the wall. He came back with an antiseptic and some bandages. "Here, let me take a look."

Randy sat back down on the end of the bunk and held his hand out for Bill, who dabbed at it with a couple of antiseptic wipes and then covered the scraped skin. Randy flexed his hand open and closed. "I don't think I broke anything."

Bill walked over to the trashcan and dropped the wrappers in, "That's good. The last thing you need to do is take a medical leave on top of everything else. Gotta try to keep it together." The way the words came out of Bill's mouth, they weren't any more exciting than if Bill told Randy he wanted milk on his cereal. Bill was like that. Never got too excited. That's one of the things that made Bill a great firefighter and paramedic. He never let his emotions get out ahead of him. Randy wished he had the same composure.

Randy stared down at his boots for a second and then looked at Bill, who'd sat back down calmly on the cot next to him. In a hushed voice, Randy said, "I just don't know what to do next, Bill. I mean, I'm the man. I should be able to protect my family and I didn't. And now Keira," he paused, swallowing. "She's a mess. Won't eat. Can't sleep. Even the anxiety medication the doctor prescribed for her isn't working. She sits for a few minutes staring at a book or TV program and then gets up and walks to Lexi's room and then comes back. She repeats the same cycle all day long. She's not doing anything and yet it's exhausting to watch her."

"So, maybe it's a good thing she sent you to work? Maybe taking a break from everything at home will clear your head. Get your mind off of what's going on."

Randy nodded, still looking down. Before he could say anything, he heard the springs from the cot next to him squeak a little, the warmth of Bill's hand on his shoulder as Bill stood up. "I'm here for you. Whatever you need. Just let me know."

Randy stood up too, knowing that it was time for them to go to the morning meeting before their shift started. Randy felt a little twitch in his stomach as he followed Bill out of the bunk room. Following him down the hallway, the tightness in Randy's stomach increased. In the common room, three other guys were sitting on the couches and chairs, Chief Bartlett standing up against the wall, waiting. He gave Bill and Randy a little nod as they came in. Randy chose a chair towards the back of the room, not his usual seat. He didn't make eye contact. Randy felt the other firefighter's eyes boring into him. He knew they wanted to ask him what was going on and how he was doing, but it was too much. Thankfully, the chief cleared his throat before anyone could look back at Randy and say anything, "Good morning. Thanks for coming in on this wet day. As you can tell, we've got quite the storm coming overhead. Based on the meteorological information I have, the storm will continue to pound us for almost the next twenty-four hours, just in time for you all to get off your shift." The chief ruffled through some papers on the clipboard he held in his hands. "You all have your regular assignments, but I think what you can expect over this shift would be some people with water intrusion into their homes or on their property that need a hand getting out. There may be some medical calls, but that's nothing new, just a little bit more challenging with a tropical storm hollering overhead. At some point, it wouldn't surprise me if we got a call from the parish asking for us to help with tree removal if they get swamped with blocked roads. That said, make sure you've got all your waterproof gear handy and ready to go. It's going to be a wet shift, guys, but we'll get through it, just like we always do. Please keep me posted if your families need anything."

Randy glanced up at the chief, knowing the last comment was just for him. Randy gave a little nod and then leaned back in the chair as most of the guys got up and walked away. He knew what they were doing. Bill would walk behind him into the kitchen and start a fresh pot of coffee. A couple of the other guys would go out into the garage and fuss with the tools to make sure they were ready to go for the shift. Normally, Randy would help with the trucks or check the medical supplies on the ambulance, but not today. Today, he felt like sitting and staring.

As the meeting thinned out, Randy realized Chief Bartlett was still standing against the wall, watching him. A second later, he walked over, "How are you doing Randy?"

"I'm all right, Chief. How are you doing today?"

"Doing fine. Anything we can do for you or Keira?"

Randy shook his head and looked down again, feeling a surge of emotion, "I wish there was, Chief. I just gotta get on with doing my job until the FBI tells me otherwise, I guess."

Chief Bartlett furrowed his eyebrows, "Well, if you need anything at all, or you need to go home, don't give it a second thought. Just let me know, okay?"

Randy nodded and then put both hands on his knees, pushing himself up into standing, "Thanks. I think I'm gonna go out and check supplies in the ambulance."

"Sounds good," Chief Bartlett nodded.

Randy didn't feel like doing anything, but sorting through

the ambulance sounded better than dealing with question after question about Lexi and Keira. Hopefully, Bill would share the information with the rest of the guys so Randy didn't have to keep repeating himself. Walking to the ambulance, he looked down, avoiding eye contact.

Randy spent the morning doing chores around the fire station. Just as soon as he got the ambulance restocked, there was a medical call, a couple of the other guys heading out to take it. While they were gone, Randy decided to mop the station floor. It wasn't a job he normally loved to do, but anything that would keep his mind occupied seemed to push the anger and fear back down inside of him where he could at least function. Running the rope mop over the painted red floor took about an hour, just in time for the wet ambulance to pull back in from the storm, the lights blinking as it backed into the station. As soon as the garage door slid close, Randy sopped up the rainwater from underneath the vehicle with the mop. The driver popped out, looking at Randy, and said, "Floor mopping today?"

Randy nodded, "You guys all make a mess. Somebody's got to clean up after you."

The guy looked at Randy, smiled, then walked away. It was normal firehouse banter. On another day, the two of them would probably have stood around and talked about the upcoming college football season or argued about what plays the New Orleans Saints should run on their home opener, But not today. Randy looked down again, continuing the rhythmic swipes of the rope mop on the floor.

An hour later, Bill came out into the garage. Randy had just finished his second mopping of the floor, the water black in the rolling bucket, "Lunch is just about ready. Think you've done enough mopping for this morning?"

Randy looked back over the floor, much of it still wet, the water refusing to evaporate with the humidity from the tropical storm floating overhead and filtering into the building. Reaching over, Randy flipped on the ceiling fans, hoping that would help remove some of the moisture. "It was dirty. I'll be in for lunch in a couple of minutes," he said, pushing the mop and bucket across the floor, the clatter of the wheels echoing in the garage. Going into the utility closet just past the door into the common room, Randy flipped on the light switch. On the walls on either side, there was extra equipment neatly displayed on shelves — two extra helmets, two extra facemasks, and a rack bolted to the wall with replacement oxygen tanks. Passing all of those, Randy pushed the bucket and mop to the back, where there was a slop sink. He spent the next couple of minutes cleaning everything out, putting it back where it belonged.

By the time he finished, lunch was halfway over, all the guys seated with plates in front of them. They took turns cooking. Nothing fancy. As Randy passed by, it looked like sandwiches and chips. All the seats were taken except for one between Chief Bartlett and Bill. Randy sighed in relief, realizing he wouldn't have to answer too many questions from the other guys at the moment. That was good, he thought, sliding into the chair between the two of them. Luckily, they ignored him. Randy stared down at the food on his plate and tried a bite. The turkey sandwich tasted bitter in his mouth, the chips too salty. He took a few more bites, trying to wash the dryness down his throat with a glass of water. As he sat there, he listened to the other guys, some of whom were talking about their families and their dogs. One of the guys was telling a story about how his mom got her hand stuck in the kitchen disposal and he had to go over and get her out, "How crazy is that?" he said. Another guy started talking about his son's baseball game. When Randy looked up at him, not meaning anything by it, the guy looked back, blinked, and then said, "Well, how long do we think the storm is going to last?" he said, changing the subject off his kids.

Randy chewed slowly, sadness overwhelming him. He realized it wasn't just sadness about Lexi and Keira, but the way everything had disrupted his life. The idea of going into work seemed like a good one when he and Keira talked about it, but nothing at the firehouse was even the same. The guys were tiptoeing around him, not sure what to say. Randy took a sip of water. He couldn't blame them. If he was in their shoes, he wouldn't know what to say either. There was nothing they could say that would make him feel better. The only words that would heal his heart were, "Randy, Lexi is home and safe."

By dinnertime, the chief called them all together again, "I just got a call from the regional fire chief. He said the worst part of the storm is getting ready to come into our area now. We should expect to start getting calls from people needing help. The ground is already saturated, so flooding is going to be an issue. We need to be prepared with multiple routes to any calls that we get in case the roads are impassable. I've got a call into the parish road manager to make sure he's keeping us updated on anything they've closed or have marked as flooded. Hopefully, that will save us some time." Just as the words came out of Chief Bartlett's mouth, the alarms overhead rang. "Bill, Randy, go take this one," the chief barked.

Randy nodded, jumping up out of his chair and running out into the garage. With the storm raging overhead, he and Bill pulled on rain gear as they jumped into the ambulance, not taking the time to fasten their jackets closed. Normally, an ambulance run simply meant work pants and navy-blue Tifton Fire T-shirt, but in this weather, they'd get soaked through in a matter of seconds. At least the rain gear would keep them dry.

As they drove, dispatch relayed more information to them. An elderly man, who lived about five miles from the station was having a heart attack, or at least his wife thought he was. Randy's heart started to race, his chest tightening. Normally, a call like this wouldn't bother him, but with the weather and under the circumstances, his nerves felt more frayed than usual. He chewed his lip and then looked over at Bill, "You think we're going to get to the hospital okay with this one?"

"We'll figure it out, buddy. Don't you worry about that," Bill said. Glancing over at Randy, he said, "You okay?"

"Yeah, I think so. Just a little worried about the transport," he lied. Sure, he was worried about getting the victim over to the hospital, but that wasn't what was lurking in his mind and heart. Lexi was. He pulled out his phone and sent a quick text to Keira and another one to her sister, checking in. He knew there wasn't any news — Keira would have called him right away if there was — but he wanted to check in with them anyway. Keira's sister would tell him how she was doing, how she was really doing.

Pulling up the driveway of an old farmhouse, the lights on the ambulance bouncing off of the wet siding, sheets of rain driving across the yard, Randy saw the front door open, the silhouette of a woman waving at them. Randy didn't take time to unload the gurney. He grabbed the advanced life support kit from behind him and ran at a sprint across the driveway and up the front walk, leaving Bill behind. Panting, he got to the front door, "Ma'am? You said your husband isn't feeling well?" Randy tried to use calming language, but his heart was pounding in his chest.

The woman stared at him, her eyes wide behind her round glasses, "Yes! Over here! I'm not even sure he's breathing!"

Randy followed the woman into the sitting room, where the TV was on in the background, a weather person showing the radar images of the tropical storm overhead. The woman's husband was in the chair, his head slumped to the side, his face pale, his mouth open. "Sir? Can you hear me?" Randy said, using his fist to rub on the man's sternum. It was one of the most effective ways to wake someone up. Randy felt for a pulse. It was there, but faint.

By the time Bill came in out of the rain, Randy had the man flat on his back on the floor, attaching AED leads to his chest. The mechanical voice coming from the machine read the pulses from his heart and said, "Normal heart rhythm detected." Randy breathed a sigh of relief. Why the man was unconscious, he still didn't know, but that was something for the doctors to figure out. At least he was alive.

Randy stood up, looking at the woman, who was standing behind him, her arms crossed over her chest, one hand covering her mouth, her eyes wide, "Ma'am?" Randy said, bending over a little, trying to catch her eye. "Your husband has a normal heart rhythm. We're going to get him packed up and off to the hospital. Would you like to ride with us?"

The woman nodded, "Why isn't he awake?"

"I don't know that part, ma'am," Randy said. "That will be something for the doctors to figure out. But what I can tell you is that for the moment, he's stable." Randy glanced over at Bill and gave a nod. The two of them worked silently, starting an IV and getting the man up onto the gurney. Bill covered the man's legs with a blanket and fastened belts over his legs, waist, and chest so he wouldn't fall off of the bed as they moved him. From inside of one of the first aid bags Bill brought in, Randy pulled out a plastic tarp. He looked back at the woman, "Ma'am, we're just about ready to go. If you'd like to ride with us, how about if you go grab a raincoat and your purse and any other information you might need, like any medication your husband is on?" The woman nodded without saying anything, turning and walking away.

By the time they got to the front door, the woman was right behind them. Randy nodded to her, "You stay right here in the doorway for me while we get your husband out into the ambulance and situated, okay? I'll be back for you in just a moment." The woman didn't say anything, standing stock-still. She looked like she was in shock. Randy would have to remember to say something to the doctors when they got over to the hospital. In a way, the woman just looked like an older version of Keira — the haunted look in her eyes, the way her lips pursed together. Randy shook off the thought, trying to avoid thinking of Lexi.

Stepping out into the rain, Randy pulled the plastic sheeting up over the man's face, laying it loosely so that the man on the gurney wasn't completely soaked with water by the time they got him into the ambulance. Once Randy heard the satisfying click of the bed as it locked into the back of the ambulance, he ran back to the door where the woman was waiting where they'd found her, still silhouetted in the lights from the house. This time, she had on a long raincoat, the hood already pulled up, her purse tucked under her arm. "You ready?" Randy said, offering her his arm.

It took a little longer to get back to the ambulance with the older woman in tow. She didn't move very fast. Randy helped her up into the back where Bill was busy adjusting monitors on her husband. Randy slammed the doors and ran around the front, glad to be inside of the dry cab. Now, if he could just get them all to the hospital in one piece.

OLLIE'S VAN was just a mile down the road when his eyes started to swim in front of him. The van swerved, the tires screeching on the wet pavement. There was a thud and a few loud bumps as the van lurched to a stop, stuck in a drainage ditch filled with water on the side of the road. Furious, Ollie pounded on the steering wheel, "For the love of God! Nothing ever goes my way!" he yelled, his voice booming off the inside of the van.

Ollie sat there for a moment, leaning his head on the steering wheel. He wasn't a hard The two shots of bourbon he'd sucked down before he left the bar were catching up with him, his head pounding, waves of nausea rolling over him. It was nearly impossible to see in the dark. He sighed. He needed to get home. Revving the engine, Ollie threw the van into reverse, hearing the tires spin underneath him. Ollie tried going forward with the same result. He pounded his fist on the steering wheel again, trying one more time to back the van out of the ditch. It didn't work. Ollie pushed the door open, having to climb up and out of the side of the van to get back onto the road. As he did, water seeped into the inside of the van. In the dark, it was hard to see. There were no lights nearby. The rain was pouring down, instantly soaking through his shirt and hair.

Ollie climbed back into the van, looking for his phone. He retrieved it out of a puddle of water, the screen cracked from him throwing it. His hands shook as he tried to decide whether to call for help or not. If he called the local police station, they'd send out someone to help him, but they'd quickly figure out he was drunk. He checked the time. It was well after midnight. There was no one he could call for help, at least not at the moment. Another wave of nausea washed over him. If I can just close my eyes for a couple of minutes, maybe I can figure out what to do, Ollie thought as he passed out.

42

By the time Bill and Randy made it back to the fire station, it was nearly midnight. Predictably, the roads were swamped. As they backed in, Chief Bartlett met them by the ambulance, "Things go okay?"

"Aside from the fact that it took us twice as long to get to the hospital as it should have been and about three times as long to get back here? Yeah," Bill said, walking off.

Randy shook his head a little. Though he and Bill were friends, Bill could be a little surly from time to time, "Yes, to answer your question, it was fine. An elderly gentleman was unconscious when we got to the house. Not sure why. Could be an issue with his heart, but we had a normal rhythm the whole way to the hospital. I'm having them take a look at his wife, too. She seemed pretty spooked by the whole thing."

Before Chief Bartlett could answer, the alarms overhead went off again. Randy leaned his ear to his shoulder so he could better hear about the call, "Van in a ditch on the side of the road in an area of flooding," the dispatcher said. "Passerby reports one individual in the van. They tried to help him out, but the man was unresponsive."

Randy turned around and got back in the ambulance, waiting for Bill. From behind him, he could hear the scurry of boots on the floor he'd mopped earlier, the other guys up and out of bed, climbing inside of the fire truck. As Randy closed the door, he heard Chief Bartlett yell, "Let's go!"

Bill got back in the ambulance and shook his head, "And I thought maybe we'd have a chance to at least have a cup of coffee before the next call. I guess not."

Randy shook his head a little bit. Keira was right. Staying busy was helping him. He glanced down at his phone. Keira had texted him while they were at the hospital, "Everything's okay. Stay at work." That was all she said. He sent her a message back, "Love you. Things will be okay, I promise." How he could say that he wasn't sure.

As he drove, following the fire truck, the chief's SUV behind him, the emergency vehicles making a line, Randy's mind slipped back to Lexi. Where was she? The surge of adrenaline at dealing with the elderly man had taken his mind off of the issues in his own house, but only for a moment. Was Lexi outside somewhere in the storm? Was she lost? Cold? Randy shook the thoughts out of his head. He couldn't afford to be distracted, not with the storm raging overhead and someone trapped in a vehicle. He needed to focus.

Randy leaned forward, squinting at the road ahead of him. The driving rain made it hard to see even with the bright flashing lights of the fire truck ahead of him. Screeching with every swipe, the wipers on the ambulance whipped back and forth in the downpour. The rain hadn't let up. Randy gripped the wheel a little tighter, easing the ambulance back a bit. Based on the location, he thought they were close, but it was so hard to see in the rain and the wind. It wasn't as if Tifton's streets were lit anyway, and especially not where the van had been reported. He breathed a silent prayer that somehow the person had been able to pull their van out and leave the scene.

Otherwise, it was going to be a couple of hours of misery in the wind and the weather.

"There," Bill said, pointing. The fire truck in front of them slowed and Randy narrowed his eyes trying to see through the rain. All he could make out was the back of a white van, tilted off the side of the road. The caller had been right -- the drainage ditch was full and running over the road itself.

"All right, let's go see," Randy said, throwing the ambulance into park and pulling the hood of his jacket up over his head. Stepping out of the ambulance, the driving rain immediately attacked his face, droplets running down his cheeks. Randy lifted his hand and pulled the hood down a little lower on his forehead, trying to make out what he could see in front of him. The other firefighters ran ahead of him, in full turnout gear, the reflective tape on their pants and jackets glowing in the head-lights from the ambulance and the fire truck.

Chief Bartlett pulled up behind the ambulance and stood with Randy and Bill, his white fire helmet one of the only bright things in the stormy evening. "We might have to winch this one out."

Before Randy could respond, he saw one of the other guys motion for him and Bill. It was policy for the paramedics to hang back while the firefighters secured the scene and did the initial assessment. Randy and Bill would do the same for any of the other paramedics on the days they were assigned to the fire truck. "Over here!" Randy heard a voice, muffled by the rain, calling out to them.

Randy took the lead, striding over to the van. "What'd you have here?"

"Looks like this guy spent a little too much time at the bar tonight and thought his van was a boat," the firefighter said. "Smells like alcohol. You guys want to get him out of here and we'll winch the van out onto the road?"

Just as Randy was about to respond, the man in the van

started to stir. "Finally!" he muttered. "I've been sitting here forever!"

Randy stepped back as the man in the van managed to get himself out, wading through what had to be about two feet of water. At one point, the man nearly slipped and fell, but one of the firefighters extended his hand as he managed to scramble up the bank. "Sir, why don't we go over to the ambulance and take a look at you?"

"Naw, I'm fine. I'd just appreciate it if you could winch my van out of the ditch. I'll be on my way then. Gotta go to work in the morning."

Randy squinted at the man, looking at him, the rain running down his face. He was large, well over six feet tall. Everything about him seemed to be square, from his head to his shoulders to his hands. He stood out in the rain like it was a perfectly sunny day, never even blinking or wiping the water off his face, seemingly content to get drenched.

Chief Bartlett walked over, "Sir? Are you okay?"

The man nodded, "Yeah, I was just telling your boys that I'm fine and good to go. Just need a bit of a pull out of the ditch."

"Well, while we get your van out, why don't you head on over and sit in the back of the ambulance. At least you'll be dry."

The man nodded, more agreeable to the Chief Barlett's suggestion than Randy's. Randy and Bill followed the man over to the ambulance. As the man climbed in, he sat down on the bench, ducking his head under a row of storage cabinets that held medications and equipment. He sniffed the air, "Sorry about the alcohol smell," he said, wiping his hands down his pants. "I stopped and got a couple of beers, but the guy next to me at the bar managed to spill. Got whiskey all over me. Nothing a little wash won't take care of, but sure doesn't smell good."

Randy nodded. At least that explained the strong alcohol smell coming from the man. Whether it was true or not, Randy wasn't sure. He could only go by what he knew. The man wasn't slurring his speech, was able to climb out of his vehicle just fine, and didn't stagger as he walked. They could call the local police department, but with the storm raging overhead, the chance that they'd get here in the next couple of hours was small. Resources always ran thin during a tropical storm. "How many drinks did you have?"

"Aw, just a few," the man said. "I've been sitting in that van for the last couple of hours. I'm good to go, don't you worry about me."

From outside, Randy could hear the noise of the fire truck being moved, the hydraulics activating as they got ready to put the winch on the van. A couple of minutes later, Randy heard a creak and then a scraping. From experience, he knew that was the van being pulled up and out of the ditch. "Well, I'm guessing they got your van out of the ditch if you want to go take a look."

The man hadn't said anything more after their initial conversation. He just got up and climbed out of the back of the ambulance, right back out into the pouring down rain. Randy followed him, giving Bill a little nod.

The man stepped into his van and turned the engine. It hesitated, but then started right up, the wipers slapping back and forth on the windshield, pushing the rain out of the way. "Thanks for the help, boys," the man waved, slamming the van door behind him. Randy saw the shadow of something fall to the ground as his door shut.

Randy stood and watched for a second, the taillights disappearing into the dark, and then looked down at the road where he thought he saw something. He hoped it wasn't the guy's wallet. Whether the man made it home in one piece or not, Randy wasn't sure. There was no reason for them to hold him, though. Getting whisky spilled on you wasn't the same as drunk driving.

Randy looked down at the spot where the van had been parked when they got it out of the ditch. He wiped the driving rain off his face as he walked toward the spot where he saw something fall. Something pink caught his eye. It wasn't a wallet. Curious, he tilted his head to the side and knelt down. It was a hair clip, one with two lavender-colored flowers attached to it. Randy stood up, holding it in his hand. He stared down the road, the van lights disappearing in the background, his hand open, his heart pounding in his chest. He'd seen that clip before. It was Lexi's.

Chief Bartlett walked up behind him, "Everything okay, Randy? Looks like Bill's about ready to get moving if you want to head back to the firehouse..." There was a pause as Randy looked at Chief Bartlett. Chief Bartlett glanced at Randy's hand. "Oh my God. Is that Lexi's?"

43

Emily was on a conference call with Mike, Flynn, and Alice, going over some of their ideas about the evidence. No one had gotten any sleep yet. The storm was still raging overhead. Alice was in the middle of talking to Emily about the bones that had been found just a few hours earlier out in the field when Flynn looked up at the screen, his eyes wide, "Emily. The FBI knows who it is."

A shiver ran through Emily's body, "What are you talking about?"

"Cash just texted his team. He's getting them all up. They think they know who it is."

"What?" Emily jumped up off the bed and ran over to her duffel bag, changing out of the leggings she was wearing and pulling on a pair of jeans, just outside of the view of her computer's camera. "Keep talking. I can hear you. I'm just changing my clothes."

By the time she got back to the screen, Mike was staring at his phone. "Randy Cooper went back to work tonight. They pulled a van out of a flooded ditch."

Emily's mind began to race. In the reports Mike had been

able to intercept, there had been the mention of a white van in the park next to the Cooper's house the night Lexi was taken, but no one had made anything of it. They thought it was just some hunters. "What happened?"

"Cash isn't giving all the details over his cell phone, but it looks like when the fire department got there, they got the van out and then Randy found one of Lexi's hair clips on the ground." There was a pause, "Wait, hold on. I guess one of the firefighters took down the guy's license plate number while they were winching it out, just in case they needed to follow up after the storm." Mike stared at the screen, "Looks like they're calling for warrants."

Emily froze. She could wait for the FBI to get their warrants and all of their paperwork together or maybe there was a way for Mike to get the information before the FBI ever showed up. Emily chewed her lip. Mike's voice interrupted her thoughts, "Em? What are you thinking?"

She sat down on the end of the bed for a minute, "If that's the guy, then I'm not sure we have enough time to wait for the FBI to get their warrants. That could take hours, especially in this storm." Her eyes darted left and right staring at the floor, her mind racing. If she went after whoever the fire department had seen, it was possible she'd run into the FBI while she was in the middle of trying to save Lexi. How that would go over, she wasn't sure. "Any chance you can intercept the information?"

Emily could see Alice and Flynn standing together behind Mike, whispering, Flynn's arms folded over his chest. They kept glancing at Mike and then at Emily. Mike was furiously typing on his laptop. He kept glancing over to the side as though he was watching his phone at the same time. "Bingo! Cash just sent the license plate number to one of the other agents. Gimme a sec and I'll track it."

A shiver ran up and down Emily's spine. There was a lot at

play here — the storm, the fact that a little girl's life was at stake, and the FBI hovering all over the case. If she'd read Cash correctly, he'd want to move as quickly as possible on the person they'd identified. His career and reputation depended upon it. What Emily didn't know was whether they had that kind of time. "Alice? Can you give me an idea how long you think this guy holds his victims before he kills them?"

Alice's face emerged on the screen, "Based on the files Dr. Wiley sent over, I'm guessing about forty-eight hours. Maybe a little longer, maybe a little shorter. With the bodies soaking in water, it's very difficult to get an exact read, but Dr. Wiley's results on their stomach contents indicate something around that timeline."

Emily did the math. Lexi Cooper had been gone just over two days. Forty-eight long hours. If the man the firefighters had spotted in the van was the one that took her, Lexi's time was running out. Emily balled her hands into fists. She walked over to the dresser and fixed her holster onto her belt. "Mike, I need that information. I need it right now."

Emily quickly finished getting ready, tightening the laces on her boots and pulling on her rain slicker, passing in front of the computer every few moments, her chest tight. She knew it was annoying, but it was her way of letting Mike know she was ready even if he wasn't. Her hands were gripped in tight balls waiting for the news. "Hold on, I've almost got it," Mike said, not glancing up from his keyboard. The only thing Emily could see was the flop of his long hair across his forehead and the tip of his nose as he bent over the keyboard of his laptop. Emily swallowed, running scenarios in her head, questions swamping her. Would she be able to even reach the site where this guy lived? The storm had been raging for hours. Many of the roads were already flooded. Sure, she had Bradley's Jeep, but even then, trying to pass over a flooded road in a strange city in the middle of the night might be nearly impossible if she was hoping to beat Cash there.

"Okay," Mike said, breathing heavily, his eyes darting back and forth in front of the screen. "Two pieces of information. First, I have the address of the guy that you're looking for. His name is Ollie Gibson. He lives on the outskirts of town." Emily heard her phone pinging in her pocket. The address had arrived. "Secondly," Mike stared at the screen, his mouth open, "Cash has pinged your truck. He thinks you're involved somehow."

Emily swallowed, a wave of bile rising in her throat. "Why would Cash think I'm involved? There's nothing in my background to suggest that."

Mike shook his head, "I have no idea. All I know is that Cash knows your truck is at Bradley's house."

"Is he sending agents over there?"

Mike stared down for a second. Emily could see him checking his phone, "No, not yet. But you'd better be ready to make a quick escape out of Tifton."

Emily pivoted on her heel, quickly gathering up the things that were left in her room at the bed-and-breakfast. It was the middle of the night. There was no one there, no way for her to check out, not that it mattered. She quickly folded her clothes and stuffed them in her duffel bag, sweeping the toiletries she'd left in the bathroom off the edge of the sink and into a plastic bag. She tossed it in with the dirty clothes. Two minutes later, she was packed. "Okay, I'm gonna head out. See you on the other side. Keep your phone handy."

Closing the lid to her computer, Emily saw Mike nod, "Good luck."

IT TOOK Emily all of another thirty seconds to exit her room. She checked both ways as she opened the door, making sure no

FBI agents were standing in the hallway waiting for her. Cash's team didn't seem concerned that she was staying in the same bed-and-breakfast, or they hadn't taken the time to check. Why, Emily had no idea, but she had no time to figure it out. She ran down the steps, her heart pounding in her chest, only taking a small second to pull her hood up over her head as she braced herself to run out into the storm. As she sprinted to the Jeep, she could feel a gust of wind push against her, trying to keep her from making any progress.

Emily threw her backpack and duffel bag inside and got the Jeep started, the engine rumbling to life as soon as she gave it a little gas. She needed to warn Bradley the FBI might be showing up at his house, looking for her truck. If she wasn't careful, it could get Bradley in a lot of trouble. Cash was the kind of guy that might charge him with harboring a fugitive, even though there was no crime against Emily they could make stick. Questions weren't a crime after all. If she could find the killer and end him, that was another thing.

Emily flipped on the headlights and put the Jeep into gear, pulling out of the parking lot. The GPS on her phone was beeping with the location she needed to get to — Ollie Gibson's house—but it wouldn't connect. There was no way for her to find her way to Ollie Gibson's house in the storm without a GPS. She wasn't sure the FBI would be able to either. The hair on the back of her neck stood up. That meant the only hope she had was to get to Bradley's and have him guide her. She hoped they could get to Lexi in time.

Turning out into the storm, the wind and rain pelting at the windshield of the Jeep, the headlights barely cut through the darkness with the storm swirling overhead. Squinting at the windshield, she picked up her phone and glanced down long enough to find Bradley's number. She tried to get it to connect, but it wouldn't. "Cell phone service must be down," she growled. Emily gripped the wheel tighter and swung the Jeep around, heading out of the center of Tifton. She knew she could get herself to Bradley's house. Maybe he could get her to Ollie's in time to save Lexi. Emily swallowed, hoping there was enough time.

THE DRIVE OUT to Bradley's house took longer than she expected, the darkness of the storm making it almost impossible to see the roads. Emily had to slow down a couple of times and navigate around fallen trees and water running over the roadways. "Why do they not stripe the roads out here?" she said to herself, pounding her hand on the steering wheel, seeing another downed tree in front of her. Luckily, it only covered part of the road. She turned the wheel just slightly, keeping focused on where she was going. The last thing she wanted to do was end up in a ditch on the side of the road with no cell phone service. She'd be a sitting duck for Cash and would be no good to Lexi.

By the time she got to Bradley's driveway, Emily could feel the tension in her chest spreading into the muscles in her back and up her neck. Her tendons and ligaments were as tight as a steel drum from the adrenaline pumping in her. She revved the engine, pulling the Jeep up the driveway, not bothering to turn it off. There was a single light on in the house. Someone was up. That was a good sign at least, she thought, sprinting to the front door. Pounding on it with her fists, her hands wet from the driving rain, she waited, hoping it was Bradley that was up and not his wife.

A moment later, the door cracked open. It was Bradley. "Bradley, I've been trying to call you."

"Emily? It's late. What's going on? Do you want to come in?" Bradley looked confused. He had on a pair of floppy gray sweatpants and a T-shirt with stains on the front. His hair was standing up in a couple of places as though he'd been nodding off in front of the television or something.

"I came to warn you. The FBI — they pinged my truck. They know it's here. They are going to come looking for me."

"Well, that's okay. I'll just come out and get the garage open for you and you can take your truck out of here. If they come by, I'll tell them I don't know anything about it."

Emily was surprised at how quickly Bradley adjusted to the information. "That's not the only problem. They have a location on Lexi Cooper. I have to go. I gotta go now, but I don't have any GPS. It's down from the storm."

"In this storm? Where exactly are you going?" Emily held up her phone and showed the address to Bradley. He shook his head, "You'll never make it out there on your own. I'm coming with you. Give me just a second."

The door in front of Emily slammed closed. There was nothing else she could do other than run back to the Jeep, waiting for Bradley. She drummed her fingers on the steering wheel while she waited. Why did he feel like he needed to go with her? Maybe the roads were unpaved or something? At this point, nothing would surprise her about Tifton. Before she had much more time to consider her options, Bradley opened the side door of the Jeep, sliding in, putting his cane between his knees. "Let's go," he said. "Turn right out of the driveway. I know where you're going."

They drove in silence, except for Bradley giving Emily directions here and there to turn right or turn left or to watch out. Emily could hear the GPS beep and then recalculate the route they were taking still searching for a signal that wasn't there. The rain pounded on the sides of the Jeep, the constant thrum of water hitting the metal roof. Emily leaned forward, using the sleeve of her jacket to try to wipe some of the steam from the window. Bradley reached into the back of the Jeep, grabbing a towel and wiping it for her. She squinted into the darkness, not sure what she was driving into.

WHEN THEY HAD BEEN DRIVING for nearly twenty minutes Bradley spoke, breaking the silence, "Listen, on the back of this street you're getting to, there's a farm. It's been abandoned for years. I'm not sure if you want to go to the front door, do you? If not, we can go up this street here," Bradley pointed, "and then you can go through the woods and approached the house from the back."

Emily took her foot off the gas, slowing the Jeep down, a little surprised at Bradley's thinking. Bradley had a point. Even though it wasn't her truck, the presence of another vehicle in the driveway if the FBI pulled up would make it nearly impossible for her to leave. In her mind, she saw the two black SUVs blocking the driveway, forcing her to wait, or worse, talk to them. "Yes, let's do that."

Bradley pointed up a side road, "As I said, the farm's been abandoned for years. No one will be there. I'll just wait for you here."

The Jeep made it through the side road with relatively few problems, bumping over a couple of fallen branches. As Bradley pointed to where the driveway for the abandoned farm was, Emily could see a couple of large buildings in the distance. They were hard to make out, the rain and the storm making it nearly impossible to see where she was going. As she got a little closer, Emily spotted a small farmhouse, the windows black. Bradley was right. There was no one home. They passed an abandoned car in the driveway, Emily's grip forcing her knuckles white in the darkness. The rear tire had a flat. It must have been left behind when whoever owned the place moved out, Emily thought. Bradley pointed, "You can park right up here, behind the barn. While you're gone, I'll see if I can get the barn door open and pull the Jeep inside. I'll either be right here or have the Jeep ready to go inside the barn."

Emily nodded and then squinted, "Where is this house I'm going to?"

Not being able to see landmarks distinctly left her feeling confused. Maybe they should have gone to the front of Ollie Gibson's house, Emily wondered. Bradley could have dropped her off. She swallowed, a tingle running down her back. This whole thing, maybe it was a bad idea.

Bradley pointed. "See that little light in the distance? That's gotta be the back of the house. You just have to cross the field and a little stand of trees and you'll be there."

Emily nodded, the knot in her stomach growing by the seconds. If she had any hope of beating the FBI and helping Lexi, she had to go now. "Okay. See you in a bit. If I'm not back in an hour, go back to your house."

"Okay." There was a pause, "Emily?"

"Yeah?"

"Be careful."

The words hung in the air. Emily knew what she was about to do was dangerous, probably one of the most dangerous things she'd ever attempted. In her mind, she pulled up a picture of Lexi with her blonde hair and her wide eyes. If Lexi was in that house, Emily knew she didn't have a choice. Getting warrants and permission from judges could take hours, especially in the middle of the night. Lexi might not have hours. Emily was her next best hope.

44

C ash pounded his fist on the conference room table at the bed-and-breakfast, where he'd been cooped up with his agents for the last two hours waiting for warrants to enter Ollie Gibson's house. Randy had given them the hair clip they'd found, plus a license plate number. It was all they needed to do a search and hopefully find Lexi. But based on the phone conversation he'd just had, the warrants weren't coming any time soon. "You've got to be kidding me!" he shouted, startling Janet, who'd been sipping on coffee the staff had brought in.

"What happened?"

"The storm has the roads clogged up so bad no one can get to any of the local judges to get the warrants signed for at least another hour. By the time they get back to us, it's gonna be another one on top of that."

"And Lexi could be dead by then..." Janet whispered, the color draining from her face.

"Darn right." Cash started to pace, rubbing his hand across his forehead. "This is when I hate the judicial system. This girl's life is on the line and we are sitting here with our thumbs in our mouths."

"Is there anything we can do?" Janet asked.

Cash slumped down into a chair next to her. "Nothing. Absolutely nothing."

45

Emily jumped out of the Jeep, slamming the door behind her, bending forward against the wind and taking off at a trot towards the light in the distance. She couldn't go too fast, the land underneath her was bumpy and rutted. If she wasn't careful, she'd end up twisting her ankle before she got there. Then, she'd be no help to Lexi, none at all.

Though the rain slicker kept the water off her back and shoulders, within a minute, the water had soaked through her jeans and was trickling down her face. "At least it's warm," she mumbled, stepping over a log halfway. In front of her, Emily could see a stand of trees. It extended around the field in a U shape, ending near where she'd left Bradley in the Jeep. Getting near the edge of the woods, she felt bad for a second, exposing him to problems with the FBI. FBI agents were relentless. When they got their eyes set on you, it was nearly impossible to get rid of them. She hoped that wasn't the case for Bradley.

In the woods, Emily stopped for a second, her breath ragged. She stared toward the house, trying to get her bearings. Pulling out her phone from her pocket, she glanced at the GPS just for a second and then stuck it back under her slicker, wiping it off just a little bit. That was the house Mike told her about. It was square and white, two stories. There was a dim bulb on, glowing on the side of the house, probably above a side door. Emily started to move again, stepping over another log, crouching low. If the FBI was approaching from the front of the house, which would be their most likely path in, the last thing she wanted them to do a spot her in the woods. As she got to the edge of the yard, Emily stopped again leaning her head right and left, using a wet hand to wipe as much water off of her face as she could. There was no use. The rain was coming hard and fast. She heard thunder in the distance. Lightning flashed nearby, sending a crackle through the air.

Emily crouched low again, half running across the yard and stopping under a window at the back of the house. She started moving to her right, scanning the back of the house and stopping at the corner near where the light was on. She couldn't go that way without taking the risk she'd be spotted. Emily turned around, hugging the back of the house, her heart pounding in her chest, the whoosh of blood in her ears. She stuck close to the back of the house, the ground squishing underneath her boots, everything soaked with the rain from the storm. She passed under one window, and then another and was just about to dart around the corner when she saw a small window near the foundation. Leaning down, Emily looked inside. It was the cellar of the house. There was a dirty bulb hanging from the ceiling. Emily squinted, her eyes searching the space, trying to focus in the driving rain. Lexi. In the back corner of the cellar, Emily could see the little girl, duct-taped to a chair. Emily's heart started pounding harder. Lexi looked like she was alive, But for how long?

Emily's mind raced. She had to get Lexi and get her out of the house. It didn't make any sense to go in through the front door. She'd be a sitting duck. Emily turned and glanced around. There was a cellar entrance on the outside of the house, a wooden door secured with a padlock that was nearly flush to the ground. Emily ran over to it and knelt down, pulling a set of lock picks out of her pocket. Fumbling with them in the damp, it took her an extra second to get the lock open, the pick dropping into the mud and then the metal coming apart with a click, slick in her hands. She twisted the lock apart and pulled it off of the phalange flipping the door open.

Just as she did, she felt something grab the back of her neck yanking her into an upright position. The force flipped her around and she stared into the face of a giant man, his face frozen and angry. Emily didn't have time to think. Ollie Gibson. Emily kicked and yelled, but he had such a tight grip on her she was unable to break free, dragging her down the steps into the cellar like she was a bad dog coming in out of the rain. Emily's heart was pounding in her chest. She couldn't see him. He had her by the scruff of her neck and the back of her coat. She felt her body being carried down into the cellar, the wind whipping into the dank area behind her, the heels of her boots scraping down the steps. He's going to kill me and kill Lexi, Emily thought, kicking and elbowing him with all she had. It wasn't enough.

At the bottom of the steps, Emily felt the man pull her up to face him, just before slamming her with all of his force into the brick cellar wall. Pain seared through Emily's back and her head as her skull cracked against the rough stone. She slid down, landing in what had to be five inches of water. Woozy, pain shooting everywhere in her body, Emily realized the cellar was flooding. Before she could move, Emily saw Ollie as he stepped back for a second, tall and square, with wide shoulders and big hands clenched by his side. He groaned and then came for her again. She ducked out of the way, scrambling to the side. Out of the corner of her eye, she saw Lexi kick her feet as if she was hoping that Emily noticed she was there. "Hold on, Lexi," Emily screamed as Ollie lunged for her again. Emily's heart was pounding in her chest. She ducked just in time to watch his fist make contact with the brick wall where her head had been.

As she reached back to pull her gun from the holster, Ollie grabbed her arm, his eyes wild. He hadn't said anything. He didn't need to. He was going to kill her. Emily's mouth was dry. Ollie shoved her to the ground. She landed in a splash, the water moving in waves away from her, feeling his hands wrap around her throat. The only hand free she had was on the left side of her body, not her gun side. Emily panicked as the breath drained out of her, black spots forming in front of her eyes. She was going to die in this basement with Lexi Cooper. Cash would find her body along with the little girl when they got here.

Without thinking, Emily fumbled in her pocket for the lock picks. She gripped the two of them in her fist and with an arcing motion stabbed the man in the back of his leg, feeling the pointed metal penetrate his pants and his flesh, diving deep into the sensitive muscle. With a yell, the man let go, falling backward.

With a sweeping motion, Emily pushed herself up and drew her gun, leveling it at him. On his knees, Ollie looked up at her. Emily pulled the trigger, the creep of red blood crawling down his forehead as his body fell face-first into the water, the echo of the shot bouncing off the walls in the small space.

Emily stood up as quickly as she could and kicked at his body, hoping he was dead. There was no movement. She looked at Lexi, whose body was wriggling. Emily ran over to her, making her way through the water that was flooding the basement. She quickly undid the tape on Lexi's mouth her wrists and her ankles, "Are you okay?" Emily whispered, seeing the blood on the side of the girl's head. The little girl nodded and started to cry. Just as she did, Emily heard a noise from upstairs. Footsteps. Yells of, "FBI, we have a warrant!" The FBI. They had gotten the warrants faster than Emily anticipated. She licked her lips and looked back at Lexi, whispering, "The FBI is coming to get you. I want you to yell as loud as you can, so they know you are down here, okay? I've gotta go. Stay here."

Saying nothing more, Emily ran back the way she came, stepping over Ollie Gibson's body with a splash, pulling the hood up on her jacket as she ran up the cellar stairs and out into the darkness. She could hear Lexi screaming from behind her and glanced back, knowing the little girl would soon be home.

From the front of the house, she could hear yells and see the sweep of flashlights. How many agents Cash Strickland had brought in, she didn't know, but it seemed like a lot more than just the few Mike had reported. Maybe he called for reinforcements? Emily didn't have time to think. Her mouth was dry. Standing at the top of the cellar in the pouring down rain she glanced left and right, knowing she had to make a run for the woods. As she started to move, she saw the sweep of flashlights behind her and heard yells in the background, "Stop!"

Crossing the backyard, Emily darted into the woods, following it to the right, knowing the U-shaped line of trees would lead her back to the barn where Bradley was waiting with the Jeep. She didn't have time to think, her breath coming in short pants. From behind her, she heard more noise, the crackle of branches breaking behind her. She was just ahead of the agents, but she had no idea if they could see her or not. The drenching rain hadn't stopped and she slipped, falling to her knees, quickly scrambling up and looking over her right shoulder. The flashlights were still coming, the light arcing through the backyard and into the edge of the woods. By their pattern, Emily didn't think they had any idea who or what they were looking for. She had to keep moving. Scrambling up, she kept going and then heard another voice, "Stop! FBI!" They'd spotted her. Moving as quickly as she could, Emily charged through the woods, veering left and right, hoping to avoid them and the beams from their flashlights cutting through the storm. After a minute or so, she stopped, glancing back. They were no longer coming as hard and as fast, but they were sweeping the woods where she'd been. If she had any hope to get away, she had to keep going. Sucking in a breath, Emily took off at a run again, turning toward the barn. She'd nearly made it out of the woods when she tripped, feeling a crack in her right ankle, searing pain running through her body, even worse than the pounding of her head from getting slammed against the brick wall in Ollie Gibson's basement. She sat for a second, stunned, then realized if she didn't get up and cross the yard to the Jeep, they would get her. She would be in Cash Strickland's hands and likely spend the rest of her life in jail.

With a grunt, tears streaming down her face from the pain, Emily got up and limped across the yard, opening the door to the Jeep and getting inside. She started it up and pulled away without turning on the headlights, without saying a word to Bradley.

A half-mile down the road, Emily turned the headlights on. Her breath had slowed, only the pain in the back of her head and her ankle still remnants of what she had just been through. Bradley's voice broke through the noise of the rain and the windshield wipers on the glass, "Everything okay?"

Emily nodded, "Lexi's safe."

EPILOGUE

Four days after she'd gotten home, Emily was reading an email from Bradley when Mike brought his computer into the living room where Emily was resting her ankle after having surgery on it. The fall in the woods when she was running from the FBI had broken it in three places and required surgery, something that happened the day after she got home. Mike had been staying at the house with her since the beginning of the case to take care of Miner. Now, he was staying at the house to take care of Emily and Miner while she recovered.

"Thought you might like to see this." Mike handed his laptop to her. On the screen was a story from the Louisiana Gazette that headlined, "Tifton Killer Finally Got Justice." There were two pictures on the screen – one of Cash Strickland next to one of Ollie Gibson. Emily smiled. At least Cash got the recognition he wanted, she realized.

Emily handed the laptop back to Mike, "I just got an email from Bradley. He said everyone is grateful and that he's been sleeping better. Even said he got rid of the murder boards in the garage and Carla has been out helping him. I guess Lexi's doing well, too. Dr. Wiley looked in on her and told Bradley about it."

"That's some progress," Mike grinned. "That's a lot of weight off of Tifton and the FBI. I think they kinda owe you."

"I don't know about that..."

A WEEK AFTER GETTING HOME, Emily limped out into the backyard, still trying to get used to the boot she had to wear after surgery. The day had dawned warm and bright, the birds chirping in her backyard through the open window in the kitchen. Emily was restless. She was used to going on walks and working out with Clarence. When she'd called him and told him about her ankle, Clarence said, "Well, there's nothing wrong with your hands, girl. Come on in next week and we'll get you working on the bag. Don't need no feet for that."

Until then there wasn't much to do.

Emily started a pot of coffee and then heard Miner whining. He wanted to go outside and play. Limping toward the door, the tap of the plastic from the boot on the wood floor, she leaned against the frame, watching her dog run out into the backyard, where he found a Frisbee and shook it as hard as he could. Carefully managing the two steps down onto the grass, Emily stepped out into the yard, waiting for Miner to bring the frisbee back. She tossed it to him a couple of times, the dog darting to chase it and then trotting back to her, dropping it at her feet. Mike would have to take him for a walk later on. Though it was nice to be outside, Emily knew Miner needed more exercise than a couple of throws of the Frisbee in the backyard.

A second later, Miner stopped, barking and growling, the hair on his back standing straight up. The back gate to her yard opened and Emily looked just as Miner started to charge.

"Miner! Stay!" she yelled, looking at the figure who opened the gate.

It was Cash Strickland. "Emily, we need to talk..."

Join the mailing list and get exclusive content! Click here and get an exclusive prequel instantly delivered!

A NOTE FROM THE AUTHOR...

Thanks so much for taking the time to read *Victim 14!*

After reading *Victim 14* I hope that you've been able to take a break from your everyday life and join Emily on her adventure to get justice for Lexi

There are more stories to come! In fact, the next series is ready and waiting for you. Curious? Join intelligence analyst, Jess Montgomery, as she searches desperately for her niece after a botched bank robbery. What the robbers wanted wasn't exactly money... Click here to check it out now, or see the next couple of pages for a preview.

Enjoy and thanks for reading,

KJ

P. S. Would you take a moment to leave a review? Reviews keep the creative juices running for indie authors like me!

GET BOOK ONE OF THE JESS MONTGOMERY THRILLERS TODAY!

The Trident Conspiracy

Twelve-year-old Abby Montgomery is gone...

A Saturday morning stop at South Ridge Bank with her aunt, intelligence analyst, Jess Montgomery, sends the family on a high-stakes rescue mission to save Abby after she's kidnapped in a bank heist.

The kidnappers want one thing, and one thing only – an invention that's so secret it's a matter of national security.

Jess has nowhere to turn. Involving the police will get Abby, and probably the rest of the family, killed.

Can Jess save her niece and protect the secret that she's been entrusted with? Can she get justice for the family in the process?

If you love Tom Clancy, L. T. Ryan and Mark Dawson, you'll love the first book in the Jess Montgomery vigilante thriller series.

Click here now to check it out!

A PREVIEW OF "THE TRIDENT CONSPIRACY"

Jess darted between two buildings, dodging the blinking lights and the police tape that had been practically wrapped around the entire block where the bank was located. Her heart was pounding in her chest and her hands were still clammy, but she made her way down an alley, darting left and then turning right behind another building before weaving her way back to the parking lot where she'd left her car. A lump formed in her throat. What if the emergency vehicles blocked her car in and she couldn't get out? As she slowed down, she pulled her phone out of her pocket. She needed to call Chase. He needed to know what happened and that it wasn't her fault.

Jess shoved Abby's phone in the back pocket of her jeans and pulled up Chase's number. Her hands were shaking and the phone bobbled. She nearly dropped it. Out of the corner of her eye, she spotted her car. With the phone pressed up against her ear she glanced left and right, trying to see if she could get out of the parking lot. There were no police cars with flashing lights or yellow tape anywhere to be seen. That was a break, she thought, thinking back to just a few hours before when she and Abby had arrived in Catalina on the outskirts of Tucson's downtown. It wasn't always easy to find a parking spot.

As Jess got in her car, she felt her heart race again. Chase hadn't picked up. Jess chewed her lip, scrolling through her contacts, trying to call Piper, Abby's mom. No luck. Piper might not even accept her call. The two of them hadn't always gotten along that well. Piper wasn't exactly someone Jess would hang out with, with all of her fancy, designer clothes and lunch dates with her friends. Jess was a bit more rough-and-tumble, sometimes even more so than her brother, who was frequently buried in books or some sort of research. Piper's phone went to voicemail. Jess pushed her shoulder-length, straight dark hair behind her ear as she left a message, "Piper, it's Jess. I was at the bank with Abby and there was a robbery. I don't know where she is. She's gone..."

Join the adventure today when you visit the series page for the Jess Montgomery Thrillers!

Made in United States
North Haven, CT
14 February 2022

16112805R00173